"SCREW OFF, TRAFFIC WATCHER," HELLFIRE SNARLED. "YOU UNDERCOVER POLICERS GIVE ME THE CRAWLIES."

In the Loophole Bar, even pirates were supposed to be able to drink in peace. Janja, glancing from Hellfire to the man standing at her side, knew violence was coming. She jammed her elbow into his crotch at the same time Hellfire's stopper cleared its holster.

"What seems to be the trouble here?" A metal cyber-bouncer rushed over on silent rollers.

"I...fell down..." the man on the floor said with effort. He flashed a look at Janja, who had probably saved his life. The robot, who thought he was drunk, escorted him away.

Hellfire scowled at Janja while the other people around the table waited for the explosion. Hellfire was a deadly guttersnipe whose sexual preference never stood in the way of murder....

SPACEWAYS

#1 OF ALIEN BONDAGE
#2 CORUNDUM'S WOMAN
#3 ESCAPE FROM MACHO
#4 SATANA ENSLAVED

SPACEWAYS #2

CORUNDUM'S WOMAN

JOHN CLEVE

PLAYBOY
PAPERBACKS

SPACEWAYS #2: CORUNDUM'S WOMAN

Published simultaneously in the United States and Canada by Playboy Paperbacks, New York, New York. Printed in the United States of America. Library of Congress Catalog Card Number: 81-83489. First edition.

Books are available at quantity discounts for promotional and industrial use. For further information, write to Premium Sales, Playboy Paperbacks, 1633 Broadway, New York, New York 10019.

ISBN: 0-867-21037-0

First printing May 1982.

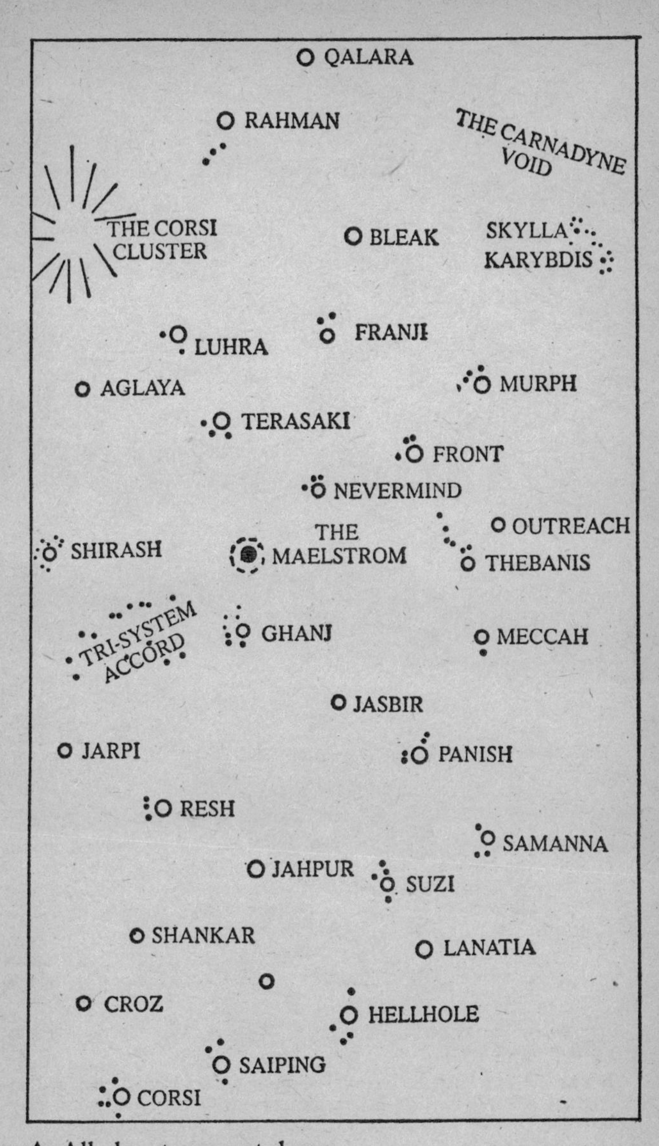

A: All planets are not shown.
B: Map is not to scale, because of the vast distances between stars.

SCARLET HILLS

Alas, fair ones, my time has come.
I must depart your lovely home—
Seek the bounds of this galaxy
To find what lies beyond.

(chorus)
Scarlet hills and amber skies,
Gentlebeings with loving eyes;
All these I leave to search for a dream
That will cure the wand'rer in me.

You say it must be glamorous
For those who travel out through space.
You know not the dark, endless night
Nor the solitude we face.

(reprise chorus)

I know not of my journey's end
Nor the time nor toll it will have me spend.
But I must see what I've never seen
And know what I've never known.

Scarlet hills and amber skies,
Gentlebeings with loving eyes;
All these I leave to search for a dream
That will cure the wand'rer in me.

—Ann Morris

1

We live on an ordinary planet, one of nine that orbit a typical, undistinguished star. And this star, our sun, is just one among billions scattered around our Galaxy.

William J. Kaufmann,
Black Holes and Warped Spacetime

Space.

Take a piece of black—something. Steel, iron, cardboard, velvet; no matter. It need only be black, and enormous. It must surround and blot every horizon. There must be no horizon. Curvature or noncurvature do not matter. It must be true black, that overabundance of color and absence of light that produce black, and true black does not show curve or plane. True Black has no shape and no depth—unless perhaps it shows infinite depth?

It is just Blackness.

Now punch as many holes into the Blackness as it will accommodate without overlapping more than a few of the holes. They may vary in size and distance from each other. Now set a light behind the Blackness.

You have created a representation of space. A simulacrum of the galaxy. If the holes are closer together in toward the center, all the better. Stars are clustered thick there, thick as flowers of white and yellow and red and blue in an untrodden meadow.

The pinholes are not pinholes. They are stars. Hundreds of millions of stars. They form a fraction of that part of the universe called the Milky Way galaxy. A ridiculous name! Herakles a.k.a. Hercules, the Greeks claimed, once jerked his infant mouth from his wet nurse's breast with such force that the night sky was spattered with droplets of milk!

Lactose and lactation; ga-lactic and galaxy; milk and the Milky Way. The Greek *gala* and the Latin *lac:* both mean "milk."

That is the panorama. That is one galaxy in a universe of galaxies. Now adjust the zoom lens and note that one of the pinholes is not stationary. One of the pinholes is moving. It is not a pinhole or a spot of milk or a star. It is a made Thing, a vessel made by men and women: a craft. It is a ship to sail the limitless ocean of milk-spattered black.

It is a spaceship, racing. The men and women now call themselves Galactics. They sail the star-splashed ocean of black and indigo that is the galaxy.

In the spaceship are Galactics and they and their created Things have detected another star that is not a star. It is not moving toward them, which would be useless at their velocity. It is racing to intersect their course. It will, too, since its velocity is greater than theirs.

They know interest mingled with some fear which becomes fear and dread. It is too late. Their craft is slow and the other is swift. In the ocean of space, they are a meandering but tasty fish, stalked by a shark. It races to intersect their course.

It intersects.

Now it is horribly near, in space, where nothing is close. Its human-created Things grapple the two craft together in the manner of an ancient pirate vessel on, for example, the Caribbean Sea of what was once called "Earth." It *is* a shark. The two ships are locked together.

Captain Harry Morgan, model for Captain Blood and others, used steel grapnels. They were curved and clawed multiple hooks at the ends of long rope or chain. They bit into wooden hulls and were tugged taut to bring the ships together, and hold them so. That was in the seventeenth century, and that was hundreds and hundreds of years ago.

Centuries upon centuries later, Captain Corundum uses a directed electromagnetic field called a "tractor field."

The target ship does not stop. It continues rushing through space. So does its new dark companion, *Firedancer.* The harpooned whale is not dragging the boat; both are whales and one accompanies the other. The velocities are matched, whale and killer whale. No human helmsman or navigator or astrogator on *Firedancer* does this, because none could. A human-created Thing does. It is a Ship Inboard Processing and Computing Unit (Modular) and is called SIPACUM. On *Firedancer,* it is called "Jinni," a form of djinni or genie. It also aids its captain's voice to travel from his ship into the other, where it crackles crisply in via the comm system of the . . . prey.

"Hail, merchantship. We are grappled to you. You have a choice. Accept us on board, losing your cargo but keeping your lives and your ship, or refuse and resist. In that event we shall not board, for you can prevent that. We will break off—and fire. We will not destroy you. We will cripple you. You will not rush on toward Murph's moon with your load of fine mining equipment and the secret small cargo you also carry. You will wallow, wounded and stripped. You may be discovered and you may not. You may survive and you may not. You may reach Murph and you may not. You may all go mad."

All this from *Firedancer* in a quiet, cultured, eerily polite voice.

"Open your airlock," that voice went on, *"to let us board, and you live—along with your ship."*

Pause, while the merchantship's crewmembers looked at each other and at their captain. Their viewscreen remained blank. There was only the voice.

"If you now expect me to restate what I have said, forget it. It is said. Over to you. Reply."

The merchant captain stared at the viewscreen before him as though it were not blank. He was sweating. His jaw worked and his lips moved. At last words emerged.

"This is—this is *piracy!*" Winged with indignation, his voice rose high.

A trace of amusement rode the calm, quiet voice. *"Of course it is."*

"We—we will not allow this!"

"You have been advised of your choices. You know there are no others."

"We will not—"

"Stand by!"

At that third voice the merchant captain jerked his head up in anger. The voice was that of his own Ship's Mate!

"We are conferring," the Mate said, and his hand moved past his captain.

"Understood," the quiet calm voice said, politely.

The captain was still sweating. His round, jowly face had gone darker at his Mate's temerity than at the pirate's.

"You—*confer!* Confer my ass! *I* am captain of *Suyari!* I will *not* yield on my knees to that pirate scum—or to you, Prith! Now get out of this cabin, sir—you are relieved."

"What's this about a 'small secret cargo'?"

Those words came in a fourth voice, and the captain of merchanter *Suyari* half-turned to stare, rearing up out of his con-chair.

"Nothing! The words of a hopeful pirate. What are you doing away from your post?"

Mate and third man looked at each other. The newcomer stayed where he was. The captain fumed. Sweat ran down out of his grease-shiny hair, black as space. He flipped aside toggles and belt to rise. Once it had seemed certain that the interceptor was a shark, he had strapped on a sidearm. Now he started to draw the slim tube.

The Mate produced his stopper first. "Sir, I relieve you on the grounds of irrational behavior." The snout of the microwave tube was lined up on his captain's chest. "Stoppers," the Galactics called their pistols.

"Because we aren't anxious to die or be set adrift," the other crewmember said.

The captain continued pulling out his stopper. "You flaining bast—"

His Mate squeezed the grip of his own tube and the captain broke off, frozen in every muscle—stopped. The Mate dropped his weapon into the big worn conchair and was just able to catch the captain as he began falling.

"Do you concur, Engineer?"

"I concur, *Myrzha* Prithvi. I'll be fried and flained if I want to die or be set adrift out here by no pirate, with no way to get somewheres else. To hell with the cargo. To hell with the captain. Tell the sharks to come onboard."

The unconscious captain was loosely seated in the Mate's chair, and Prithvi was kind enough to strap him there. His stopper had been set on Two, which was called Freeze and which was paralysis by direct attack on the nervous system. The One setting would have set the captain to dancing helplessly; Three was called Fry, and killed.

"Stand behind him, Tetsu, and be sure he stays put. Most likely he will be out long enough for them to board, transfer cargo, and leave. But—"

"I understand."

Prith settled into the control chair and opened the comm-link to the other ship, including Visual. His screen showed only the restless writhing of cosmic static. Star noise.

"First Mate Prithvi 712-90-4119 of *Suyari,* acknowledging an act of piracy. We have conferred. Signal when you want the outer lock opened."

"Thank you, Myrzha *Prithvi,"* the quiet, calm voice said. *"We shall arrive spacesuited and bearing arms. Would you be kind enough to place your own sidearms in the airlock, please? It will be so good for our mental state."*

"Uh—agreeable, but they will be drawn out into space and we could use—"

He waited. There was no reply. He sweated. Damn the damn pirate! At last he spoke.

"Very well. We are a crew of four, with four sidearms and another locked up in the captain's cabin. Be assured that we are not stupid enough to try using a cutter onboard ship!"

Again he heard the amusement in the polite tones of the other man, who continued to refrain from activating his Visual send. *"One is glad to hear it,* Myrzha *Prithvi. Not actuating even a short-beam laser onboard a spacer is a lesson learned by all good farers along the spaceways. One of us* will *bear a cutter. It is not to be used except in emergency, you understand! Place your arms in the airlock and be certain that the inner lock is secured. Open outer port once you have accomplished that. Two-plus-two taps means close outer port. One more signals you to open. Three of us are now leaving ship. Evil pirate out."*

"Evil pirate!" Tetsu repeated incredulously, while Prithvi shut off and sank back with a sigh. Damned fancy-talking *polite* pirate! He looked over and up at Tetsu. The captain continued inert. Prithvi sighed again and opened internal comm.

"Suki? Meet me at the airlock. SIPACUM and the shark have everything in control. They're boarding.

We are going to be very very still and polite. If they want your earrings, pass 'em over. Better than losing your lobes!"

He buttoned off and waited a moment for a reply that did not come. He rose. A glance told him that the console was placid. All systems were stable. Locked together, pirate and merchanter plunged on, oncourse for Murph and its fourth moon. Prithvi looked at Tetsu.

"We're in trouble, of course," he said, holding out his hand. "Doubly."

Tetsu placed his stopper in the other man's palm, cold blue cylinder on warm beige skin.

"Horrible thing to say, but—better we set that thing on Fry and used it again." He jerked his hairless head at the captain. "Once we reach port we'll just tell 'em the pirate done it."

Still again Prithvi sighed. "We can't. I know it and so do you. Everything we've said has been recorded. We'll have to take our chances." His smile was pallid. "Maybe he'll decide it's smarter not to press charges, once he thinks it over—and accesses that part of the record."

"You believe that?"

Prithvi shrugged. "We'll be alive."

"Either way, we're through. Even if he decides to let it go, we can't stay on *Suyari*. And he won't be giving us any gold stars!"

"We'll be alive," the lean Prith said, and left the con-cabin.

Suzuki, big in shapeless gray coveralls, apparent-age forty, Indian blood evident amid the Oriental, waited at the airlock. She looked at him and the three stoppers he bore. She proffered hers.

He opened the airlock, explaining. They put the four cylindrical pistols inside, closed the lock, double-checked. And buttoned to open the outer hatch. They heard it. They waited. Ship's aircon was working fine, but both of them sweated just the same.

"You bring any secret cargo onboard, Suki?"

She shook her head.

"This shark talks like an edutape and thinks we haul contraband."

She shook her head. "Captain Ota, maybe. I *know* he's run contraband before. We'll have that evidence anyhow, won't we—I mean, we're in trouble."

"What would you have done?"

"Approved your action on the spot. I'd not have been able to do it, though. But I concur, First Mate." She had no more epicanthic fold than he, and not quite as much nose.

He touched her shoulder, which was less bony than his. "We'll be all right, Suki."

"Sure."

Both of them jumped at the sound of clanks in the airlock. They waited. They jumped again at the *rap-rap, rap-rap* on the other side of the hatch. Prithvi swallowed. He pulled a lever, turned a wheel, pushed up a toggle. They heard the closing of the outer hatch and automatic pressurizing of the airlock. Now it had the ominous hollow sound of a dungeon door.

Thump!

Prithvi set the inner hatch to open and stepped well back. He kept his hands in plain sight. His and Suzuki's big weapons belts and empty holsters were pathetically obvious. Nervously, they stared at the hatch.

The hatch opened. The three pirates entered *Suyari.* Their spacesuits made them even more menacing, despite the fact that any spacefarer was used to them. Strange that these were one each white, pastel blue, and yellow! Prith might have expected pirates to wear black spacesuits.

(Sure, he thought, *and if one slipped or something happened out there,* they'd *be next to invisible in space! Of course they don't wear black suits, dummy, with or without a skull-and-bones insignia!)*

Considerably more disconcerting was that these

boarders were faceless, even eyeless. All three suits had opaqued viewports.

Prith knew these sharks were far from blind. They were seeing as well as he.

Above each helmet's viewport a little device was mounted, no larger than the last joint of his thumb—A TP optic or camera. Long available to the unimplantable blind, telepresences served as eyes. Their double feedback system enhanced their further use as reach-extenders and grip-strengtheners—the safety devices once called waldoes. With electronic help, they were marvelously effective even over long distances. While direct retinal attachment was possible, Prithvi assumed that these had viewscreens mounted inside the helmet viewports. He was seeing the backs of those screens. A TP's scan could be set as high as 4x1, which meant that the wearer could move its head as far to the left as it would go—and see to the right. More common was the two-to-one setting, in which the wearer looked to the side and saw behind its back.

Suyari First Mate Prithvi 712-90-4119 rather imagined that the pirates had their TPs set at one-to-one. Simple. They saw him as well as he saw them. Better, perhaps.

(Later reflection would remind him that opaqued helmet viewplates were more *sinister*, fearsome, in addition to being an effective disguise. This shark captain had a sense of style, of drama, of creating effect.)

About the one in the yellow suit, though—that was a shock. The first two seemed normal. But their companion, with that adjustable-beam laser repair unit cradled in three of four arms! Had a new race of aliens been come across that Prithvi didn't know about?

The pirates were daunting, made far more menacing by their silent entry with leveled stoppers aimed in two directions along the ship's corridor or tunnel—and by the third boarder's height and obvious *alienness*. Prith would not dream of hampering or challenging this trio of spacefaring thieves.

Suzuki was staring at the yellow-suited one. It was definitely 215 or more centimeters or "sems" in height—above seven feet. And four-armed. And two-legged, two-footed. And . . . its TP eye was on a level with her face! Suzuki was 157 sems tall. Had she worn a TP in a corresponding area, it would have been in the center of her chest!

The calm, quiet voice emerged electronically hollow, and made both *Suyari* crewmembers jump.

"Are you carrying knives? Are there blades in your boots?"

Both shook their heads and both said "No," as well.

"I believe you. I spoke with the captain and with the Mate. Which are you?"

"Mate," Prith said. "Prithvi."

The white suit bowed slightly. "*Myrzha* Prithvi. And your captain?"

"Unconscious," Prithvi said. "He was not going to let you board. Engineer Tetsu and I decided that was irrational, and told him so. He began to draw his stopper. I stopped him."

"Second setting?" There was that amused tone again.

"Of course."

"And where is Engineer Tetsu? Pardon, but that is not a woman's name."

"Here," Tetsu said, having come quietly along the tunnel from the con. The speed with which two stoppers were leveled at him was genuinely shocking. Prith also noted that the alien did not move. The cutter was aimed at Mate Prithvi.

They all heard the banging, scraping noises on the hull.

"You are a dangerously quiet man, Engineer Tetsu," white suit said. "Potentially dangerous to yourself. Were we not professionals we might have given away to the urges of adrenaline and squeezed these stoppers. In that event there would have been no more Engineer Tetsu.

"You are hearing others of my crew transferring your external cargo. Where is the captain?"

"In the Mate's chair. Unconscious."

The white helmet nodded stiffly. "That is unfortunate. Captain Ota brought onboard some contraband. One assumes that only he is cognizant of its location. We cannot wait hours for him to awaken. Engineer Tetsu: pray escort us to his cabin. Number Three: remain here with the cutter. *Myrzha* Prithvi: do go and revive your captain. An injection . . . whatever you have to do."

"But—"

The white-suited shark had already begun moving away. It turned back. So did the stopper in its gauntleted hand. The stopper was a most sinister black. Prith nodded and went forward. The others went to the captain's cabin. The banging noises on the hull continued.

Naturally Captain Ota's cabin was locked.

"Engineer Tetsu, one assumes this cabin is coded to the captain's thumb or voice or both. Is there an override card?"

"Not that I know of, sir." Tetsu heard himself add that last word automatically, and wished he had not. Still, perhaps it was best.

"Before we open it with the cutter, Engineer Tetsu, is there—in your opinion—an electronic override? In the con, perhaps?"

"If . . . there is one, *Myrzha* Prithvi would know of it—probably."

"Secretive sort, your captain."

"Yes, sir."

Suddenly, the white spacesuit swung to Suzuki. "I have been remiss in my manners, computrician. What is your name?"

"Su-zuki," she said slowly, and couldn't help asking, "How did you know my function on *Suyari?*"

"First Mate said there were four aboard *Suyari*. The captain does not seem sufficiently stable to double as computer interfacer and maintner. The first mate does not seem to possess that sort of personality. Number Two: go to him and advise that we desire this lock open, now, or we shall be forced to employ the cutter."

Breaths were sucked in. Tetsu and Suzuki watched while white spacesuit stepped back to allow azure suit to pass. Walking awkwardly, clumping, azure suit went forward. Apprehension slithered in like a constrictor serpent and twined about the two *Suyari* crewmembers.

Presumably it would be necessary only to set the laser beam to its shortest range and burn a semicircle out of the captain's cabin hatch, at the latch. That seemed simple; however, no one quite breathed while any use of a cutter was made on a ship in space. Vacuum surrounded them, an inimical demon lusting for their very existence. One slip, one technical error on the part of tool or user, and the hull could be sliced open with the ease of cutting into zucchini. The consequences of that were unthinkable.

White suit resumed his explanation: "For an engineer also to be computrician is unusual—and indeed most unwise, on a ship of limited crewforce. Both talents might well be simultaneously required in entirely different onship locales."

Tetsu nodded while the golden-skinned woman stared at the invader, impressed. A *pirate!* And the language he chose to employ; the measured way he spoke . . . a *shark,* she reminded herself again, with incredulity. What had he been? What might he have become?

"Would you please now precede me back to our yellow-suited friend?"

And his politeness! A *pirate!*

As they paced along the corridors that on spaceships were called tunnels, Tetsu turned his head to one side to ask over his shoulder, "What—what sort of being is that in the yellow suit?"

"One with six limbs and an oddly placed visual

organ, obviously," the pirate said from behind him, and added no more.

Nor did Tetsu ask anything else. The exterior noises continued, the banging of the ghostly revenant come for Don Giovanni. The sounds were interiorly transmitted as eerie gonging sounds they all knew originated on *Suyari*'s hull. The ship bristled with a sort of spacegoing Spanish moss: long flexible cables made rigid by braces between them and the variable charge running through them. They trailed back from the ship to make it resemble some monster squid of the spaceways. To the end of each cable was attached a crate. Some were big enough to serve as small houses. None was so small as *Suyari*'s con-cabin. Each contained a piece of heavy equipment, factory fresh. In space, such parasitic trailing appurtenances had neither weight nor drag. Unless it had a nice small but rich cargo it carried entirely interiorly, a merchanter on a run between the stars was no pretty sight. Even more than a squid, it resembled a big ungainly bird that had flown through even bigger cobwebs laden with insects and had flown on, untidily festooned and trailing all that detritus.

Now, Tetsu and Suzuki knew, cable linkages were being detached from their *Suyari* and transferred to receptacles mounted on the hull of the sharkship. Assuming at least two for that chore and another standing by inside the ship, white suit's crew must include at least six persons.

No, make that individuals. Surely no *person* was standing there so silently and unpleasantly menacing in that yellow spacesuit made for a giant!

Suzuki and Tetsu stayed well away from it while they waited the few minutes necessary for Prithvi to find the proper cassette. He did, and inserted it. SIPACUM took note and a tiny part of its capability released every lock on *Suyari*.

The white-suited pirate ushered everyone into the captain's cabin. It was quite small, a serviceable spot of privacy on a business ship designed to devote all possible space to the double-P engines, internal systemry, and cargo holds. Their captor bade the three crewmembers of *Suyari* to sit side by side on their captain's bunk. He directed his Number Two to go and relieve Number Three of its—yes, he said *its!*—cutter and bid it bring the captain along.

Then the pirate began searching. No one knew what he sought.

It did not take long. The captain's standard old yellow go-bag still held a few items and the pirate emptied them out. It was obvious that the bag remained heavy. In a fine show of confidence—or contempt for his captives?—the shark in the white spacesuit holstered his stopper and snicked his suit-knife free. He knifed open the base of the go-bag. They watched him withdraw a flat packet almost precisely the size of a human hand. The simple fold-over was of soft, opaque plastic. He unfolded it, peered in, shook it, nodded, and refolded it. The three crewmembers stared.

"TZ," they were told, while he kneaded the bag. "You know it?"

Engineer and first mate frowned; ship's computrician nodded.

"Very illegal," she said. "Dangerous; very expensive and very profitable. Tetrazombase."

"One hopes that you have not been made forcibly acquainted with the foul substance."

Suzuki shook her head in a jerk. "No!"

"A substance everywhere illegal," the faceless pirate said, "inasmuch as no person would take it willingly. Therefore it is to be employed only on the unwilling. As the name implies, it makes the recipient take on the appearance and some attributes of a *zombi*. That's an ancient word of Homeworld and has unknown linguistic origin—it means the walking dead. A human automaton or a badly programmed robot, you see. Your external cargo is telecybernetic mining equipment.

Heavy machinery for those poor lonely pnamprum miners on the fourth satellite of Murph. This," he said, hefting the bag, "is worth about as much as two-thirds of the crates outside—combined. It is true that your captain's backer is in financial trouble, but it is also true that your captain knows that he is hauling this evil substance. Nor did he object to transporting it, for a percentage."

He had reclipped the knife to his suit. Now he opened the suit's knapsack and slipped in the folded little plastic bag.

"Now the tetrazombase is where it belongs—in the hands of a manifestly evil man! In which case we shall not bother to look into your holds. Whatever is there will pay for your trip, surely, and we are not after all pigs—ah."

The alien was entering, half-walking and half-dragging the captain. The paunchy fellow with the side-worn single braid was only partially recovered from the nerve-paralyzing effect of Prith's stopper. He came to life at sight of the crowd in his cabin—and the ruined go-bag. A wordless little cry escaped him and his elbow slammed back to rob the impossibly tall alien in the yellow suit of its grip and its breath. Captain Ota glared wide-eyed at the white spacesuit, and the business end of the tube pointed at his chest. If it occurred to him that this seemed his day for being helpless at the wrong end of a stopper, the thought did not make him philosophic.

With his stopper persuading the captain against further unwise moves, the pirate made a gesture that stayed the alien from retaliating.

"You *knew* I had it! You've taken it!"

"Correct, Captain ´Ota, both times. Consider. You are a respectable though hardly likable merchant-ship's master, while it is telemetrically obvious that I am a pariah, an unclean untouchable, a bloody vicious murdering *pirate*. Ptui." All of them heard the tone of suave amusement as white suit pronounced the satanic litany. "You have no business with TZ, Captain Ota. Obviously such an outlaw as I, however—"

"You filthy rotten sisterslicer! I *need* that! I need the income it will bring, the stells—" Ota was spluttering, his face dark and eyes bulging. Yet he could not attack the pirate and it was always safer to let such a flainer revile himself. Helpless, therefore, Ota turned his rage on his crew. "You flaining *bastards!* You will never work again! *None* of you! You—you *mutineers!* MU-TINY! I'll see you all minus your *eyes!*" He spat the threat of that barbaric punishment for theft with such venom that had he been a cobra they might have lost their eyes then and there.

Tetsu looked nervous unto fright. Suzuki stared grimly at her captain. She who knew about tetrazombase knew also some insouciance, some control. Prith said, "Captain, Suki had absolutely nothing to do with—"

"That cow!" Ota exploded. He was obviously beyond reason and restraint—other than that of self-preservation, for still he restrained himself from attacking the real villains. "So *val*uable in her speciality she wouldn't even share a bit of my bunk now and again. No no—you were all in on it! And you know that's what will be believed before any board of inquiry, you rotten mutinous flainers! I'll see you all *eyeless!"*

"That," the white-suited pirate said quietly, calmly, "is a threat that is most personally abhorrent to me, Ota, you cowardly venal little swine."

His thumb moved on the setting of his stopper and calmly, quietly, he squeezed. Captain Ota made only the beginning of an outcry. There was, briefly and horribly, the aroma of cooking. Then Ota was no longer present, save as minuscule components. The odor was not pleasant. It never was, when a man was fried by a microwave projector set on Three, and vaporized within seconds.

The pirate in the pale blue spacesuit had started

sharply, but said nothing and made no further move. The others, seated in a forlorn little row on the captain's bunk, resembled chastised students in a disciplinarian's school. They stared. Perhaps Suzuki and Prithvi were trying to measure time and distance, considering a jump at the shark before he turned his stopper on them. Tetsu was beyond thinking.

The white-suited pirate gestured to his companions, who held stopper and cutter. *Suyari*'s seated crew understood. Holstering his weapon, the killer paced to the captain's bedside comm. He buttoned it to life.

"Record," he bade the comm, which he obviously knew was linked to SIPACUM. A button flashed yellow then green and stayed green.

At last Suzuki said, "It . . . it's a visual acknowledgment. That flasher means it is standing by to record." She wondered whether this strangest of faceless men had a fully vocalized computer on his ship. Was he so successful, so aesthetic? Had he conferred with a visual program before intersecting *Suyari*'s course? Who might such a man choose as personification of a mentor-counselor program?

He nodded and thanked her before speaking clearly into the comm.

"I have just fried Captain Ota, a swine who has been stealing from his crew and who reviled his computrician in my presence for her refusal to spread for him. I do not applaud his taste, but I do hers. The spaceways and this crew are better by far with Captain Ota having joined his doubtless dishonorable ancestors —all pigs and small yellow she-dogs. Evil pirate out."

He buttoned off the comm and favored the shocked trio with another of his astonishing little bows. He might almost have been a courtier in the throneroom of one of the monarchic planets. His voice and demeanor had continued level and quiet before, during, and after the slaying of Ota.

"There. You three are clear. Evil pirate came onboard and did a good deed: he murdered the captain.

I made no mention of *this,*" he said, slapping his suit-slung bag, "and if you are wise you will not either. If one of you would like a lasting bruise to show Murph-side authority, handle its infliction yourself. Any such marks, obviously, would fade long before you reach your destination. You should, however, be fully in the clear. I shall now put a stop to my outside operations. Whatever remains is yours to carry on to Murphstation. It is my hope that you all remain on *Suyari*—with you as master, Acting Captain Prithvi. It may be of interest to you to know that this ship's backer is in turn backed by T.M.S.M. Company, of Murph. My ship shall not again detain *Suyari* . . . unless of course it comes to my attention that none of you is longer aboard, and opportunity arises."

"Name—name of Gri," Prithvi said. "Who are you?"

"Ah, you swear by the god of Resh. Did you know that Gri's absolutely and totally evil old retired high priest Sicuan, with his venal son Chulucan, are no more? A gift to the spaceways—like Ota's demise! My name is Corundum, Captain Prithvi, Corundum; and Corundum now departs your ship. Best wishes for an uneventful continuance of your run to Murph."

"Th-that was c-cold-blooded murder," Tetsu said, and he was shaking.

"Not quite. Corundum's blood was heated by Ota's threat to have you convicted and deprived of your eyes. Corundum liked the ones he was born with better than these optics he has now worn for some years. Sometimes they itch, or seem to, and the center of vision is dead ahead, which is wrong; you see just a bit more clearly to the side, as you must know by seeing distant stars just a bit better by not quite looking at them. In hot blood or cold, however, Ota's is a death that you will long appreciate."

The three crewmembers stared at him from the bunk of their late captain.

He touched the black handle of his stopper. "This will be left in the airlock. It is Corundum's suggestion that you leave it there if possible, so that you may pretend it and Number Two's were left for you. As they will be. Your own were of course sucked out when you opened the hatch for us. Now of course you will facilitate our departure, for should we become trapped in the airlock we should merely have to cut our way out. Or, worse still, back in." Again that satiric amusement freighted his tone.

Prithvi nodded. "Of course, Captain Corundum. May we rise now?"

"Do."

As they trekked to the airlock, Prithvi asked, "Captain Corundum . . . once you gave your name, you referred to yourself only in the second person. Do you always speak so?"

"Yes. I also lie shamelessly."

After a moment, Prithvi chuckled. A good man, Prith of Resh. Had Corundum need for a crewmember, he might well converse with the fellow. Still, one so bold and decisive might well be unhappy on *Firedancer*, and, too, might not be onboard long.

Less than five minutes later the three invaders had departed *Suyari*.

Three people were left to take the ship on to Murph, to wonder about the unaccountable alien in the yellow suit even while they got their stories together so that they were one, and to think and talk about Captain Corundum for the rest of their lives.

Outside, the unlikely pirate saw to the completion of the transfer, in progress, of a hut-size crate's towing cable to *Firedancer*'s external cargo attachments. Nine such crates remained indecorously attached to *Suyari*. Two spacesuited figures—an orange and a pale turquoise—had been working at the transfer. They were happy to call it off and join their three cohorts at *Firedancer*'s airlock. It was equipped with something Corundum had read about: he pushed the doorbell, in a code-sequence. The hatch swung noiselessly open.

The pirates entered their ship.

2

CORUNDUM: *an esp. hard mineral of the composition Al_2O_3, forming the valuable gemstones ruby and sapphire. The massive, abrasive, non-transparent forms are known as emery.*

Universal Edutapes

Quite comfortable in the spacesuit and with full vision, Corundum went directly to the con-cabin, which he referred to as the "bridge." In less than three minutes he was assured that all systems were just fine and so was the situation. With his right gauntlet in his left hand, he slipped a course command cassette into the slot. The cassette was not commercially available, though many were. This one had been programmed by Corundum and a woman he still regretted losing.

The cassette was tailored to his own habits and use, and thus to the present situation. It bade SIPACUM (which he called Jinni and which was fully cognizant of their situation with regard to *Suyari* and space itself) to break off, ease away from *Suyari,* move to a safe distance for tachyon conversion, prepare for subspace entry, and sound a fifty-second warning.

Manually and vocally, he also set SIPACUM/Jinni to plotting a subspace course for the vicinity of the fourth moon of the planet called Murph.

Captain Corundum returned to the others in time to see the yellow spacesuit slide down Hing's body.

The Saipese was nearly the same color as the suit and was far from 215 or even 200 sems in height. Hing stood about 175 and his two brown eyes and two gold-hued arms were in the usual places. He was strictly a Galactic, born and raised on Saiping.

Hing's TP "eye" relayed its image to the self-lit screen built inside the chest of the gigantic headless suit. The extra arms were controlled by a separate telepresence which Hing operated most expertly indeed. The suit served its purpose. It was intended to add a bit more menace and mystique and thus fear to in-space boardings. No four-armed beings had yet been encountered among the hundreds of contacted and/or colonized planets. Thus far.

Stripped to a temp-controlled coolsuit of Ming blue, tight as the skin of youth, Hing grinned at his ingenious captain. The suit and its use were Corundum's concept. It had been made meticulously to order by a talented individual on Jahpur. He was, regrettably, no longer alive.

Bearcat was already peeling his turquoise suit and Sakbir his orange one.

Corundum's newest associate was far less experienced and thus slower at unsuiting. The helmet came free to reveal the small, well-molded head of an astonishingly pale woman whose short straight hair could not be real; it was the almost white of a distant GO sun. Until Corundum had brought her aboard, none of his crew had ever seen anyone of such hue with (undyed) hair so nearly achromatic. Nor, computer-link had informed them, had 99.789 percent of all the people of the galaxy—including the small (estimated) populace of her planet. The skin and hair colors were real.

No less startling were her eyes, and even more so when one knew they were her own, and genetically unadjusted at that. They were lighter than her spacesuit. Their light gray showed only a hint of blue. No such eyes had been seen in the galaxy since the destruction of the majority and absorption of the rest of such a race on Homeworld, centuries and centuries ago. The galaxy was bronze, brown, and browner, and a few who could be called yellow or almost-black. The color of eyes was brown. The color of hair was black, though now and then a dark brown turned up.

When the vast majority of the peoples of Homeworld-once-Earth had seized the planet and gone into space as Galactics, speaking Erts, they had done a thorough job of destroying the old ruling minority and overwhelming its genetic lesser pigmentation. Even Universal Edutapes did not contain the word *Caucasian.*

Corundum knew that the colors of the hair, eyes, and skin of this unwrinkled and sparsely haired woman were real and inborn. So did the Accord that Protected her "backward" planet. So did the slaver who had snatched her from it and sold her on Resh.

Corundum also knew her pride. No one offered to help as she struggled to unsuit. She was militant about that. (*Firedancer*'s twitchy lurch was tiny and not even the new crewmember staggered. All knew that they had just moved free of the other ship—incidentally freeing it.)

At last the sky-blue suit dropped. Its wearer was revealed as short, compactly lean, and definitely female. Obviously firm of skin and well-toned muscle. In a tight gray breast-band rather than bra or bandeau, and skimpy briefs of the same unattractive gray. She stepped out of the suit. Her muscular, taut-skinned legs showed no sign of jiggle. Her calves were outstanding, perhaps overdeveloped. That was a tendency of the calves of anyone from a high-gravity planet. Their thighs ranged from unusually rounded to massive. The pale ones just revealed were not massive.

"You did well, Janja," Corundum said. Both he and the (quite young, both in appearance and reality) woman ignored the appreciative stares given her by the other crewmembers of *Firedancer.*

She shrugged, then flipped her fingers in the gesture she had learned from *them:* those not of her planet. The gesture meant "so what" or "I don't care" or "beats me" or "no use talking about that," and other things.

"My first time," she said. "I did nothing but stand around in that Hing-size suit and be the mysterious Number Two, silent and inactive. The filter made my voice sound awful, but if that Prithvi has any sense, he knows I'm a woman." She heaved a sigh, crossing her arms to rub them. "I suppose I'm glad that nothing else was necessary. Should I mention that you are still fully suited and faceless, Captain?"

It was their agreement that in the presence of others she called him only captain, or Corundum. Just six days-standard ago she had come up with a perfectly awful nickname for him—which Corundum rather liked. It was better than Ruby, or Sapphire, or even Blue-eyes. And certainly preferable to Dum-dum. He knew he was called that, though never within his hearing.

"Corundum is comfortable," he said from within his white spacesuit. "That ship has no converter and therefore no subspace capability. Thus it is a long, long run from Murph. We shall be there in a few days. Or rather at its fourth satellite, tastelessly named Dot. One fears that places us a good while still from vacation and celebration—which we shall *not* take on Murph! But then it will be the better for our anticipation." He patted his suit-bag with a gauntleted hand. "Bearcat, Sakbir: here is approximately two kilos of tetrazombase."

The smile in his voice prompted Hing to ask, "Whose is it, Captain?"

"Ship's shares," Corundum said, and watched the flashing of teeth in delighted smiles. "Perhaps we can analyze it before we reach a buyer, Sakbir?"

"Immediately, Captain!"

"Good, good. Hing, you charming four-armed mysterious alien, you, do please go and tend the con. Subspace entry after fifty-second warning; Jinni is plotting course. There is both a pulsar and a collapstar to avoid between here and Murph. We are now honest but poor merchants, hauling needed equipment to those needy pnamprum grubbers on Dot. Corundum shall unsuit in his cabin. Identity Beta, comrades, if need arises. Janja?"

The others—except for Hing—gazed after the two. One lithe and short and nigh naked, the other tall and baggy-bulky in the gleaming white coverall. Corundum's ungauntleted hand moved easily and without pressure to her buttock, a taut oval of moving muscle hard as the front of his—flexed—thigh. Sakbir licked his full lips.

"So. Your first boarding, Janja. Your first act of piracy, that impossibility of the spaceways. Now you *merit* being called outlaw, and deserve your position on the wanted list. And was it exciting?"

"Of course! You know that, my dear. Here, get your hand out of there—at least while you're suited up!"

"What an inducement to unsuit! And was Milady Janja disappointed that all was so routine, so dull?"

He's asking for compliments on his planning and handling, Janja thought, for she felt or *cherm*ed it from him.

She could not read minds, Janja whose people were not truly human. But she had the *cherm*ing, the *feel*ing of emotion and intents, of others. It was more than *they* had, those she thought of as the Thingmakers. A month (thirty twenty-five-hour days-standard) with Corundum had heightened her ability where he was concerned. Otherwise the hard toughness of corundum, with a hardness of nine to diamond's ten, made it difficult to work. They shared a common enemy and the common goal: Jonuta's destruction. Their eventful meeting had taken place in a spacefarers' watering hole on Franji. There Janja had used him, meanwhile fascinating him with her looks and her ruthless resourcefulness. He had impressed her with his own surpassing resourcefulness, quick thinking-unto-action, and enormous courtly charm. Since then they had also shared life, his cabin, and his bed.

Janja of Aglaya was Corundum's woman, and more. And perhaps less.

She was answering his question: "Perhaps, but not truly. A battle would have been their error, and ours. I was impressed with the smoothness of the operation. I *am* impressed, evil pirate."

Behind her brow, she frowned. *But why did you kill that man?—and how easily, coolly you did it! How long before I bring up that subject—murder? How long before you, my ally and my mentor and my lover with that lovely ever-ready slicer of yours, disrupt my infatuation and force me to find you abhorrent?*

And then what?

He thumbed the door of his cabin, said, "Open, sesame," was ignored, and with a chuckle he undogged his helmet and spun the seal.

She took the helmet from him; a man who was very dark even in a galaxy of dark peoples. Black hair hung in waves nearly to his shoulders, framing a nose that was large; a beak. It was a lean face, with sensuous lips. The eyes were arresting, and more. Without the huge black contact lenses he had affected the night of their meeting, his eyes were a blue that was far more striking than hers, with her coloration. They were sapphire eyes; royal blue eyes, the more startling and *blue* against his dark hair and skin.

Of course that was by his choice. They could have

been brown. They were not his eyes. That is, they were his, but they were not *eyes.*

This time he spoke the code-phrase in his own quiet, medium-range voice without the electronic distorter built into the suit's speaker. The door of his cabin recognized him and opened.

"Ah, the wonders of technology," he said, with his peculiar urbane and over-sophisticated air of amusement and satire. His sweeping gesture, an ancient courtier's, bade her enter before him.

Janja did.

Still she marveled at the fantastic opulence of this man's shipboard home. He was a pirate, lean and seemingly ascetic while courtly in his far-out-of-fashion way. He wore unrelieved black—except for the spacesuit, since a black suit in space would have been stupid. But his cabin!

She remembered the first time she had seen it, a month ago shortly after their hurried departure from Franji and then Franjistation, and she tried to see it that way again, as if for the first time. (The year or so since her kidnap and enslavement now seemed a decade. Her month with Corundum seemed a year—in the most positive way.)

On her third day aboard *Firedancer* she had risen from his bed, naked, to examine his cabin. . . .

One three-meter-long wall—never a *bulkhead,* as the bed was not a *bunk*—was a hologram of what he told her was a medieval tapestry. It was alive with color. With animals and richly dressed (and poorly painted) people and flora, the vista seemed to stretch away a kilometer. That wall commanded one's attention on entering the cabin, and the spacious feeling was there to stay.

The adjacent wall continued the illusion. To Janja of ever-warm Aglaya it was at once beautiful and eerie, gaze-demanding and frightening. The title was the subject: Icebergs.

She had never seen icebergs and never dreamed of

their existence. She still had yet to see snow. The beautifully blended colors of this wall were many, and hardly chill, so that somehow this oddly hued, jagged mass rising out of water seemed not too harsh and cold. It seemed to be stone. It was not. The artist was Frederick Edwin Church—a most strange and unfamiliar name, and without I.D. numbers! He had painted the scene centuries and centuries ago on Homeworld in a year then designated as 1861. And no, Corundum's researches indicated that icebergs had never truly looked so beautiful, even at sunset, all in yellow and gold and pink and lavender and rose and purple and blue and . . .

A *pirate!*

This scene, too, stretched away for kloms and kloms —kilometers and kilometers. Its shadows and depth were ghostlike and magnificent. Here was majesty, and no person had had anything to do with its creation. (Yet one had, for this was a painting; not reality but human fancy and vision.) Janja could stare at *Icebergs*. Three meters long by 215 sems tall, it could become the universe. Staring, she felt a part of it. Losing herself in it. Joining it; going away into it. Shudder and fear it even while loving it, with a feeling close to reverence.

To promote a feeling of security, the wall a meter or so from the foot of the (large! firm!) bed-not-bunk was covered with cork of a warm deep gold hue. Corundum had hung it with various smaller holograms made from paintings.

He had to tell her what that one was—a "horse." And that strange city of domes, that was most ancient indeed, he told her, and had been called "Al-Madinah." There were twenty-one "Medinahs" now, on twenty planets, but that one was gone. And that ferocious-looking man sitting his "horse" atop a hill and gazing out across a vista that ran out to meet a planetary horizon. That was Jenghiz or Chengiss Khan, he told her; *Jen*-ggis, staring at a place he would conquer.

It had been called Khitai and Cathay then, China much later, on that cerulean-sky planet, which was Homeworld. Khan was about the color of Hing, Janja noticed.

The painter of this beautifully idealized space scene —a woman and a man striding in lockstep across planets—was an artist who signed itself only "Jean." Homeworld, Corundum said; twenty-second century. Its title was *Oneness*. From conquest to oneness.

And there was this strange thing in heavy shades of red, yet not harsh reds. Its title was *In the Underworld.* A man and a woman—she with yellow hair and pale skin!—had their backs to the viewer. Neither wore much. The man was brandishing a rather short sword. They faced a giant *thing,* a hairless, massive, winged, horned being that Corundum said was fanciful. A demon, or shaitan. (Who?—An ancient embodiment of evil.—Oh.) The woman's legs could have been copied from Janja's: solid-looking with overdeveloped calves like smoothly doubled fists beneath the skin.

Why that one? she had asked. It was so menacing.

"Because hers are the most magnificent legs and posterior Corundum has ever seen," Corundum told her, and after a while she chuckled. Why not? That was a reason, and it was his cabin, his home in space.

Here was another by the same long-dead artist, with the single name "Boris." It was called *Primeval Princess.* Again it showed a nearly naked woman. Again she was blond. This one faced the viewer in majesty, staring coldly *down* at the viewer from the heights of her beauty. She had a hand on each of two perfectly horrible lizard-monster-things that flanked her. Various pieces of entwining metal jewelry visibly cut into her flesh. She was beautiful and she was imperiousness itself; a face that looked down upon the universe in general.

Why this one? (That stare, Janja thought, would make her nervous. Self-conscious. And the beasts looked ready to come slithering out of the painting.)

"Because she is a magnificent and desirable woman and Corundum is a man," Corundum told her. "And now she reminds me of you."

(Janja had some understanding of that, now. Then, that third night, she had reacted with incredulity and some scorn.)

"Her? With those big meaty thighs and those great sacs on her chest? That thick waist? How can you say so?"

"I can say so. She is that artist's concept of the ideal —and *not* thick-waisted! She comes close to Corundum's. You approach perfection, Janja; *she* is idealism."

"*Male* idealism."

He finger-flipped. "No fine sub-ancient Greek athlete ever looked as good as that same artist painted men." Before she could ask the meaning of "Greek," he went on, "This is Corundum's home. You may have noticed that Corundum is male."

The sound that came up from her throat united a purr and a chuckle. She had noticed, yes. He gave off more male *feeling* than anyone since Jonuta, whom she wanted only to kill. She considered, staring at the meter-tall painting in golds and other connected hues, with that weird yellow foliage behind the—behind H.R.H. Primeval Princess.

"And do you think you would like me so . . . so . . ."

"Imperious," he provided, from just behind her.

"Haughty and almost sneering, looking *down,*" Janja finished.

"Imperious," he repeated. "Perhaps. How can one be sure? Corundum likes the work. It is intensely sensuous, to a definite male who definitely loves definite females. I may be a bit in love with her."

A *pirate!*

"And with this one's—posterior and legs." Almost she touched the full firm-looking backside of the blond in the other painting.

"And yours, Milady Janja."

She poked it back a little and wiggled it, just a little,

but he was not that close behind her, and chose not to respond. *I hope I am not expected to twine too-tight metal jewelry about my arms and legs,* she mused. "You are not understandable, Corundum."

"Perhaps my name should be Conundrum? Of course I am not, Milady Janja. Corundum is unique, and no one-sided fictional creation. Corundum is a mix. We would not accept many of the people we know personally, if they were characters in fiction, because they are too many-faceted. Corundum is many things and belongs only to Corundum."

"Sapphire, and ruby, and emery."

"Yes. Though none of those has the softness of estheticism that you know is in me."

Yes, she did. A *pirate!* "And Corundum answers . . . does he answer only to himself?"

"He does."

"Oh," said willful Janja who had been enslaved and bloodily freed herself, "I do like that!"

He was close behind her as she examined another painting, a long one. "Hmm. Is this on old Homeworld, too? All in blues and those weird greens?"

"No." His voice was even more quiet as he looked over her shoulder at the landscape she regarded. "No. That is a scene on a small planet named Meccah, and it was painted only thirteen years ago."

"It is lovely. Why is it so—flat?"

He chuckled. "It is a painting, Milady Janja. That is the original. A painting. Hand and oils on canvas. No computer, no laser. It is not a hologram or a holo-projection. Its depth is its own; the artist's."

"It is beautiful and I would like to be there." Janja was staring at it and into it. It bore no title and was signed with the single word or name "al-Addin."

"Now?"

"No," Janja said, and put back a hand to touch the man in black. "Not quite now. It is lovely and inviting and yet it makes me . . . uncomfortable. Doesn't it you?"

"In a way. Only in a way." He was close behind her and his hands came onto her hips.

"Meccah," she murmured, not handling the little growl-sound well at all. "Do you think it has changed a great deal, in thirteen years?"

"I know that it has changed, but very little," he said, only just loudly enough to be heard. "And that area has changed even less."

"You *know* that."

"Yes. I own that land. It is Corundum's land. Corundum will not allow it to be changed. The mineral rights under it might be enough to buy everyone on Meccah. They are not for sale."

"Everyone on Meccah?"

"No. The mineral rights. Many are for sale on Meccah, and everywhere else along the spaceways."

"Oh. Mineral . . . oh." She did not have *their* language completely, yet. She had many words and phrases yet to learn. "Valuable things in the ground. Platinum? Oil? Gold?"

"No. Corundum."

"Oh! Rubies and sapphires. And emery."

"Yes. Corundum."

"And it is yours and you will not sell it," she said in delight, standing in his cabin with him behind her, his hands on her, only three days-standard after their violent meeting in the Parallax Lounge on Franji.

"Pos," he said; the standard word of assent and agreement.

"Now I know that you are sentimental and probably I know where you are from. You bought the picture from the artist itself? You know it, the artist? Is it a woman or a man?"

"Pos. I know him."

From behind, his fingers were on her breasts and her breasts were naked under his fingers and his fingers were moving. Three days after their meeting, she remembered the first time she had felt them there. A few hours after their meeting! She had been encased in shining silver then, a skinnTite over which she wore a little skirt and bandeau, both of a deep red. Burgundy, he called it, the cultured Corundum. The word was unknown to her, then.

She had rushed off the street of Franji's capital and hurled herself against the first man she saw, a stranger. Corundum. She had no idea who he was. He was standing conveniently, and he wore a sidearm that instantly gave her an idea. She had embraced him and pretended to need rescue from Jonuta's man Srih. Srih had not spotted her, for she was disguised. She had called out to him, then run, knowing he would follow. Srih followed. He entered the Parallax Lounge behind her. Clinging to this black-clad stranger she had cleverly drawn the stopper he wore on his left hip, pivoted, whirled, and fried Srih. All in less than a minute.

Srih was the murderer of Tarkij. Tarkij, with whom she would have spent the rest of her life on peaceful, "Protected" Aglaya. Srih and Jonuta's Jarp crewmember, Sweetface, had snatched her off Aglaya. She wanted Jonuta. That was her purpose now, her Mission.

She had begun. Srih was dead.

The charming Corundum had bade her keep his pistol and urged her to depart the Parallax. He joined her in an electricab. They quickly discovered their shared enmity for Jonuta, and their fascination with each other. (And possible use to each other? Best not to think about that.) Corundum suggested immediate departure from Franji.

"Since you are most definitely female and Corundum male, however, you may well question the motivation. My ship *Firedancer* is above, docked at Franjistation. If Jonuta is onplanet, he will soon be warned, and seeking you. Best to leave now, and believe that

another and better opportunity will present itself. If you have valuable possessions here, Corundum will happily replace them in honor of these two salutary occasions."

Janja was less grim than she had been in a year. Inside she was smiling, perhaps even grinning. What great good fortune to have run into this courtly co-enemy of Jonuta! Question his motives? No. She handed him back his stopper, which had now served doubly as a symbol.

She asked, "Two great occasions, Corundum?"

"Two, yes. The occasion of the entirely timely demise of Srih, left hand of 'Captain Cautious'—Jonuta! And the equally felicitous occasion of our meeting, Janja."

Janja's *cherm*ing told her that what he said was precisely what he felt. Along with sexual desire for her, of course. She decided to respond.

He had drawn her to him then, in the cab, and she had responded, liking it and the way he did it. A few hours later they were in space and his hands were on her breasts, from behind. She did not stiffen at the intimate touch. She shared his yearning . . . and she had a Mission.

And besides, Janja was excited. She had killed, and found this man, and fled. She was free, with a friend and ally—who was a fascinating and more than attractive man.

The fingers of that friend and ally were moving on her breasts. The hands were not harsh, and not arrogantly possessive. That was good and better than good. Janja liked it and she appreciated it. During her months as slave of Sicuan and Chulucan, she had received no tenderness. None. She had been *used*.

Now she made tiny throaty noises and let herself soften, for Corundum. She had *decided*.

That first time they had not got around to taking off all their clothes for quite some time. But by then they had long been horizontal and were panting and practically tearing at each other.

Three days later she gave close examination to his cabin, and asked questions, and again his hands were cupping her breasts from behind. This time she was naked. Once again she was beginning to feel that combination of happy languor and excitation, need. Already she had felt it—and removed it temporarily—with him, eight times in three days. What a lover he was! What wonderful patience the man had; how he loved to please a woman! And he knew how.

"Is the artist, this al-Addin . . . handsome? Young? Uhhh . . ."

His fingers were scissoring her nipples with just the right pressure, making them grow, pressing, pressing. She squirmed and pushed back against him. Her naked bottom found his groin, found a firmness there that was growing, becoming a hardness.

"Is he handsome?" she repeated, staving it off a little, gazing at the painting of Meccah through lowering lashes like a lace veil. Her arousal was a lovely pink mist rising around her.

"No," he said very quietly, very close to her ear. "Neither handsome nor young. Perhaps he was, thirteen years ago. What is young?"

"He lives, still? Is he alive—uh!—Cor-uhnn-dummm?"

A long silence; a long sigh. He was pushing her tight breasts upward, his hands a warm living bandeau. "No," he said very very softly. "I believe that he is dead. As a painter, I believe he is dead."

That was cryptic and aroused her curiosity. Her mind was aroused, but . . . her nipples were burning tight knots and a hard hot bar was pressing at her from behind, inveigling itself unassisted between the tight ovals of her buttocks and she did not want it that way from Corundum, not Chulucan's preferred way of . . . *using* a woman, ignoring her femaleness in favor of that orifice she had in common with his sex. Janja did not want Corundum to enter her there, not unless *she* decided.

Suddenly she turned to him. Her eyes were excited. "Corundum, who—"

His mouth closed hers. His mouth and tongue and hands changed her excitement to the purely sexual. His tongue explored her mouth and she met it with hers. Painting and artist were forgotten as her hips writhed involuntarily.

They went at each other with mouths and tongues and hands and fingers and lurching, writhing bodies. They went at each other's mouth, and buttocks and their cleavage, and at each other's genitals. They wallowed on the unlikely: a carpet on the floor of a cabin of a spaceship moving at thousands and thousands of kloms per second. They wallowed and sucked and chewed and the seemingly sprawlingly spacious cabin grew warm. They panted and moaned and she had an iron bar of penis in her and two fingers, all at once. She clutched at him and hunched to those three probes. There were no frigid women on Aglaya. Aglaya was not a selfish planet of selfish men. Both sexes were circumcised, on Aglaya. The clitoris was not buried in a sheath, on Aglaya, but freed, bared to attract and excite and receive direct attention. There were no frigid women of Aglaya.

And Corundum knew what he was doing, loved what he was doing and what she was doing, and they both did it well. She did not hold back her cries. It was good that he liked them and said so. Restraint and reserve lay beside the bed with their clothing. He was in deep, with that iron bar *they* called a "slicer," slicing her, and within her his two fingers moved in the adjacent channel to heighten her arousal and her delight. He was striving ever for more depth and so was she, bucking, upthrusting.

Furthermore, he came in her like a cannon and like a boy in need of solace.

She liked that very much, and the fact that he did not try to cover up his explosive orgasms and instant weakness. It was . . . gratifying. She held him to her, in her. She stroked him while he gasped and valiantly kept his full weight off her for he was a more valiant and gentlemanly lover than anyone in that medieval tapestry. As if he were heavy, this Corundum who looked forty and must be older and who sliced—the current euphemism for fucked—like a boy, though longer. She liked that very much, too.

I deserve it. There's no pun in saying that I have it coming.

She did deserve it, after that rapacious flainer Jonuta and his raping bastards Arel and Srih and those raping flainers Chulucan and wizened evil old Sicuan—former High Priest of Gri for all Resh!

Sicuan, Chulucan, their slavemaster—and Srih. Dead. She had slain them, one by one. *They* had taught her to kill, and instilled in her the rage. Now *they* wanted her, as a criminal. Oh, she was wanted, Janja of Aglaya was. But not nearly so much as Corundum the pirate was wanted, or Jonuta the slaver!

Before Corundum, her first and last truly and totally voluntary and enjoyable sex had been with Tarkij, her Promised. Then Jonuta's spaceboat had come down, though neither of the lovers on the Aglayan savannah knew what a spaceboat was. Tarkij and Janja did not know what a stopper was, either. Srih had unnecessarily shot Tarkij with his stopper on the third setting. Then she had been taken, unconscious, up to Jonuta's *Coronet.* She had not known then what a coronet was, or a spaceship—or space, for the matter of that.

After that had come the horror and pain and use.

Months and months of it, months that seemed years. And escape at last, because she was Janja, worthy of Aglii and worthy of Aglaya; worthy of the spaceways! Then had come knowledge, her days in the library dredging Retrieval like a manic fisherman dredging a river's depths. A torrent of information inundated her brain. And then Corundum.

A *pirate!*

Three days later she lay beneath him and held him, on her and in her, and she welcomed his weight. She told him so. He told her that he welcomed hers, on him.

Now a month had passed and Janja was truly a pirate, entering the fantastic opulence of his cabin: his home on *Firedancer,* which was now Janja's home.

"Scientists who study such things say that we are excited after danger, and that the excitement is sexual," he said.

"They are right," she said, low and throat-thick.

"Perhaps that is a partial explanation for our human history of post-battle raping."

"They are right," she said again. "I hated it when you stood and so coldly killed that pitiful sponge of a man. But I understand it and I am not civilized and so do not have to pretend horror." She whirled. "Get out of that spacesuit, Emery!"

"Ah. You sound imperious, Primeval Princess."

"And you sound sarcastic! Strip, evil murdering pirate, or I'll loose my lizard-monsters on you!"

She elevated brow and chin while lowering her eyelids, in the manner of the Primeval Princess he "might be a bit in love with." With a jerk she tore the dull binder from her chest. She gasped at the pain and wonder and wondrous pain of the sudden freeing of her breasts. Warheads, *they* called them. *They* had names for everything; euphemisms. Warheads and slicers and slicing. She was a *cake,* with a *stash,* and into it a man put his *slicer* to cut a *slice.*

She clamped her hands to her warheads. She saw his stare and knew her nipples had been too long warm and compressed and were celebrating their release into coolth by erecting. Aureoles became goosepimply and smaller, feeding into the nipples they surrounded. They were subcutaned a pale lavender color, because it pleased him. The same nonpermanent subcutaneous dye turned her lips the same exotic hue.

She stood as tall as she could and gazed imperiously and rose onto her toes to tauten her calves and bulge them because he loved them. Her pubis bulged too, against the skimpy gray briefs.

Corundum stared at her with those glittering, eerily blue implanted optics that were not eyes, and Janja knew why he had slain Ota. *They* called Aglaya a "barbarian" planet because it was not only pre-technological but pre-steel—and *they* punished several major crimes by blinding. It was accomplished painlessly. They were *civilized* barbarians!

Still, the concept of such a cool, easy killing had not occurred to her. She had slain to escape death, and for Tarkij, dead Tarkij. She was not civilized. The retrieval encyclopedic display she had accessed had told her so. Had she been civilized, one of *them,* she'd have known about casual murder. Janja had learned to kill, since *they* dragged her among them. *They* had hurt her and taught her and used her and hurt her and killed Janjaheriohir of Aglaya, so that now she was reborn, partially, as Janja of *them.* A new Galactic who was as alien, though *they* did not know it, as a Jarp. But she had slain only in vengeance and in self-defense. (Oh, that night on Resh when that so-clever couple had tricked her in order to sell her anew! She had done them violence, but had not even thought about ending their lives. They were out of business.) These barbarians, these Thingmakers, *they,* proudly called themselves Galactics and smugly called Aglaya "uncivilized" and "barbarian"! Aglayans stole no people. Aglayans sold no people, killed no people.

Yet I have killed, and I know that I am worthy of Aglii and Aglaya!

Now I have seen cold killing—murder. And I want him. The killer! This pirate! *O Aglii, O Sunmother . . . help your daughter Janjaheriohir-who-was.* They *are dark and call me "white" though I am not. But I am becoming one of* them *. . . becoming gray!*

Can black and white exist at one and the same time in the same object?

And . . . just now . . . who cares—I lust!

While she watched with luminous, excited eyes. Corundum's bulky white suit dropped from him. Under the protective coverall he wore a skintight one, a coolsuit that fitted tighter than the skin of youth. It covered him from neck to wrists to ankles and it was black, black as his hair and the hawkish brows aswoop over eyes that were not eyes.

He bulged beautifully in the skinnTite, she thought, if she was thinking. Perhaps she was thinking with her vagina, as that long-ago writer Stendahl had put it. The heat was in her and her eyes glittered, staring at the bulge of his genital triad. His slicer. A slicer to slice with. Her stash wanted to be sliced.

He was not a tall man, but his leanness made him appear tall. (Everyone was tall to Janja, who stood 156 sems, barely over what used to be called five feet.) He was well-muscled and in tone, so that he would be considered rangy. Dangerously rangy, rather than just lean. Not thin. She knew his strength and had felt it, though he would not use it on her, against her. He used it to drive into her. Dark and black-haired, he was. Aware of drama and effect.

A *pirate!*

He popped the single polarizer control of five seams and the suit fell from him and the Primeval Princess became not imperious but predatory.

She pounced, she mouthed and chewed, she ate. She gnawed and teased his dark little twigs of nipples until they were swollen and hard and would be sore tomorrow. Her eyes were aglitter like gemstones as she squeezed his balls until he gasped and his hands tightened reflexively on her buttocks, then dropped from her. She rode and was ridden. Neither of them noticed Jinni's fifty-second warning for her mouth was agape and she was sweat-sheened, swiveling her hips, plunging up and down, listening to the wet slappy sounds their bodies made on impact, feeling the thumping of her rearward cheeks on his thighs and the thumping of his ferrously hard slicer against her cervix. His hands rose for her breasts and all glittery of eyes she slapped them away, then bent a little to let his nipples feel her nails again. She loved it, loved it, screwing her gapingly distended body up and down on him with swift jogging movements. Goring herself. Gorging herself. Her breasts bobbed only a little. Their muscles had developed on a high-G planet, like those of her calves. She was giving herself a constant salvo of extremely deep thrusts, right up to the mouth of her womb. Hot little carnal thrills surged up into her tauntening belly and she was a happy animal.

"I can actually feel it, feel it! That bulging knob all the way up me, up me! And it feels *nice*. I love it. Uh—and uh, and there! I've got you, I've got it, I've got your slicer trapped up my stash, jacko!"

She had, and she ground on it. It didn't break in her, and his groans were not of pain. She jogged on it. Slicing, slicing, being sliced. Her driving hips plunged and swayed while she listened happily to his moans of delight and rising need.

Milady Janja, was it? Primeval Princess, eh? Imperious, hmm? Loved it, didn't he! Loved being used, ridden.

Again she bent to give each of his nipples wicked little scratches and tweaks—and paused while his fingers tried to sink into her hips. Straightening again she began rocking slowly back and forth on his lap with what seemed about a half-meter's worth of hot stiff very male flesh-club stuck up her somewhere in the vicinity of her lungs.

Feared and courtly, menacing and deadly, swiftly offended and swift to shoot, he lay on his back. He smiled at her while enjoying the fleshy caresses of her haunches on his thighs while this incredible woman sliced herself happily. Raping him!

"Let me—uh!—know when you tire, Primeval Princess! I'll—"

Her face was straining but she smiled almost ferociously and ground down. "Not—until—you've shot—*me,* you evil murdering cold-blooded *pirate!*"

He laughed aloud. His knees rose and he pushed to thrust sharply upward. They squirmed and hunched and wallowed their way right into subspace. Down the Tachyon Trail they went: ruby, sapphire, emery, and diamond. Short hair and long; white hair and black. At one area they mingled, black hair and white, dark skin and fair. Tachyons in rut.

3

The breeding concept, the concept of the "Be Fruitful and Multiply" mandate, had never really taken, on Sekhar. Sekhar was an unfriendly planet plodding around an unfriendly sun. The sun was blue-white and it was too close. It was said that Sekhar's colonization was accidental, in desperation. A dying ship on its way elsewhere, forced to duck past that nasty sun and bang down on steamy little Sekhar. Sekhar extended no welcome mat. The standard pioneer instinct and mandate had never surfaced, much less prevailed: breed to survive. On Sekhar, the situation was dreadfully obvious: *Don't breed all that much! We can survive here but where in hell on Hell is there for more of us to go?*

Had Homeworld, old Earth, been anything like Sekhar, humankind would never have risen there to settle here. And good riddance!

Still, pride and roots being what they were, the Seks called it home. Once they were found, a century after their arrival, most of them refused to be offlifted. Centuries later they were still here, mostly clustered in and very close to the spaceport city, Refuge.

Verley 2197223SK was born in Refuge. She had

never been off Sekhar. She had been out of Refuge only twice (Sekhar didn't really have much else), and Jarps were something she had only heard of. She didn't believe what she'd heard and didn't know the difference between Jarp and Jarpi any more than her ancient ancestors had known a djinni from a genie. She married at sixteen, to get away from home. That got her six years with a husband hung up higher than a solar-power satellite and tighter than a banker's fist. She worked, tried to be the best of wives, bore a child, and learned nothing.

Dat was a good Sek. His idea of a woman's role in sex was that she must be a lady. That meant she did not think about It. That also meant very little touching, indeed; and turning out the lights, undressing, getting into bed, and lying still while he did It. His idea of his own role in sex was to put It off as long as possible, since It was an unworthy, animalistic but unnecessary Thing.

That was Verley's 2197223SK's first sexual experience. Over the next six years-Sek of 298 days-Sek, that described her other seventy-one sexual experiences. Since he always put It off so long, as long as he possibly could, Dat always came fast. That made Verley (who knew nothing and did nothing in bed, really) think that she must be great in bed.

It had to be just that bed wasn't great; It wasn't great.

Still, she did get all excited. How many nights had she lain awake long, long after Dat came and his mouth came open and his uvula dropped so that he either snored or breathed as stertorously as a water-cooled engine on the Great Sekhari Desert? (There were no water-cooled engines on the deserts of Sekhar. No one was that stupid. It was just a saying. Besides, neither Dat nor Verley knew a uvula from a vulva anyway, or a clitoris from a clepsydra.)

So Verley got a divorce and now Dat was doing the same thing with someone else young and dumb and likely to remain the latter, and she seemed to thrive on it if not on It. She was happy on her pedestal, and she was happy to lie still while he did It to her. Sometimes she prayed, during.

As for Verley, she was still looking for another orgasm, of which she'd had three. All since the divorce, eleven months-Sek ago. She had added twenty-two sexual experiences in the past four of those eleven months, Seeking. She was at least touched, held, seemingly cherished when she was in bed with someone. Otherwise she hadn't found much, or learned much either. She had found three orgasms. All they were, were great. *Great!* Starbursts and novas, and enormous, happy lassitude after. And happy, proud males. (And twice, females, for by Sekhar's tight standards Verley was a very wicked woman indeed and in deed.)

Verley, Seeking. She still wasn't learning anything about the making of love, but she was trying a lot of things and a lot of bodies. She thought she had tried everything. Bodies, that was where it was. She proved she was wanted and worth something if she ran up a good body count, didn't she? Bodies. Attracting him and giving It to him; letting him do It to her. Proving her attractiveness, her femaleness. *Pumping*, in Sekhari terms. He put his *pump* into her *oasis*, and pumped. Pumping. Wow.

She loved it, or thought she did. She thought she was sexy. It all meant that she was wanted and worthy, didn't it? She had after all had three of those wonderful experiences whisperingly called "orgasms," hadn't she?

Verley, Seeking. Strangely, it was easy for her to continue moving from body to body. She was seldom asked twice. In bed, Verley was a willing body with a convenient hole in it.

So, naughtily for a woman on Sekhar, she walked into the Imperial Hotel's bar, the Cosmoasis, on this particular night and the weirdest creature she had ever seen looked at her and kept looking. It was hard not to stare back.

It had great big starey eyes, eyes about twice the

size of Verley's, which were large. And they were *round,* this creature's eyes; really round. They were set well apart in a face with a broad forehead and cheeks above a little chin that was almost pointed. The skin was not tan, or brown, or copper or bronze or brass or yellow, but *orange.* Not cupreous orange or brazen orange. This was a true most-definitely-no-mistake-about-it *orange.* And the hair was not redhead red or Titian, but a deep dark glowing impossible wine-like *red.*

The mouth in that sort of heart-shaped face had semi-everted lips of a paler orange. The nose was a bit broad of septum and of nostrilar flare, but was without the slight downward tip of almost every Galactic's. The creature was tall and lean, broad of shoulder and rather lean of hips, with long limbs. The hands at the ends of those long arms were different too, but all Verley noticed for a while was the strangely childish *sweet-faced* look of this creature. And its body.

It wore no kaffey or the usual full Sekhari robe; not even a cloak. Some sort of lacework "helmet" webbed the head with straps. The straps were equipped with more than one . . . dial? Verley realized that she was seeing a spacefarer, a genuine "alien," meaning non-Galactic. It must be staying here at the hotel with no intention of going out. Or did orange skin not burn?

What it did wear was a short-sleeved sort of shirt that was slashed in a deep round-sided V or set of parentheses, which ended just below its breasts. There it snugged tight.

Breasts, yes. Therefore it was female, and could be called *her* and *she,* rather than the standard no-gender singular pronoun *es:* it. And that abbreviated shirt was a most un-Sekhari scarlet.

But . . . well, there were the dark brown boots that sheathed the legs without wrinkle to a point higher than mid-thigh. The couple of inches of laces at the top must be ornamental. There was the low-slung belt, broad and matching the boots, that supported a holstered stopper slung low on the left hip. And there were the tights. Like the upper garment and the hair, they were scarlet, vanishing into the boots. They began low on the hips, so that a long expanse of narrow-waisted abdomen was left orangely bare. (There was a navel, yes.)

The thing about those supertight tights was that either the orange creature had a large and protuberant vulva or oasis, or, as appeared a lot more likely no matter how incredible: a pump and scrotum!

While Verley was wondering if it was possible that the creature really did possess male primary and female secondary sexual characteristics, it uttered a strange whistling sound. It was still gazing at her, as she entered the Cosmoasis. It, with fresh drink in hand, was apparently returning to a table from the bar.

She shrank back a bit. "What?"

It raised a weird six-digited hand to do something to the weird strap-work helmet and said, "My name is T'leetl-Wheee'tT!, and this is my first time ever on Sekhar. Had I known about you, I'd have been here before. Do you mind if I stare at you the rest of the evening?"

She stared at T'leetl-Wheee'tT!, which she could not hope to pronounce. *Tweedle,* she thought. "I . . . I . . . eyes that stare are no insult to her who dresses so as to attract stares."

The enormous eyes seemed to send forth rays that went through her, all through her. "Is that a Sekhari saying?"

"Yes," Verley admitted, and lowered her gaze, ashamed that she had not been able to think of something original.

"Well," Tweedle said, "I like it, and your honesty. I wish you'd have a drink with me."

How exciting! A real . . . something else. "You are —you are a spacefarer?" *Oh that was dumb,* she told herself miserably.

"Oh yes. No one resembling me ever grew up on Sekhar."

"Well, uh, what are—I mean, I'd love a drink. And—" She tried to smile but failed and looked down into her cleavage, which was more substantial than this exotic spacefarer's, if not as fully revealed. "What did you say your name is?"

It gestured her to a table. Lots of people were watching, and Verley was really aware of that. They didn't all look happy, but she certainly was getting attention!

"You heard but can't pronounce it," Tweedle said. "Non-Jarps do have trouble talking Jarp. As a matter of fact, no one I've ever met can pronounce Jarp. People usually just call me 'Jarp.' That's about the same as calling you Sek, really."

"You're a *Jarp!*" she burst out. "I mean—excuse me, but I've heard of Jarps but never saw one. Is it true that—I mean, are Jarps . . . are you really—"

"Pos-for-positive: we really are. I really am. Breasts and penis and vulva. One ovary, one testicle. One egg, one nut."

"Here," a male voice cut in. "We don't talk to ladies that way hereabouts, Jarp."

The Jarp stared at the man, a nice-looking Sek with a gut. "You are not being bright, big-ears. I am wearing a stopper and you are not. Interrupt us again and I will start an interplanetary incident."

"Not to mention an interracial one," someone else said.

Neither Verley nor the male Sek nor the Jarp glanced in the direction of that voice. They were busy being caught up in tension. The Jarp and "big-ears" were trading stares. The Jarp's eyes were huge and it did indeed wear that stopper on its hip. The Sek kept staring and so did the Jarp. Its face did not look quite so sweet. Verley had not been so uncomfortable —or so thrilled—for months and months.

Around them, a lot of conversations had broken off, in mid-word.

The man broke. "Yer right," he said, looking away.

"I don't have a stopper and I'm not stupid." He turned all the way away, and Verley thought that he had shrunk visibly.

The Jarp returned full attention to Verley. "I am sorry we never exchanged names," it said. "I dislike telling anyone what I am called by my captain and crewmates, because people laugh."

Then the Jarp—T'leetl-Wheee'tT!!—presented Verley with its untasted drink, and departed the bar. Many stared. The man who had challenged it began to grow to his former size. Verley felt disappointed. Also abandoned and nervous. The bar was normal again, and dull.

The man who had challenged the Jarp, now regrown to his full size, turned toward Verley. His voice swaggered.

"Sorry you had to hear that, beautiful. Now that I've relieved you of that thing's presence, why don't you join me?"

She looked at him, glanced at the doorway, looked at him.

"No," Verley said, and hurried to the exit.

"Good thing," she heard a voice say in an un-Sek accent, " 'cause if she'd joined you then we couldn't've. You got room for three spacefarers, haven't ya, jacko?"

Verley glanced back. The three spacefarers were pulling out chairs to join the man. The middle one was a native of the planet Jarpi.

Someone said, "What'syer hurry, Oasis?" as Verley passed, and someone else corrected sarcastically, "What's ya hurry, *Sunflower?*" But that was wasted on Verley, who was not familiar with the pejorative for Jarp-lover. Someone else reached for her as she hurried past, and some crude spacefarer said, "Lookit them warheads swing and bounce!" Verley, large unfettered breasts indeed alive and lively within her jallaba of beige, yellow, and pale blue, ignored the voices and thumped away the reaching hand with a large swinging hip.

She passed out of the bar into the little tunnel-like corridor, eyes searching, and followed the loop-and-ramp to the lobby. Eyes seeking. Verley, Seeking. And there was the smiling Jarp, facing her. Waiting for her, smiling!

It extended an orange hand. Four fingers flanked by two long thumbs.

Since she couldn't think of anything to say and *had* been following the most exciting, uh, being she had ever met, Verley took the hand.

It felt nice. Warm, large, long-fingered. A nice hand. The orange digits did look strange overlapping her sort-of hazel ones, but that was part of the excitement. She felt no difference in pressure from its two thumbs. That must be very . . . handy.

Sekhar was so *conservative*. This person was not only from off Sekhar but a spacefarer, a ship's crew-member! And altogether different as well; excitingly different. She loved the way Tweedle had faced down that man in the lounge. Big-ears! The man was a bigot. Verley had vowed never to be a bigot. And besides, this non-androgynous man/woman combination was sexy.

(All conservatives were dull, Verley's liberal friends told her. That's what *conservative* meant. And they were all bigots, her liberal friends assured her. All of them. They hated all dull conservatives or were contemptuous of them, at the very least.)

Verley and the Jarp were in the hotel's sprawling artificial-planty lobby. Some people were looking. Two were staring, including that woman in the scandalous scarlet-and-gold "skirt" that was cut on the bias and showed one hip and most of her un-Sekhari legs. And almost everything else, too. Most of these people were spacefarers. They had better things to do than look at a titsy Jarp and a titsy local holding hands and looking moony at each other.

"Tl'l-loodl'l—" the Jarp began, and touched or turned something on its helmet of straps. "I am on Sekhar," it began again, "and neither Sek nor human,

nor man nor woman. It is definitely best that I quit the bar tonight and forget it. Perhaps you would show me the town? First I will need to go up to my room and take a pherinotal, against the heat. Will you come along?"

"Will you tell me all about space, and—Jarps?"

"Of course not. We have a sexual interest in each other, and no time to talk all about space and Jarps or Jarpi, my planet."

It was turning, slowly. Their hands were still entwined. Verley moved with the Jarp. Staring, astonished, affronted, impressed, charmed. Her eyes were bright. Verley, Seeking.

"Please pronounce your name again," Verley said.

They were ascending the first broad carpeted set of stairs. Powered elevators would be a silly luxury, on Sekhar. Besides, the Imperial Hotel was only three storeys high. Since there was hardly anyplace else on Sekhar for anyone to come from, the hotel's business derived almost exclusively from spacefarers. Not many of them came, either, to Sekhar.

"You still couldn't pronounce it," the Jarp said. "But I have not heard your name at all."

"Verley," said Verley, and was distracted by a man bounce-running down the stairs toward them.

His skin was the color of excellent bronze and his eyes slightly atilt. His hair was intensely black and vehemently straight. He was human, a Galactic, but not of Sekhar. He wore black tights in black boots under a silky-shiny yellow tunic emblazoned with a wonderful dragon. And he wore a stopper. Few spaceport cities dared tried to prohibit the wearing of sidearms by spacefarers. Perhaps some men and women were more arrogant, for that. On the other hand, manners and politeness were back in vogue. Sekhar prohibited nothing to spacefarers. Not many of them came to Sekhar.

Verley saw this one's eyes take her in and saw herself pass the appraisal with high marks. That was life to her: being found desirable, being found wanted. She saw the man's tilty eyes swerve toward her tall companion.

"Ho, Sweetface! Already found the best-looking woman on Sekhar, eh?" Grinning, he swung his black-eyed gaze back to Verley. "Be careful, little girl! You know what they say about Jarps!"

Then he had bounded on by, grinning.

"A . . . friend?" Verley asked. They reached the landing, turned, and started up another purple-carpeted flight.

"Shipmate. His name is Sakyo."

"S— What kind of name is that?"

"A name-name, Verley. He's from Terasaki."

That's a planet, she remembered. "And he called you Sweetface?"

"Pos." The Jarp sighed, still holding her hand. "It's what I am called. They can't pronounce my name. Are you laughing?"

"No." After a moment, "Why should I be laughing? They can't pronounce your name so they give you a nickname. He's a—a shipmate," she said, tasting the exotica of it and liking the flavor. "And besides, you have a sweet face."

"So have you. Would you be offended to be called Sweetface?"

"No." And Verley, who had heard herself called a number of things, said, "Really. It must be hard then, being a Jarp? When no one can pronounce your real name and everyone else is . . . is . . . not Jarpese?"

"Just Jarp. From Jarpi. The planet Jarpi. In some ways it's hard. Not in all ways. Do you prefer women or men?"

"What?"

"Since I combine both sexes, I am a true hermaphrodite. All Jarps are. I can be what some people call 'all things to all people.' It isn't true, but it sounds good."

"Oh. I . . . I prefer . . . I like both . . . uh—"

"Say it?"

". . . Men."

Her hand was squeezed. Four long orange fingers, two thumbs. "Good. Think how nice to be able to suck each other's breasts and have penis in you too!"

She made a sort of attempt to reclaim her hand. The Jarp did not allow it. It was a half-hearted attempt, anyhow. "You are . . . forward. Outspoken. That is not the way we are, we Seks."

"I just say what everybody thinks and wishes it had nerve to say. It isn't that Jarps have so much nerve, Verley. We are just straightforward. So, everyone thinks we are horny all the time."

Verley had never heard such talk. While she was trying to be Sekly affronted, she was giggling. "But you're not?"

"I am," Sweetface said. "This way."

About forty seconds after they were in Sweetface's room she was being kissed, and she was kissing back. Red, *red* hair and her black waves; orange skin and hazel; breasts against breasts—except that the Jarp was taller, of course. So she stood on tiptoe, and its hands on her buttocks tugged her loins against its bulging tights. It was a long kiss, and the hands were never still on her bottom, through the jallaba. Vanity made her hold the cheeks taut.

"I . . . I believe," she said, a little short of breath, "you said you needed to take a . . . a—"

"Pherinotal," Sweetface said, "if I'm going out. I probably should, although it was also a fine way to bring you up here. You *smell* good, Verley. You *feel* good." It kissed her forehead. "Please do wait."

"Oh I will," Verley said, as it left her.

Sweetface returned to find her staring out the window at Refuge's lights. It came up behind her, but did not touch her. That surprised Verley. She was available; didn't her vulnerable back show that? Untouched, she did not know what to do. After a long moment she moved just a little forward before she turned, so that her prominent backside would not rub the bulge in its tights.

"Please tell me about space. Spacefaring, and what it's like. What is the name of your ship?"

"Coronet," Sweetface said, and made a call downstairs, and over the lukewarm beer it had ordered they talked for a long while.

Eventually, their coming together was natural. They knew each other. Feeling possessed by long arms, feeling a tongue demanding entry to her mouth, Verley decided to think of Sweetface as "he." (It was a slender, unusually sinuous tongue, more than a little pointed at the tip.) She was intensely aware of the pressure of his very male organ against her loins, despite the softness of anomalous breasts. The kiss lengthened and she was grinding against breasts and penis alike. Her garment's velcro fastening proved neither mystery nor obstacle to the spacefarer. Just as easily he wiped the jallaba from her shoulders. As the fabric began sagging from her body, she set her hands to his halter. Their hands eased onto each other's breasts.

Then she was marveling that Sweetface really did have these nice firm-soft feminine lobes. Just like hers, except for color and size!—and too this real true manful pump that she just had to bring out of his trunks. It became sensible that they pause long enough to strip. Yes, it was real, all right! It was slim, and not long. She realized that his oasis would be small, too. There was, after all, only so much room down there. She hated to ask silly questions and despite her marriage and subsequent experience, Verley remained shy about sexual matters and talk. She'd have to look up Jarps. Tomorrow. She was not one to touch, to explore, to fondle. Dat had taught her to be a lady.

She was aroused and as a lady she was ready to be stretched out and pumped. They became naked and in bed and for a long while her lover's hands and mouth delighted themselves with her breasts. Eventually that smallish mouth lifted from nipples grown dark and fat. Orange hands stilled their lovely stroking of her.

"I love your warheads."

"I'm glad," she said lazily, also liking the spacefarer's slang.

He looked at her for awhile, and was still, so that she wondered if something might be wrong. Then, "You don't like mine, Verley?"

"I *love* them, Sweetface!" The name came naturally to her tongue, and it sounded fine and was all right.

"Then . . . come alive. We are not children. I am not a boy, and *girls* I ignore. You have my hands and mouth on you. Give me yours. I'll love it."

To Verley such a statement, such a thought and implied criticism, were more a blow than a challenge. It hurt and frightened her. Her heart pounded and her brain whirled. Her stomach threatened to knot. And she had thought everything was going so well! She had been enjoying so much.

She considered, and chewed her lip, feeling desolate . . . and asked some questions and revealed some things. Talking almost mechanically, not quite looking at Sweetface, she talked of herself, and of Dat. She revealed how much experience she had had—with bodies. Without quite saying the words so cruelly, her Jarp lover let her know that she was not experienced; she had "made love" with a lot of bodies, doing the same things—or rather not doing the same things—over and over, without ever really learning anything. For instance: how to be a lover, a participant, rather than merely a willing object.

And then Verley changed forever. With an alien, she learned that lovemaking was far more than different *bodies,* and being done *to.*

At twenty-four she reached the end of her girlhood and began to work at being a woman. It had never occurred to her that it was not automatic, even though she realized by now that Dat was more boy than man. He was also pitifully repressed. And now she knew that she was too and had been right along, while she had thought herself all free, a modern sophisticated woman!

She changed. And she began acting as a woman. She liked it. She loved it! She liked the taste of the Jarp, and the way it licked and sucked and fondled. Sweetface kept making happy noises that encouraged her. After another time Sweetface suggested, urged that she too provide feedback signals, support or positive reinforcement, by making happy sounds. She did. It was nice to let go and let the sounds emerge! She overdid it, but she was learning.

They wallowed naked, rather noisily, while they made love mutually in celebration of each other, and it was wonderful.

Dat had expected her to be a lady, the epitome–or, rather, nadir—of Sekhari repression. An object to which he "made love"—briefly, in the dark. That she became, and that she remained, after the divorce. She had felt that it was working, with a succession of partners. Bodies. Now . . . this spacefarer was a lover, sophisticated and accustomed to lovers, not objects. It expected a lover and Verley became one. She opened up more and more. She dared more and more; did and enjoyed more and more.

What fun to seek its/his approval and pleasure while she knew that Sweetface was seeking hers!

In a room of the Imperial Hotel, with a non-human who had been a stranger only hours before, Verley popped open like a seedpod. She would never be the same. She was sucked and fondled and she fondled and sucked breasts and, for the first time, a (small, slim) pump. (Slicer, the Jarp called it.) And she was fondled and sucked and sliced as well, and she loved it.

She also came twice and enjoyed herself more than she ever, ever had. With an orange non-human. In one night it increased her lifetime orgasm total by two-thirds! She would never be the same and she was more than glad; she was ecstatic. She was also proud. This because of a non-human being called a Jarp, which dared talk and suggest, and which was a true lover rather than a . . . pumper.

She stayed. She slept just wonderfully.

She was still there in the morning when the other Jarp came in.

That was shocking and sort of scary. Verley had not considered that Sweetface might have a companion, a Jarp roommate who spent the night elsewhere. (With a Sekhari man or woman? Verley later remembered to wonder.)

Clutching the covers to her, she soon learned that the two Jarps were lovers, shipmates on *Coronet*. The other seemed somehow more feminine than masculine, as Sweetface was a bit more male than female. The other gave its name as Whistle, but Sweetface reminded it that its name was Tweedle-dee. Tweedle-dee, Verley realized, was not too bright. Verley remained terribly uncomfortable. . . .

Then Tweedle-dee stripped and came smiling to join them!

Verley was ready to jump and run, naked or not . . . for about four minutes. She wasn't being raped or attacked. It was more lovemaking, now extended laterally. Now it was Sweetface and Verley and Tweedle-dee, and it didn't take Verley long to begin to feel unfortunate, being a human and having only a sexual receptacle. The Jarps had both plug and socket, each. (Small, both and each.)

Never had she been kissed and licked and caressed so much. Never had she done so much kissing and fondling and licking and palpating not to mention palpitating! When it happened, he was wet and open everywhere and it was natural and wonderful. Only after a minute or two did it occur to Verley that she had never before contained two pumps, either.

She loved it, and just kept on sliding her fingers in and out of a small alien oasis while two alien pumps glided in her and she fondled and sucked a swollen red-orange nipple.

4

A man's success in business today turns upon his power of getting people to believe he has something that they want.

Gerald Stanley Lee

Sekhar was a planet Kenowa would be happy to forget and she wished she had stayed on the ship.

Outside the sun was blue-white, and Sekhar was too close to it for comfort. Some Sekhari said it was true that Sekhar's colonization was an accident, result of near-disaster that forced their ancestors to land here, and remain. Some said other negative things about their hotbox world. Let offworlders complain or denigrate the planet, though, and those same Seks took offense. Sekhari were called "Seks" and they were called "testy," among other things.

They were a lot testier in summer.

Those Galactics who now considered themselves native Sekhari, after several hundred years' worth of generations, had adapted eventually. Too bad that ship hadn't been loaded with those darkest brown people most of whom had originated in the vanished black race of Homeworld. The ship had not. Those it had brought here adapted, and their descendants adapted and coped and now seemed not to mind. Sekhar was their planet.

Some few wore optic filters and put up with them inside. Even fewer wore glasses at all times. The photoptiks darkened immediately upon exposure to ultraviolet, and to any desired degree, and cleared as soon as one returned inside or turned from a window not made of photoptik plass. Such glasses were not popular because of human vanity and estheticism. Who wanted to wear spectacles all the time when no one had to wear them to see, ever?

Most Seks, then, and all visitors wore dark glasses outside. One learned quickly to cover the eyes before stepping out. There were laws about the composition and tint of windowglass, on Sekhar. Glassmaking was a major industry, on Sekhar.

There was lots of sand on Sekhar.

Dark glasses were called "darkeyes." There could be no confusion as to what one referred to, since there was no such thing as eyes other than dark. Darkeyes were of many hues and styles right up through ornate and into ludicrous. They tended to eclectic shape and ornamentation unto over-ornamentation. Styles and popular colors in darkeyes came and went just as they did in cosmetics and furnishings, sashes and boots. Many were clipped to the long duckbills of *Sekcaps* or *Waynes,* the broad-brimmed headgear some remembered to call ten-gallon hats, without knowing why. (Everyone knew "ten" and "hat"; but what sort of creature was or had been a "gallon"?) Darkeyes snapped up or down at the touch of a finger to a button or tiny lever.

Most Sekhari wore the "native" headdress called a kaffey. It had begun simply as a circle of cloth with a section cut away. The center of the circle was plopped onto the head. The rest of the cloth formed a skirt around the head with the cut-away area, of course, at the face. Any sort of band or piece of rope held it in place. Over the years a stiff bill had been added, to facilitate the snapping up of darkeyes. Sekhari kept their heads covered inside, because it was convenient. One uncovered when one was at home at day's end. Over the years that, naturally, had gotten all caught up in custom and taboo. Now many believed that heads really weren't meant to be seen by anyone save one's own family. Fanatics removed their headgear only at home and in the dark.

Kaffey bills—called beaks—were stiff and slightly curved in a sort of jaunty quarter-circle. Every beak had two standard attachments for darkeyes, of which everyone except the very poorest had more than one set and usually more than three.

Seks tended to have pale circles around the eyes, and darkish marks on either side of their noses.

Under any circumstances, Sekhar's sun was just too much for the eyes to take.

Men and most women wore their hair short, on Sekhar. Not that much of anyone ever saw it.

Most people wore loose robes, on Sekhar. There was a great deal of white and yellow and the pallid turquoise of readout panels and ALL CLEAR buttons, and white-shot skyblue, on Sekhar. And beige, too much beige and the color called "sand." Only the rich and ostentatious wore dark robes, so that everyone might know they wore coolsuits beneath. Seks laughed at a dark-robed person with a sweaty face; that person was faking it, trying to appear wealthier than it was.

Kenowa thought Sekhar was really dull.

Also hot. Temperature on spaceship *Coronet* was maintained at twenty-four degrees—usually, almost always, except when glitches occurred. (It was frequently upped to twenty-five in Captain Jonuta's cabin, and when Kenowa was present it tended to run up another degree Celsius.) A nice gentle winter temperature on Sekhar was thirty-two, which would have been about ninety on the ancient scale some still liked to joke about. Summer on *white*-clouded/cloudless, electric azure-sky'd Sekhar was not even discussed.

Some hotels strove to maintain temperatures of twenty-six or twenty-seven for their idea of the comfort of offplanet guests; locals complained and staff dressed warmly.

The Wet Sand Oasis saw few spacefarers but, ever in hope, maintained a nice twenty-seven-degree temperature. Too many centigrades. Way too many. Alcohol raised the body temperature and was better consumed in nice cool places. Maybe about a shade over twenty-two degrees, Kenowa thought. So she happily gave the locals something to look at on *Coronet*'s mercifully infrequent visits here. Some were scandalized. So? It was a free planet in a free galaxy. No one had to look at Kenowa.

She and Jonuta had arrived in the Wet Sand over an hour ago, wearing kaffeys, darkeyes, and the voluminous white cloaks all non-Seks called Sektents. They had entered a couple of minutes after the arrival of *Coronet* crewmember Sweetface, in company with last night's conquest. Kenowa liked the large bosomy woman and the way she was so attached to Sweetface. Yet she—her name was Verley, she said—knew that he would leave this lounge and then this planet without her. She just wanted to stay with him as long as possible. Kenowa knew about that kind of attachment, and it made her wonder idly just how great Sweetface might be as a lover. He was at the bar now, which had a human attendant, and Verley was right there with him. It.

The two Union Security men—locally hired bodyguards—turned up one minute after Jonuta and Kenowa. The rent-a-guards affected not to be together. They took seats on opposite sides of the room. The one on the right side was, as Jonuta had specified, left-handed.

"I should make liars," Jonuta said, "of those who call me Captain Cautious?"

Both rent-a-guards wore large nasty guns, low-tech high-noise things that hung in holsters on their aisle-side hips. Both men were fast, good, and surly. They were an additional expense, a hopefully needless precaution. The heat tended to make people short of temper and downright mean on Sekhar, and Jonuta had already set a record for survival. Nearly eighteen years as a slaver, alive and unimprisoned. The record was the result of brilliance, attention to details, keeping up with technology and the opposition, luck, and constant caution. Captain Cautious.

Presumably no one had any hard evidence on him. Jonuta would have to be caught in the act. That had been tried. There had been assassination attempts, too. Jonuta assumed that most of those were backed by a certain Corundum, and he was sure about several. Word got around. So did Captain Corundum.

In the dimness and so-called coolth of the Wet Sand Oasis, Jonuta and Kenowa had snapped up their dark-eyes and peeled their Sektents. The tall Jonuta was dramatically and romantically attired in a long swash-buckling coat of scarlet with ornamental buttons of brass-imitating prass, and tights. And a stopper. His boots were tall.

But it was not Jonuta the Wet Sand's patrons were looking at. Kenowa did like to dress up, or undress down, and there was quite a bit of Kenowa to be spectacular in the spectacular and often frankly kinky attire she preferred.

The thing to wear on Sekhar, Kenowa naturally decided, was Dark. Anything dark in color, to contrast with everyone else's light hues.

Her SpraYon body stocking was a metallically scintillant plum. It covered her from insteps to third or fourth ribs in front and rose all the way up in back to circle her neck. Jewelry of silver and violet covered seven-tenths of her otherwise bare arms with a seeming angry desire to bite into her brass-hued skin. A cerulean kaffey covered all her head except for her face.

Her gown, a clingy Saipese slink, fell to her insteps but was slit all the way to the crucial areas fore and aft. Above, it dived to display a tiny portion of the skinnTite and a larger portion of bosom.

Kenowa had a lot of bosom to display. She was a big woman and a shapely one, with a lot of everything to display, one way or another. Displaying it was her pleasure, and Jonuta's.

It was sad, she felt, not to be able to wear spectacular earrings and a Terasaki coil, a purple wig twenty-five sems tall.

Mighty men, truly superior men from Maddog Joshua through Xerxes and Cyrus and Julius Caesar, Napoleon and Takashi Subarishi, Jorvis and Yakubu Mpale, tended toward the kinky. Captain Jonuta tended toward the kinky. The woman who called herself his aide positively wallowed in it.

For the past hour Jonuta had been negotiating with Arsane er-Jorvistor, a very large Sek with a very large credaccount. Jonuta had come here with six walking units of merchandise. He wanted not just money, but the TDP the Seks had rather necessarily developed. The TDP was the best anti-glitch device in the galaxy. Both men wanted to deal, so both remained throughout long negotiation that now and then bordered on exchanged insults. Since each knew the other wanted to deal, both bargained hard and kept the peace. Jorvistor had inspected the merchandise in *Coronet*'s hold up at Sekharstation, but he insisted on bargaining here, onplanet.

Kenowa sighed and punched in an order for another sugarless non-alcoholic drink. Neither she nor Jonuta trusted anyone on Sekhar. It was just that Jonuta liked to keep his hand in everywhere and move around a lot.

Things were warm for him on Shankar and Lanatia. Even their last visit to his own world of Qalara had ended with a murder attempt. (Jonuta refused to use the politician's and "news" mongers' word, *assassina-*

tion.) That had shaken him badly. Then on Franji—where he had gone, damn it, because Kenowa knew he just couldn't forget that pallid little barbarian stash—Srih had been killed. Word was a blue-haired woman did it, but Corundum was there. She left with Corundum. By the time Jonuta learned of Srih's death, Corundum and the unknown woman had left the place and Corundum had departed Franji.

In only a few months Jonuta had barely escaped a murder attempt that had cost him his trusted long-time crewman Arel and had lost Srih as well. He was left with Kenowa and Sweetface. Necessarily he took on Sakyo and then Shig, but who could be sure of new people? (The half-wit that Sweetface had taken on as "companion" was no help.) It was time to vanish somewhere for a nice long time, Kenowa thought. Now she knew that Jonuta agreed.

The trouble was that first he wanted a Sekharese TDP. Unfortunately, their sale was controlled by the government here, and tightly. The devices were being gobbled up by military/policers, med-research, and big spaceliner companies as fast as they could be manufactured and tested.

So. A quick deal for some human merchandise, just the type wanted and even needed on Sekhar. A long and expensive run here. And now . . . Arsane er-Jorvistor was being as difficult as possible. It was dragging on and on and Kenowa had to make a deposit in the restroom of all the sugarless non-alcoholics she had been trying to sip slowly, but she was not about to make a move to interrupt the flow or the tension, to throw off the pace of this bargaining. She sighed, crossed legs, and tried not to listen.

Besides, she had just come up with a brilliant idea. Jonuta could acquire a TDP without all this hard labor on this hotbox world!

"But I really do not want the sixth unit," Arsane er-Jorvistor said. "Only the five, and we both know that my offer for them is a good one. We have been working at it long enough!"

Jonuta, who sat almost casually with his left elbow on the table's wood-imitating glastic top, did not move a muscle. "I have six units onboard and I brought them to sell on Sekhar." His voice rumbled vibrantly up from his chest. "I do *not* want to leave Sekhar with the considerable trouble, worry, and risk of one unit still in my possession. I could be detained at Sekharstation and my ship searched. I could be overhauled out in space by any countryboy policer and searched, or ordered onplanet for search. We both know my risks, Arsane. I have no wish to increase them."

The very dark Sek in the virginally white jallaba and broad-brimmed hat leaned just a bit more forward. "I can't believe you are truly worried about being caught in space with a piece of cargo, Captain. There is more here than that. You could and would, if necessary, merely—jettison cargo."

Kenowa began tapping her fingers. Jonuta sat up stiffly and the brass-imitating buttons flashed on his long red coat.

"I am Jonuta," that chesty bass said. "The sort of thing you suggest I leave to such as Corundum!" And he spat. Several other patrons turned to look. No one was concerned with the spittle or crudeness, and Jonuta knew it. All, including Jorvistor, understood the extravagant gesture of a man's wasting moisture on such a planet as Sekhar. It was an extremely meaningful expression of offense taken.

"I should not have suggested it," Jorvistor said, glancing in the direction of the tapping noises. Purple fingernails, metallically aglitter at the ends of fingers the color of old brass. "I retract it, Jonuta."

Jonuta looked at Kenowa. "What is it?" His voice was as stiff as his posture. She knew better than to interrupt. He had just gained on the Sek, and Jorvistor had backed a pace.

"I—I don't feel well, Captain," said Kenowa, who never called him captain. "I wish I could confer with your friend Daktari Kita at Hakimit, back on Qalara."

Jonuta stared at her. What she had said was idiotic, and Kenowa was not an idiot. Eumiko Kita was not a physician. She was in charge of computer maintenance and repair at Hakimit Med Center on Jonuta's home world. The three of them had scheduled a nice three-way session a few months ago, for one reason because Eumiko had quite a case on Kenowa. Unfortunately they'd had to break it off when her wrist-pager summoned her to the phone. Glitch in the Hakimit transplant monitoring computer, and—

Jonuta blinked. He reached over to pat Kenowa's hand—*tap-tap; tap-tap: understood.* To hell with the recalcitrant *Myrzha* Jorvistor. They would get the scut off this heat-tank of a world, streak straight for Qalara and Eumiko Kita. Money from the sale of the six walking units of cargo would be divided with the med center, as donation. It wouldn't take long to set up 'Miko's order for a Sekharese TDP—except that she would actually order two. Jonuta would pay full cost of his, if necessary. He had enough cred and holdings on Qalara to buy the damned med center!

Besides, he had a . . . very personal project under way, there.

"You're right, Kenowa, and I'm sorry we've been too long." He drained his glass decisively, carefully not-watching the drop of Jorvistor's jaw. "Arsane, I'm sorry we could not come to terms. We have to go, and now."

It was Jorvistor's turn to sit up very straight. His face showed his shock. "But—she can be treated here . . . what—what—but you just stated your fear of being inspace with one sla—unit, much less all six!"

"As you assumed," Jonuta said, pushing back his prestglass chair, "I was bluffing. My own world needs those six as much as Sekhar. True, all six are conditioned to high temp. But then, Qalara isn't exactly a cold planet, most of the year, and they'll be happier there."

"But—"

"You know I'm sorry, Arsane. What I really wanted was the TDP. I was about ready to say keep your money altogether and I'd settle for it—and, oh, a favor owed." He stood. He turned to Kenowa, extending a hand. "Let's—"

"Done," Arsane er-Jorvistor said.

With Kenowa's hand in his, Jonuta swiveled his head, only his head, toward the Sekhari.

"Done," Jorvistor repeated. He knuckled the table with a rap, which on Sekhar was as good as a recorded vow. "I agree to those terms. It is not fair to you, though, and makes me feel bad. I also insist that in addition to the item you mentioned and a firm vow of favor owed, you accept—oh, a few items to be appreciated by your ailing lady."

On Sekhar, every female was a lady. At least verbally.

Kenowa was rising. Jonuta's nails dug into her hand and she groaned. It was perfect.

"Damn," Jonuta said, low. "Arsane—we've *got* to get offplanet. Oh, I can put her in ship's daktari, up on *Coronet*. But only the people at Hakimit on Qalara are fully competent to deal with the internal fungus she picked up on that damned soggy—well, never mind where. It can't be done. You can't get your hands on that item so swiftly and—"

"You do indeed underestimate me and overestimate the honesty of Sekhari officials," Jorvistor said quietly, also rising. "If you can see your way clear to waiting two hours from this moment, I shall be up—with the item."

Since the moment Jonuta had risen to his feet, a tall very thin *being* at the bar had turned to watch him. Its face was orange, true orange, and its eyes enormous, sweetly childlike and innocent in a face drawn down to a childish point at the chin. (The Sekhari woman beside him turned, also, but she did not watch Jonuta. She looked up at the orange face, and she looked sad. Strange, since a young woman that good looking and well set up didn't have to go taking up with an *alien!*)

Jonuta released Kenowa's hand to slap and scratch his shoulder. Immediately the being at the bar half-turned to the bar's human attendant. Squeezing the arm of the woman beside him, the creature nodded, made a whistling noise, turned again, and snapped down its darkeyes. It had already paid, drink by drink, in real Sekhari scrip. It was a Jarp, a being seldom seen on Sekhar, where of course one Jarp looked the same as another. The woman's hand remained on its arm as it moved from the bar, Sektent whirling about its long booted legs. When its motion broke contact, her arm was outstretched. It remained so, lowering very slowly, as if reluctantly. She was one of several who watched its departure, though a few in the Wet Sand—males—watched her. Their expressions were interesting mixtures of disapproval and hopefulness.

The rent-a-guards watched those who did not watch the orange humanoid.

The Jarp's name was Sweetface and upon Srih's death it had become Captain Jonuta's oldest crew-member-associate.

Outside, it ignored stares, crossed the street between tricyclists in their temp-controlled bubbles, and turned casually. Its gaze swept the street and the buildings flanking the Wet Sand Oasis, as it had already scanned the windows and doorways on this side of the street. A four-fingered, two-thumbed hand hung near its stopper, which was in an open holster.

A two-person cycle from the outspace shuttle area drew up in front of the Wet Sand and its passengers emerged. Offworlders. Before they had closed the bubble, Sweetface whistled shrilly and started for the cab. The timing was just about right; it had to stumble only once before Jonuta and Kenowa, both white-cloaked and with darkeyes in place, emerged from the lounge.

"Here you," Jonuta said, pointing. "That's my trike!"

"D'lee!" Sweetface said. The warble meant "mine" but its translator was off and the sound was one no human throat could duplicate.

"Want to toss for it or fight for it, *Jarp?"* Jonuta and Kenowa had reached the taxi. It began to hum more loudly, its mechanism bidding it return to the shuttle area a few blocks away.

"Twe'eedl'-oo-oeeOOT'l wheet'l-ll!" Sweetface said, and shook a fist as it backed away.

"You and your parent!" Jonuta snarled in a continuation of the sham for anyone who might be observing. As he rounded the trike he muttered, "Turn your damned translator on, Sweets, dammit!" Only the three of them heard. Sweetface claimed that the frequency of the translation helmet interfered with one of its teeth. Neither it nor Jonuta remembered which tooth.

One of the rent-a-guards emerged from the lounge. He waved at a passing two-person trike and was in it almost before Kenowa and Jonuta were on their way. The rent-a-guard also knew Sweetface, and he also pretended not to do.

"Want a ride, Jarp?"

Sweetface joined him. Jarp and security guard swung and hurried to circle the block and pick up Jonuta's cab on the way to the shuttle. Woe unto any who more than glanced at Jonuta's vehicle, much less sought to stop or attack it.

Arsane er-Jorvistor emerged from the Wet Sand, hurrying. The second rent-a-guard followed with seeming casualness. Without looking, he noted that Jorvistor was heading for the parking area across the street. The other Sek assumed his client needed no help. That was good, but the rent-a-guard stayed on Arsane anyhow.

"Brilliant, Kenny," Jonuta was grunting between

breaths, "Just brilliant." Their weight had shut off the trike's automatic return mechanism. Sekhar was miserly with its yielding up of energy, and its people were just as miserly about its use. Jonuta and Kenowa provided their own.

"I—didn't know it—would close the deal!" she gasped, pedaling with all she had. "It just oc-whew-curred to me that we didn't—need that downer! Da-*amn* these damned trikes!"

"Let's assume it did. Not that I trust Arsane. But I'd rather leave the cargo here than risk hauling it through space again. This way we leave clean—and I don't have to go back to Qalara just yet."

She remembered how angrily he had left Qalara, after an angry speech and withdrawal of considerable credbacking from a number of Qalaran firms. His anger stemmed from the policers' inability to turn up anything there on the assassin who had missed him but succeeded in destroying Arel. Could that slime Corundum have agents even on Qalara?

"Dam' trikes," Kenowa muttered, feeling her leg banged by the pedal when Jonuta braked for the traffic light she hadn't even noticed.

She knew the reason for these miserable excuses for vehicles. That didn't make her like them any better. Or anything else on this flaining downer of a world! The only beasts of burden on Sekhar big enough to ride were too big to bestride, and so were ridden in howdahs. They were also too big to allow inside the city. Bicycles had been tried, but not for long. Too many people keeled over from sunstroke. Their bikes then caused traffic accidents. Cyclists could not be encased against the heat. Tricyclists could, and were safer besides. Running water on Sekhar was almost as scarce as cool air and dark clothing. That made water power extraordinarily expensive. Sekhar seemed to have no oil to speak of, other than vegetable, and what vegetables could be grown under the blue-white sun were needed for food. Years passed before Sekhar managed a single orbiting solar collector, and the whole world was in offplanet hock for that. There were far too many other things the Seks needed to do with that energy. More had not been constructed simply because of expense.

Bullsnot, Kenowa thought uncharitably.

Seks were born and raised Spartan, that was it. No one needed to be in a hurry! To have powered vehicles was just to add heat to the air! Besides, it was just . . . sybaritic. Sissy, to these religiously hung-up, over-manly Sek males. (*Bullsnot!* Pedaling was hard work, even inside a bubble temp-controlled by the same power source that drove the vehicle: human legs. Bull-snot!)

And *traffic lights,* for shitsake! As if cyclists in a city of a whole big hundred-nine thousand couldn't dodge each other on these awful sulphur-yellow streets! No, they were all masochists, Kenowa thought. No feelings, these sun-baked people. Fried brains, probably.

(A young woman sat at the Wet Sand bar and ignored male importunities while she tried to be quiet about her weeping. Her name was Verley. The greatest thing that had ever happened to her was gone, way too soon and just as suddenly as it had appeared. All she had was the rest of her life.)

Kenowa was too busy and breathless to make her little suggestions until they reached the outspace shuttle area. They did, without untoward incident. Still, a shuttle was just seconds from departure, and she and Jonuta had to run to avoid waiting twenty minutes or worse for the next one. See Kenowa, with her tongue hanging out.

On the way up the chute to the synchronorbiting space station/docks, all she could do was work at re-gaining her breath. And listen to the tingling in the muscles of her calves! That this fact gave her a flash of that fat-calfed barbarian, Yanya of Aglaya whom Jonuta just couldn't forget, only added to Kenowa's unconditionally negative mental attitude.

Beside her, Jonuta was smiling—and calculating, planning. It all looked just wonderful. There had been no incident at all, much less another attempt on his life. Sweetface would be up on the next shuttle and Tweedle-dee was already onboard, with the others. The rent-a-guard company had been paid in advance, by card. Kenowa was the hero of the hour and would soon recover from her present morose petulance. And Arsane had even said he would delight her with a gift or three.

The only problem was that Captain Cautious trusted Arsane er-Jorvistor just about as far as he could throw the man—who outweighed him by a good twenty or more kilos.

5

AGLAYA (N175-2Gs13 a,u,p) PROTECTED/
UNDVLPD. XANTHOCHROID (CAUCASOID?)
INHABS: LT. IRON AGE. TOP.F. 2/3 LAND.
SPARSLY POP: HVY RAIN FORESTS.
UNIRELIGIOUS: SUN + PLANETARY EPONYM.
THOT TO BE FORM OF GYNECOCRACY.
ONLY KNOWN VALUE: *Phrillia* (Q.V.).
Standard Universography Edutapes

Janja awoke beside a sleeping Corundum and stared up at what appeared to be the parsec abyss of space. It was not. A small switch beside the bed could project one of two holographic effects over the whole of the ceiling of the captain's cabin, which was one huge mirror. One bathed it in warm pink light and tended to split the images. That was nice for lovemaking, though disconcerting and sometimes distracting, and not so much fun on wakening. The other holoprojection turned the ceiling into that deep, deep hue called Prussian blue. In it, thousands and thousands of twinklepoints represented the over 300,004,000,000 living stars of this galaxy. (It did not attempt to show the billions of collapsed stars once called Black Holes.)

She squeezed her eyes shut. Looking into the deeps of space was not the best way to awake.

In her was Corundum's seed. It did not matter. To begin with, she had been inoculated. Her body would consider sperm an invader to be destroyed until she chose to receive the counter-shot.

In the second place, Janja had reason to believe that she would not be cross-fertile with *them.*

They—the Erts-speaking Galactics who had originated on Homeworld that had been Terra that had been Erth or Earth—were about the only race there was. Or seemed to be. The galaxy was presumed to contain over ten billion habitable planets. How many had been scanned, even noticed? As many as a million? Probably not. At least this worlds-teeming galaxy seemed to hold no other spacefarers.

They had found the jelly blobs of Shirash. Those highly intelligent creatures compensated for lack of tendrils, tentacles, or even pseudopods by being powerfully telehypnotic and mildly telekinetic. Shirash was dangerous. It was quarantined. An orbiting cybercraft warned ships away from that watery planet of abominations.

They had found Jarpi—and the hermaphroditic Jarps had happily used the visitors, sexually—both sexes. *They* were angered. Though not at the technological level, Jarpi was not Protected. Slavers took Jarps at will, prevented only by the Jarps themselves. No one gave a damn about the Jarps except the Jarps. They couldn't even form human sounds, much less words, but sounded like a bunch of whistling, tootling birds.

Humankind was still not certain whether the Crozites of Croz were human or not. None had cross-bred, but no differences had been isolated, either. Study continued.

Since Aglaya was Protected (the raids by slavers

were at the slavers' own risk), no one had taken note that the few Aglayans scattered about the spaceways had not reproduced. Nor did any of Them know about Aglayan *cherm*ing, much less *chonce*ling.

Janja opened her eyes, squeezed them shut. And They thought the lovely blue phrillia was Aglaya's only known value!

None of Them knew that every Aglayan could *cherm:* know or feel or sense the basic mental attitude or disposition/disposal of another. That ability was effective within a radius of one to two meters. It was more effective when the object of cherming was relaxed (as with drugs, which were unknown on Aglaya but most definitely not among Them). It was even more effective when a rapport existed between chermer and chermed. Groupthinking, or the collective intent or emotion of a group—such as an attacking force—could be chermed within one and a half or so kloms.

If these arrogant, so-superior Thingmakers discovered that ability, Aglaya and Aglayans would become very important very quickly.

Valuable, Janja thought, with the grimness she had learned from Them. *Aglayans might not be liked or trusted, but wouldn't we be used!*

Janja kept her ability to herself. And waited. She had learned that gaining the ability to choncel would come to her only with a male of Aglaya, not one of Them. There were *very* few Aglayans on the spaceways.

Chonceling was beyond cherming. It accounted for female dominion, on Aglaya.

The ability was gained by the deepkiss: the drinking of male seed. Aglaya hedged that act about with taboo and ritual and restricted it to a couple who were lifemated. With that ability a woman could know much more than merely the underlying attitude and intent of another. It was not quite the "mind-reading" that continued to elude Galactics except for occasional genetic accidents called *sports.*

In that case, Aglayans were a race apart.

They were not a part of humankind, though they were human in every way, lacking nothing, and could be Galactics. It was the invisible extra genetic factor that made Janja realize she was of a different race. This she had learned from the edutapes in the main library of Velynda, capital of Franji. She had corroborated the knowledge with another stolen but free Aglayan.

He was Flash, or Whitey (who concealed his Aglayan name as well as his hair, under a dark brown wig), a crewmember on a tramper much like Captain Ota's.

Janja, who had been Janjaheriohir, daughter of Sunmother and Aglii of Aglaya, was not displeased to discover that she was not human. Not inasmuch as They were human and so arrogantly proud of it. As a race, as Thingmakers who preferred drugs to the use of the mind, people who spoke in terms of "conquering" nature and space, Janja had only contempt for the Galactics. Humans; Them.

She wondered if They, sometime long ago, had made a sort of racial choice. To open the brain to its potential of controlling and healing self and body or—to make Things. To "conquer" their world and turn its flora and chemicals into drugs.

First one makes Things, Janja reflected, *and then one uses them and uses them and grows dependent . . .* addicted *until the Things become more important than oneself. After that one is truly serving them; the Things one created to serve oneself!*

She assumed herself to be of a different race, then, and superior.

They thought just the opposite! That was their error and their—their problem! It made her more dangerous, as she had already learned; more able to cope among Them. She lived now to find and destroy Jonuta of Qalara . . . and to find and deepkiss another Aglayan. If only Whitey had allowed it! No. He was a crewman among Them, striving to pass among them and *be* one of Them, and yet he still preserved belief in Sunmother and the taboos and customs of Aglaya.

Already Janja had learned too much of that. Her mind was a superb absorbing sponge with an ability to assimilate and synchretize. Whitey had been on the spaceways for years, and Janja was ahead of him in knowledge and even understanding.

The man beside her stirred and a smile touched Janja's lips, which had not smiled for so long. Corundum! A gentleman outlaw! And this courtly gentleman outlaw with his odd pet-word for her had assured her that his secondary focus in life was the destruction of Jonuta.

Naturally that had prompted Janja to ask, "And the primary?"

"Ah," Corundum had said, "Corundum's primary aim has ever been his own pleasure!"

Happily she had said, "Corundum, my dear, let's pursue both."

For the past month they had focused on the primary, and on Janja's further education. Now it became specialized.

She learned about computers. SIPACUM itself taught her its use and even the rudiments of simplified programming. She learned about *Firedancer* and ships in general. Daily she had her weapons training. She aimed and "fired" a harmless beam of light at shifting and increasingly smaller targets. She pretended to use the (inoperative) cutter with full instructions as to the deadliness of its laser beam, both to people and to spacecraft. She learned to tolerate Corundum's pet, Topaz, and slowly learned fondness for the golden-eyed miniature dragon. Immediately it showed corresponding fondness for her. That was more than instinctive response. Topaz was mildly telepathically sensitive: an empath. Janja dared not let it know they shared that ability; Topaz could also talk, and cherming remained Janja's secret.

Corundum awoke with such suddenness and thoroughness that Janja could fancy she heard an audible click. He put a hand over to feel her thigh, high up, and squeezed it lightly. Then he turned onto his side to check in with the con and SIPACUM/Jinni.

He was assured that all systems were P for Perfect. Messages zero. Occurrences zero. Good. Corundum ordered Jinni to check itself for glitches. Despite the heavy shielding around the guts of computers on spacecraft, that remained a worse problem in space than onplanet. Glitches were a consequence of solar flares and seemed unavoidable. At least a genius or three had devised the failsafe whereby a computer could check itself for errors, losses, or damage. (Call it almost-failsafe.) Corundum had Jinni check itself out every "morning." Morning on *Firedancer* was when Captain Corundum awoke.

Corundum turned and eased onto his back. With his hands on his hairy stomach he lay there, deep-breathed, expelled and held, held, held . . . inhaled as he sat up again, hands on stomach. A good stomach, Corundum's. A nice heavily haired chest, Corundum's, with nipples a woman could get her teeth into.

He came down to turn onto his side, toward Janja. His hand moved to lie on her pubic bulge, which was pronounced and (sparsely) white-furred.

"Silk, pure silk," he murmured appreciatively, as he had before, again and again.

She drew a deep breath, exhaled in a sigh, and covered his hand with hers. That nice gesture also kept his fingers from moving. Most people had inhibited the growth of hair below the face; it was simple bioengineering or a simple later process-by-choice. It was nice that she and Corundum had their hair, and that each appreciated the other's.

"Corundum, my education is lacking." She spoke to the ceiling.

"Horrors! Dare Corundum ask in what way?"

"May we be serious?"

"So early in the day and so naked! Very well then." He returned to his back and pushed up the small toggle beside the bed. The deepspace abyss vanished. The ceiling became a mirror. They looked up at each other looking down at each other. "Perhaps you would be kind enough to draw the sheet over your best parts."

Despite her stated desire to be serious, Janja gave that only a moment's consideration. Then she pulled the multi-hued paisley topsheet of Jahpurese satin up over her head. She heard him laugh, and she grinned, under the sheet.

"A point well taken indeed!" he said, chuckling. "How *could* one choose the best parts of the divinely molded Primeval Princess?"

She uncovered her face, smiled up/down at him, and let him see her face go serious. She looked at his best parts in their nest of hair and wanted to reach over and fondle or at least pat. She did not. She wanted to talk, not start another of their superb sexual sessions.

"One of the things I was studying on Franji was TGO."

"Ah," he breathed. "The Gray Organization."

"Umm." The mysterious and seemingly amoral order-keeping body named TransGalactic Order was more commonly called The Gray Organization. TGO claimed to work for the good by doing bad. In Aristotelean terms, that mixed black and white. TGO was gray, as They had grayed Janja. She had killed. She had set morals aside as being less important than Purpose.

She said, "It told me about Arti—uh, Arti-something Muzuni." She paused to let him supply the name: "Artisune," and went on. "It looked as if he was on his way to becoming a sort of galactic dictator. He was collecting 'protection' from many sources, including whole planets. A bribe to keep from being raided by Muzuni's pirate fleet of nineteen ships. Then he and those nineteen ships simply vanished."

"Apparently," Corundum said quietly, without his usual underlying note of satiric amusement. "It gives one to think that TGO possesses a spectacularly extraordinary fleet and power, does it not?"

"A preposterous fleet!" she agreed, and he squeezed her leg in an expression of pleasure at the term. In love with words, Corundum was. "At the same time, I learned that piracy is not only dangerous but a back-breakingly difficult . . . undertaking. It is inclined to be unprofitable and even harder than straightforward hauling."

"One would hardly expect edutapes to extol its virtues, would one? Edutapes are subject to TGO approval, surely. However, piracy as a trade seldom leads to the wealth-laden retirement so many desire or even foresee. Indeed, it more often results in early demise."

"You are not dead and you seem . . . prosperous, Emery."

He chuckled once again at the nickname she had devised for him. A form of corundum, emery was a hard abrasive, used for polishing. "Averages include but do not allow for the occasional brilliant member of any occupation, Milady Janja. Obviously Corundum is brilliant. Still . . . perhaps he inherited wealth or once achieved it and continues because his primary focus in life is his own pleasure, and this life pleases? Another we both know is called Captain Cautious. Yet Corundum truly takes few chances when that which is at stake is life itself!"

"I was not asking how you stay alive. We have just committed an act of piracy—by the way, what is the punishment?"

He flipped his fingers. "Oh, loss of eyes, long imprisonment, death. One or all of those." The slightly sneering vocal smile was back, to indicate his contempt for the unthinkable horrors he stated so easily.

"Oh, is that all," she said, feeling a wave of gooseflesh and glad the topsheet prevented him from seeing. "You knew Captain Ota had TZ. You must have been to the planet where he got it, and you must have left about the same time he did. You could have hauled the same cargo he did—the legal cargo, I mean. Therefore, you must have an informant there. That tends to indicate that you pay people on many other worlds to keep you informed of . . . certain things. And that is expensive."

"Milady has a very good mind," he said. "And further, uses it."

"A very good mind for a *girl* off a 'Protected, undeveloped' planet also called 'backward and barbaric'? —for an ex-slave?"

"No, for anyone at all. Milady Primeval Princess has no reason to be defensive. You manifestly know that the galaxy is full of people who may or may not have minds, but who do not *think*. You think, Janja. You reason. Corundum is not sensitive about being a pirate and called murderer. You must not be sensitive about being from a planet called barbaric, or a former slave. After all, you effected your own manumission! Remember that I surmised your identity as that slave who so spectacularly ended her slavery on Resh? Even then you commented that Corundum had his sources. He does—and a vaunting ability to add two and two and arrive at the accepted mathematical answer, rather than the silly answers that are the games of the 'scientists.' "

He stopped, or paused. Janja said, "Please do continue."

"If one's reasoning seems to lead to a paradox or a statement of contrariety, a contradiction, one has probably reasoned from one or more false premises."

"Try that on me again, lover."

He rubbed the side of her thigh. "If your conclusion is unsound or seems to be, check your premises. Corundum was not on the planet from which Ota departed. Corundum was far, far away—we had just left Franji. The message was sent from Ota's origin to . . . interestingly . . . Murph! Ota would have been in a great deal of trouble, on Murph! Further, when his ship at last reaches Murph's moon, Dot, the Murph policers will be most disappointed."

"Captain Ota was set up? Why? By whom?"

"Perhaps Corundum does not know everything. Still, tetrazombase is illegal even for policer use. If it were seized, however, from a smuggler such as Ota . . . why then a policer force would have a large and long-lasting supply on hand, wouldn't it!"

"Why, that's positively evil. He was being trapped!"

"Perhaps doubly. The word also came to *Firedancer*. Is it possible that legal officials were tricked into making an *arrangement* with legal officials on Murph, and using Ota—in order for *Firedancer* to receive the word and come into possession of a couple of kilos of TZ—without charge?"

She came up on one elbow. "Corundum! How deliciously devious! Is that the way it happened? You were behind it *all?*"

He could not resist palming one of her bared, enticing breasts and drawing fingers and thumb out along the cone, lingeringly. His smile was one of lazy mockery; a Corundum smile. "Was I?"

She jerked his hand from her. "Damned nasty mocking evil pirate! Hmp!" She flopped back into the supine position and dragged the topsheet up to her chin. "All right. *Perhaps* Ota was being trapped. *Perhaps* policers set the trap. *Perhaps* you instigated it—and certainly profited from it! All right. Then how did we find him in the vastness of space?"

"Ah, a ringing poetical phrase, that," he said, for Corundum was unable not to chastise the users of clichés. He loved saying, with sonorous portent, "into . . . the . . . gathering dusk" and "he turned on his heel," and rolling his eyes—after which he held his nose. This time he winked at her overhead reflection.

"Like many freighters not owned by corporations or

wealthy combines. Ota's ship is not equipped with capability to enter subspace, in defeat of an ancient postulate stating the inability of objects to exceed the speed of light. Long ago our ancestors found a way to circumvent that troublesome 'rule.' Otherwise we should never have peopled so many planets, and created what it pleases us to call an intragalactic civilization. Now. Here, near the galaxy's center, stars are many and close together."

"Proximitous," she said, happily pandering to his love of words.

"Indeed! Thus even though many freighters move at sub-light speeds, cargo may be hauled at profit. In months, not years. Hence: Captain Ota. Corundum knew his point and time of departure, and his destination, and knew that Ota would not be stopping save in the event of emergency. A direct run to the system of Murph's sun, so far as any runs can be direct in such a crowded meadow of stars."

"We followed him, popping in and out of subspace?" Janja's eyes were bright and her brain was at work, greased and smoothly running at the game of second-guessing.

"No. Corundum and Jinni played a most interesting game. In leisurely manner, you will recall, we popped over to Ghanj and purchased some clothing and toys for you—and me, be assured."

"Even though you like me best naked."

"No, Corundum probably likes you best in the black skinnTite and highboots—and in that swishy garment that is yards and yards of polyweave and yet clings to your every salient curve in the manner of a cloying lover."

She smiled, snuggled, felt it safe to pat and rub, just a little, his best parts. Swiftly she said, "Please go on about finding Ota."

"Shameless tease! We also, by the way, turned a profit on Ghanj—and discovered a buyer for a certain illegal substance."

"TZ!" She practically clapped her hands in delight at his cleverness.

"TZ," he said, with a sort of horizontal nod. "Then we departed, still in manner leisurely, and entered subspace. As you know, we have popped in and out a number of times. We were searching for Ota."

"In what you call this meadow of stars and planets, a single spacer is smaller even than a needle in a haystack!"

He paused to chuckle. "So. And how would you find a needle in a haystack?"

She thought a moment, and then she shocked even Corundum. "Assuming that I really wanted that needle, it would be more valuable than the hay. I'd merely burn the haystack."

He showed that he was shaken by the piercing solution, the ruthless one still called Gordian. "Musla's holy Eyes and Prophet—what a mind!"

Realizing that she had thought of something he had not, Janja showed him a smug smile—a Corundum smile. "And your solution, lover?"

"To begin with, it was in the earliest part of the twenty-first century when a certain individual employed a computer and a cybernetic rake, and found a needle in a haystack in 7.19 minutes." He paused, and after a moment he chuckled. "An eloquent silence, proclaiming that such information is irrelevant. Janja, pragmatism deals with the practical and assumes that thought exists to direct action. An advanced form is called enlightened self-interest, which means simply intelligent selfishness. Self-*less*-ness is manifestly stupid and innately self-destructive."

"Does this concern Ota's ship or am I going to have to jump up and down on your stomach?"

He laid a staying hand on her thigh, letting her feel its strength.

"Corundum is a pragmatist," he continued. "He uses those tools available to him. Corundum acts as he must. My primary concern is me. You," he said, pointing to the Janja looking down at him from the ceiling, "are your primary concern and your thoughts lead to shockingly direct action. We are pragmatists, Janja."

Strange, she mused, *that I never thought of pragmatism as an ugly word, until now.* Yet she knew that she was complimented.

"Back to the needle in the haystack, Milady Janja. Corundum had these givens. The ability to leap about, which Ota did not. Knowledge of his time of departure, estimated time of arrival, probable course, and maximum velocity. The knowledge that his old ship is a ram-scoop, not solar-photonic. The ion exhaust of a ram-scoop ship with a double-P drive radiates a great deal of 'noise'—electromagnetism. Sensitive instruments perceive it as entirely different from the magnetic field surrounding suns and most planets. *Firedancer* is equipped with the best and most sensitive instrumentation and systemry. QED."

"What? Cue-ee-dee?"

"QED—we found Ota. We plotted probable areas and checked them until we detected an EM field that was probably a spaceship's. We then had only to come in closer to read and confirm him." He allowed himself a satisfied smile, and said, "Are you not hungry? Anxious to aid the water recycling facilities?"

"Are you weary of telling me how truly brilliant you are?"

"Ah, how Milady knows me!"

"What I want to know now is how all this is to be profitable."

"Milady, among all these stars power is the cheapest possible commodity. The cost of a spaceship is prodigious. The cost of moving and maneuvering in space is minuscule. Aside from the fact that Corundum serves his own pleasure, the machinery for the miners on Dot is to be paid for on delivery. Since it cost us nothing, we will charge them less than the stated price, less than they expect to pay. They will ask no questions. Everyone is happy. Perhaps the machinery can be said only to cover our costs: overhead. The TZ, then, is pure profit. Everyone is happy. Except the police officials on Murph, who will be awaiting Ota's arrival . . . in two months."

"And except Ota."

"Be assured that his *crew* is not unhappy!"

"I suppose I see. It does seem that being a merchant captain is less trouble and far less dangerous, in this sort of . . . business. With your mind, you could—"

"—Worry the same but about things Corundum does not care to worry about! Being a merchant captain lacks the excitement—which you have just called danger. They are the same, to some of us. It has been so throughout the history of humankind. Still"—he smiled—"there *will* be a Corundum shipping line," he said, almost dreamily. "Ships of red and blue—ruby and sapphire. Corundum."

Corundum revels in excitement, danger, calling himself wicked names others had better not dare in his presence . . . and dreams of legitimacy! Janja considered that for a time, scratching idly. "But then—why aren't you stealing *whole ships?* That would be easy!"

"And isn't that thought exciting to you, Milady pirate!" Corundum laughed aloud. He rose on an elbow to look down at her with ridiculously ingenuous eyes. "But that would be evilly *dishonest!*" He watched her roll her eyes, and he smiled. "To take merchandise is one thing; there is plenty. To take a man's *means* of earning his livelihood—that is another matter!"

And what, she thought, *about taking his life with such relish?*

"Besides," Corundum said, running his hands over the mounds in the topsheet over her chest. "Besides, let a few ships be seized and one might apply the impetus to unite the shipping lines, and policers. To start them *seriously* seeking pirates, with true assiduousness! Who can forget Artisune Muzuni?"

"Deterrent!" she said in a flash of revelation. "That's why TGO removed him so mysteriously; the memory of his disappearance—with *nineteen ships!*—is a constant deter—uh!"

She felt the unpleasant sensation as they again entered subspace.

Suns, live and collapsed, did exist in subspace. It was not truly somewhere else beyond the rainbow or the yellow brick road. Here, far in toward the center of the galaxy's ever more tightly coiled spiral, suns living and dead were plentiful. If SIPACUM could not dodge one in subspace, it "knew" it and kicked out to cruise past at sub-light speeds. They had just done so, avoiding another of the trillion-plus non-sentient dealers of death in the galaxy. She and Corundum had been too occupied with brain stimulus and talk and each other to pay attention to the s-s entry warning. On automatic to convey them to the little fourth moon of Murph, SIPACUM/Jinni had returned them to subspace for another long jump. The ship was no longer a ship. Its crewmembers were no longer people. They were on the Tachyon Trail. There was no "subspace" or the old dream of "hyperspace"; still, humans had learned to defeat Einstein and infinity. What they saw was subjective. To an outside observer they were . . . unobservable.

As *Firedancer* conveyed them at unholy velocity, Corundum flipped away the topsheet. He brought his mouth down on Janja's breast.

In subspace! she thought, still experiencing disorientation and the bit of nausea that always accompanied this reduction to mere particles. *The man is both mad and insatiate—uh!* "Uh-ummm," she sighed. She watched her hand glide up his hair to the back of his head. Watched her other hand strive to reach his small tight buttocks. Felt his moving tongue and began to writhe, moaning.

Far out in space, far in toward the hot, bright galactic center, they moved at never-conceivable speeds and were every nanosecond an instant away from spectacular death. And he did just what men had been doing for centuries and eons, in war and in peace, in danger and in safety. He sucked eagerly swelling nipples into his mouth and bathed them with saliva. His tonguetip moved and moved, a flickering serpent over the tips of erectile flesh. It felt good, good, and muscles and nerves tensed throughout every centimeter of her body.

Squirming, she gained his butt with her hand. She rubbed, squeezed, began a light rapid smacking while he feasted on her breasts. She felt him squirming, felt his slicer growing against her thigh, and she knew her cleft would be ready for it when it came in, centimeter after centimeter of hard flesh. Slicer slicing into stash was ancient as the race. Slicing in space was centuries and centuries old, very old hat indeed. Slicing in free-fall, in null-G, had come first, before the employment of spin to create artificial shipboard gravity. But . . . smiling, squirming, moaning, rubbing and slapping, Janja wondered just how common this was—slicing in subspace!

6

Oh Time! Of all the dwellers here below
You elevate only buffoons or fools.
The Perfumed Garden of
Shaykh Nafzawi

Long and long ago the honorable word *selfishness* had been weakly distorted into *enlightened self-interest*. Long ago nervous cretins had subsumed and vampirically drained the study of history into a husk called "social studies." It was not strange, then, that the euphemism for guns (weapons; armaments) should no longer be any of those terms:

"Stand by defense systemry."

"Standing by DS and ready, Captain."

"Ship Coronet! *You are locked to our docking station in synchronous orbit of Sekhar! We read your armaments unbuttoned."*

The first voice had been Jonuta's. The second, that of his loyal crewmember Sakyo. The third, oncomm: Sekharstation Control, shocked. The fourth was Jonuta again:

"You read true and well, Control. When menaced,

"Captain!" the shocked voice came back. *"We are* Authority*!"*

"Me too."

"As constituted Authority of planet Sekhar, we propose a routine check of spaceship Coronet," the reply came, as if perhaps a return to cold and arrogant anonymity, that magical word *Authority,* might gain its ends. The clerk sitting at Sekharstation Control was supposed to cow people. It had always succeeded before. This was too incredible. What was *wrong* with this Jonuta person?

Jonuta had more shocks in store. "I respect authority, when it is respectworthy," he said, and with seeming calm added, "You are a liar. There is nothing routine about this. I did business with Sekhari citizen Arsane er-Jorvistor—stop interrupting, clerk!—and the swine has slipped something incriminating onto *Coronet.* Now he has paid someone to detain me and worse. Bribed someone, you understand. Your superior, perhaps, nameless Control? Your superior's superior, perhaps? I am to be boarded, searched, found guilty of something false, and detained or worse. That is the official exercise of unwarranted power and intimidation: IRS. Also called 'piracy.' Well sir, I refuse."

"Captain—"

"Believe me, Sekharstation Control," Jonuta thrust in, still with seeming ice in every vein. "We shall not open for the piratic boarding you suggest. We—"

"—piratic! Captain! *We are the* Law*!"*

"Not mine.

"Captain, you will proceed to—"

Jonuta closed comm, counted seven, opened comm. "We will not admit your robots or you either. If they attempt to gain entry by violent means, we will resist violently. Obviously it would be stupid to do violence on mere cyber-searchers! Our first target, Control, is you. *Release us."*

"Captain! We—"

"Shutting off comm and manning guns. Programming SIPACUM to commence firing and breakaway attempt in sixty seconds. *Mark.*" Jonuta flipped the toggle with a sweaty finger. "Set our sensor-reading of their tractor field on Visual, Kenny. Give us an alarm when it releases us."

"Jone—"

"We're not going to be boarded, Kenowa. We're not going to become prisoners on this skungeball world. I gave that creature sixty seconds to try to do him a favor. Think of the marvelous feeling for him if he makes a decision, accepts responsibility once in his life! We have to push and keep pushing. I'm sure they're calling in a ship or two to tangle with us a few seconds after we're released from this damned station. Inslot Cassette six-three bee, but don't activate it. Be prepared to shove 63C in . . . and to activate."

Jonuta's course guidance cassettes were prepared by Jonuta. Cassette number 63B ordered SIPACUM and other systems to prepare the ship for subspace transition and take her in to defeat infinity with only a single *ping* as twenty seconds' warning. Sixty-three cee was considerably more serious and was last resort. Sixty-three cee seized everything and *rammed* the ship into transition phase with no warning, within ten seconds after its actuation. Spacefarers had a name for that desperate action, aside from jam-cram. They called it "Forty Percent City."

The probability of survival of such an unprepared subspace entry was just above seventy percent with (undefined) damage. Probability of survival intact was 59.7731-to-infinity percent. What remained was a 40.2269 percent probability of . . . non-return.

If those ships that had jam-crammed onto the Tachyon Trail had survived (somehow, somewhere), no one knew it, for none of them was seen again. Less than a year ago the pirate captain, Tomo, had been desperate enough to go Forty Percent City. Tomo's ship had departed the spaceways with Tomo and all hands. He was presumed destroyed; extirpated.

"Jonuta," Kenowa said, obeying. "What—what if—what if they—"

"Hold it," Jonuta said. "I'm busy. Sakyo: do not fire. Hold on target but do not fire under any circumstances unless I say 'Fire, Sakyo.' Shig: stand by to lay a one-second burn on the base of the controller's bubble, one meter above its stem. Forty-four seconds remain." He heaved a sigh and half-turned to lay a hand on Kenowa's shoulder. "You know I won't endanger an entire planet by wrecking or downing a whole station." He saw the sagging lowering of her shoulders and knew he was watching the release of a great deal of tension. She had not been sure.

"I couldn't do it, Kenny. No, if that controller doesn't act or someone doesn't tell him to, a one-second flash with the ten-megawatt laser will go right through the con module. That should convince them what a ruthless monster I am. It may also scare that fobber into slapping off the tractor field he's pinning us with."

"We—we'll never be able to return to Sekhar!"

"You never wanted to, did you? Booda's eyes, who does?" He was watching the chronometer. "Shig! Hit the control module with spotlights, all power!"

Digit after digit spun past on the decaseconds gauge; seconds jumped while Shig doubtless threw a real scare into the controller by making him think a multibeam laser was right on him.

"But—Jone! What if they—mightn't they—"

Jonuta said, "No, Kenny. They won't use armaments. They have that much sense—someone has to have. Not up here on Sekhar's one station." He wiped his palms on his long scarlet coat. "Eleven seconds remain, crew. Nine. Eight." He jerked his head and Kenowa felt the droplet of sweat that flew from him. "Six. Open comm, Kenowa. Five. *Stand by to fire,*" he rapped sharply, for the benefit of the reopened communications link with Sekharstation Control. "Three. T—"

The alarm sounded and a panel flashed turquoise/white, turquoise/white. *Coronet* was freed to go. Turquoise/white, turquoise/white. Tractor field lifted. Three armed, wheeled cybers zipped away from the vicinity of the airlock. Freefall prevailed. Kenowa swallowed heart, stomach, and a sour taste.

"Inslot cassette thirty-nine! Redshifting repeat redshifting."

Kenowa, breathing with her mouth open, had the cassette ready. She double-checked its number because she knew she was barely functioning. A nod, and she pushed it into its slot with a sweaty hand. Sixty-three bee floated above the slot. SIPACUM was ordered to crank up and depart Sekhar.

Coronet shuddered and began a familiar vibration. Kenowa snatched 63B out of the air before it gained weight under acceleration and fell.

"Guess we won't be needing thirty-nine anymore," Jonuta muttered, watching his console.

Anxious to say anything at all in this release of tension, Kenowa suggested, "Maybe we can sell it." That was facetiousness. She assumed that she would be ordered to give the cassette the usual treatment of superseded tapes. She would wipe it, then record music on it. An unnecessary double procedure. Captain Cautious intended to provide his carefully prepared guidance cassettes to no one.

"Stand by 63B. Stand by. Stand by. Offstation, all! Stand b—oh shit. *Shut down DS!* Off spotlight!"

"Defense systemry shut down, Cap'n," Shig reported, obviously relieved. "Congratulations, Captain."

"Shut down, Captain," Sakyo reported. Disappointed?

"Anticipate subspace entry." Jonuta tapped two keys. SIPACUM advised that *Coronet* was clear of Sekharstation.

"Captain Jonuta, you are considered an enemy of Sekhar and we will report it."

Jonuta's face went stormy. He banged in a key and the comm mike swung to his face.

"Register and record! Complaint lodged by Qalara-citizen Kislar Jonuta, captain, *Coronet*. Follows: Sek-harcitizen Arsane er-Jorvistor set me up by means of a bribed Sekhari official. I have no notion what he put on my ship. I do refuse to be set up by a desperate individual of a desperate planet. My congratulations to controller on-con, who refused to give its name, for its responsible decision in terminating piratic clutch on *Coronet*. Request foregoing be sent to TAI, TGO/TGW, Qalara, Resh, Tri-System Accord, Shankar, Franji, Panish, Jahpur, Jasbir. Jonuta out for good."

Snick. Communications ended. Good riddance.

"T'lood'l wheet—trr-ee-eed'l-l-leet!"

"Booda's eyes! Dammit, Sweetface, turn on your damned translator!"

"Sorry, Captain," the Jarp's translated voice said. "Two ships closing. Both on intercept trajectory. Captain."

"Odtaa," Jonuta sighed.

Kenowa looked up at him. He had acronymously expressed the ancient lament: One Damned Thing After Another. Yet already he was responding decisively to this new Damned Thing:

"Inslot 63B. All: subspace entry as soon as SIPACUM finds a hole to take us through. Usual twenty-second warning. Stand away from the guns and hold onto your stomachs."

"Klee'ee'eed'l-ooot't!"

"Sweetface, dammit—"

"Sorry, Captain. Not me. That was Tweedle-dee."

"Uh."

The Jarp that Sweetface had named Tweedle-dee was a halfwit Sweetface had showed up with, on Resh. It/she/he was still onboard. That was against Jonuta's good judgment, but he felt empathy for Sweetface, and he did, after all, forbid the possibility of sexual activity among Sweetface, Sakyo, Kenowa, and Jonuta. (His with Kenowa was another matter. Captain's prerogative.) He could only hope that Sweetface soon tired of Tweedle-dumb, as Kenowa called it. Now Jonuta knew he had erred in agreeing to Tweedle-dee's presence on *Coronet* and eventually trouble would result. Jonuta was for calling the second Jarp "Argon"; the creature didn't react with anything or anybody. Except Sweetface. An inert element.

"We're being scanned," Kenowa said, having replaced guidance cassette 39 (Depart: Sekharstation: Jonuta's Way) with 63B. She racked 39 without thinking. The rack was a better place than any, until Jonuta decided what to do with it. "One of those ships has tractor capability."

"Armaments showing on bandits, Captain," Sakyo reported. "Man DS stations?"

"No."

"Captain: suggest we leave defense systemry off but let 'em track," Sakyo suggested, "so those bandits will notice."

Jonuta repeated, "No. No hostile act. With my words on record Sekhar may decide to wipe and forget the events of the last ten minutes. If we fire on a policer, though, or stir up one with a nervous dee-esser onboard—"

"SIPACUM has compared emissions, blip-silhouettes, and EM fields," Kenowa reported. "Both approaching ships are Sekhari policers."

Had an inexperienced person been onboard—Verley of Sekhar, for instance—she might have been dizzied not only by the rush of events and Jonuta's seeming cool ability to cope, but by the terminology she heard.

Kenowa had reported that Coronet's SIPACUM-directed cybernetic detectors, constantly on the alert, indicated that they were being snooped upon. Explored by electronic scanning devices mounted in the two oncoming ships. Those same detectors indicated that one of the "bandits" on their screens was equipped with systemry to seize *Coronet* in an electronic attraction field: a tractor "beam" that operated just short of the level of molecular bonding. All three spacers were equipped with automatic tracking equipment for their DS/defense systemry/guns, of course, as only idiots would rely on humans to aim and fire in space. Sakyo had suggested that he actuate his DS trackers so that the guns would remain leveled menacingly at the other craft, though without firing. The threat would be implicit and constant. That Jonuta forbade, lest one of the policer ships have an inexperienced or nervous person in charge of DS. "Dee-esser" for DS-er was current euphemism for "gunner" all along the spaceways.

Next SIPACUM recorded the emissions of the other ships, and the shapes and sizes of their radar silhouettes or blips, and the electromagnetic fields created by their engines. Those SIPACUM compared with its microfile storage, and found that the combination of such "signatures" was peculiar to the spacecraft employed by Sekhar World Defense: Sekhar's policers. This news Kenowa announced to Jonuta:

"My my," Jonuta said. "Fifty percent of their entire spaceforce!" He opened his dramatic coat on which the double row of flashy prass buttons was purely decorative. He wiped sweat off his forehead. "How important we are!"

"Coronet. Coronet. *Sekhar Security SSS-four-zero here. Captain Berbistor oncomm. You are not repeat not cleared to leave Sekharstation and must be considered outlaw. We will fire repeat fire.*"

"No you won't, Sek-Sec ship number four," Jonuta said, ignoring the "zero" the Seks had added to make their four-ship force sound more imposing. "We are too close to your only station. Can it withstand the mini-nova if you blow this ship—or we do? We will not repeat not fire because we are not repeat not outlaw, but traders who refuse to be set up by your planet's criminal element." *Come on, SIPACUM,* he was thinking. *Find us a hole!*

"Captain Jonuta, we are law enforcers. We do not decide. We enforce. There is no use trying to reason with us. Break off flight and return to Sekharstation One."

Pinng. It was the twenty-second warning. Just now a voice pronouncing full pardon and amnesty for all Jonuta's transgressions would not have sounded more beautiful.

"Keep your distance, Sekhari Security Ship Four Million," Jonuta said, drawling to drag it out. "We are about to take a ride on the Tachyon Trail."

Ten seconds remaining.

"Stand by to fire," the comm said, because the Seks weren't kept busy enough to be all that experienced, and because Captain Berbistor simply forgot to button off before he issued the ill-advised order.

"Don't shoot!" Jonuta yelled fearfully into the mike. Kenowa looked sharply up at him. His chesty voice had positively squeaked. *"Coronet,"* he went on, "all crew stand by to return to dock! Cancel subspace entry." That, in the same desperate tone, was also shouted into the communications mike linking them with SSS-40 and presumably the other ship as well. Their blips were getting mighty large onscreen.

Both Jonuta's apparent panic and his words were sham. Inasmuch as he had not touched the override switch, SIPACUM continued to obey the directing cassette. Inasmuch as it had taken him eight seconds to make those breakdown noises, SSS-40's Captain Berbistor didn't get much said.

"Very wise, Coronet," his surprised and relieved voice said. *"We will follow you in. All w—"*

The voice was gone with the onset of the eerie sensation. Stomachs lurched and every nerve in every body onboard felt as if it had gone to sleep. Ears popped. Tingles beset them all. Jonuta released a lot of breath, trying to do it slowly. His heartbeat was imitating a pulsar and he knew he had just vanished off all screens. He no longer existed. He had been reduced to that tiniest of motes called a tachyon. Many tachyons.

Coronet was on the Tachyon Trail; in subspace, streaking right through Einstein's Law.

Captain Berbistor, along with Sekhar, was . . . somewhere else. Captain Cautious, rather incautiously and close to the edge this time, had done it again.

Jonuta's hand was heavy on Kenowa's shoulder. To their subjective perception, they existed unchanged. He killed the outside link and the mike swung away. Onship comm links remained open:

"Sweetface to the con," Jonuta said.

He heard a whispered *t'eeetle* and knew it was Tweedle-dee. Thought it/she/he and Sweetface were going to make it in subspace, huh? Tough. Their captain was drained.

Kenowa's hand came up onto his. "D'you think there's danger in those bales Arsane brought on?"

"Maybe a snake or a Sekhari scarlet sand-scorpion. Nothing that's going to foul up the ship, no. I'll even bet the TDP works."

"How can we be sure?"

"Pretend we don't have it available until we have it tested on Franji. And installed." He blew out his cheeks as he gusted air. "Whoof. Booda's smile, what a lot of trouble and hard work it is, being self-employed."

Kenowa was smiling. *Good!* She liked Franji, where Jonuta was presumed to be some sort of wealthy heir to something or other. "I don't want to bother with those packages now, either," she said. "Sweetface is taking the con?"

"Sweetface certainly is."

"They won't be happy about that, Sweetface and Tweedle-dumb."

Jonuta's anger rode his voice in crimson waves of heat. "Too damned bad! I need relief."

"Good. Ready to go and get out of those sweaty clothes?"

He grinned. "Pos! And into a shower instead."

She smiled, squeezing the hand on her shoulder. "What shall we get into then?"

"You," Jonuta said.

7

Dot was a satellite, not a planet. A little space-scouter or a basketball would be too, in the proper orbital entrapment. Dot was a little bigger. Murph was no large planet and its fourth moon was a mere dot in space. So it had been named. The dot in space was called Dot. It was not even sufficient to eclipse Murph's sun, Aristarkos, when the hurrying little satellite was between planet and star. It certainly was bright, though, and hot as well, on Dot's sunward side. And at its closest proximity to Murph—its Perimurph—Dot positively wiggled.

On Dot, the horizon was just right over there. The curvature was easily visible. Claustrophobia awaited anyone on Dot, with space all about and stars clustered thick as blossoms of white and yellow, red and blue in an untrodden twilit meadow.

Starlight provided plenty of visibility, even when Aristarkos was on the far side of Murph. Nevertheless, Murphside mining interests had seen fit to provide big well-mounted lights. The mining machinery and dumps of ore and waste were festooned with lights, too.

Firedancer made contact with T.M.S.M. Company's Dotside operations manager, from space. He—someone named Aaron—had to alopogize for the static in his transmission. His data terminal was presently receiving and recording an information transmission from the onplanet central processor, he explained, and Dot was almost at Perimurph. After a little electronic conversation, Corundum and a single aide were invited to "come on in and discuss business."

Janja, with no idea as to why Corundum had identified himself as "Captain Tojuna of Qalara," became the accompanying aide.

The others—Hing, Sakbir, and Bearcat—would remain silently on *Firedancer*. They would stand ready to free and offload the cargo, and for any of the other less prosaic duties a pirate had to be ready to perform. There were various occupational hazards, constants, and an emergency was always just around the corner.

Corundum explained the purpose of metacerebrinene, known along the spaceways as Stand-up, and insisted that Janja take one when he did. She allowed herself to be persuaded, despite her antipathy for drugs —things of Them. The Galactics, the Thingmakers.

In spacesuits, the two of them left the ship and made for the big bubble decorated asymmetrically with solar collectors and sensor clusters.

Walking was not easy, despite the Stand-up, a vestibular correction drug. They moved slowly. The stars seemed to lean on them.

Dot was an ugly little wart on the nose of the universe. Its gravity was 0.24 standard, with even less oxygen. Humans hardly floated at one-quarter G, but strides became long flotatious adventures. A dropped object could be caught easily before it drifted to the surface. A heavy spanner would fall with all the hurry of a leaf on a one-gee/1G planet. Should a person slip and fall, Janja knew without quite understanding, she would ease down to bounce, gently. Sortabounce, the miners of Dot called it.

Those employees of TMSMCo signed on for three years up here. The benefits were great but only after return to Murph. The duty was lousy. Somebody at TMSMCo felt that women on Dot would lead to trouble. Male or female, that person might have been right with such an old-fashioned attitude, but the decision and the reality of its implementation didn't help matters.

TMSMCo's employees here were called miners although they did not mine, on Dot. Machines did. The miners—all males and all on the pill, sooner or later—directed the machines, one to one, by means of telepresences.

Janja did not know these things. She was surprised to see no spacesuited men out laboring on the little ball that had so gingerly caught *Firedancer*.

Dot merely looked barren, untenanted, and small. The visible curvature and all that gem-flashing space were far from pleasant. Still, there was the bubble to herald human presence. Here and there she saw definite heavy equipment tracks, and now and again a gleaming smooth area of metaliferous stone sliced or scraped too neatly to be the result of any natural process. Dot was tenanted, though there was no settlement. Just the bubble. It must enclose both working and living quarters for a score or so of Galactics. Males.

A port opened to admit them to the bubble that was large and sprawling, a gigantic walnut shell, and yet that did not seem large enough to house work areas, computer terminals, telepresence equipment, mess, bunks, and living area. . . . Since they stepped into a small chamber that faced another hatch, they knew that the bubble was pressurized. This was an airlock. The hatch closed behind them. The interior one opened. Only a voice greeted them.

It bade them enter what it called the phone booth—in a bubble empty of people!

"They're down inside the satellite," Corundum said, as much to himself as to his "aide."

They knew they were in air, now, but they retained

their helmets while they float-walked over to the tall rectangular box. A phone booth—or an upended coffin.

It was neither. It was another airlock!

"They are most cautious," Corundum muttered. "Wise men."

Janja glanced at him. They were being monitored, surely. Why had he troubled to say that? For her benefit? Merely to be talking? Or was it a deliberate compliment, a sort of early opening of his sales talk?

They entered the strange little structure, an airlock within an airlocked bubble with presumably breathable atmosphere. In the steel or cyprium floor was a trapdoor of steel—or cyprium? Corundum depressed a wall-mounted key, as directed. The wheel atop the trapdoor spun, rose. The trapdoor came up to stand as a thick slab over a flight of narrow plasteel steps. They were painted turquoise with luminous white stripes that were safety treads. The vertical shaft, about a meter and a half on a side, was brightly illuminated.

"Safety precaution after safety precaution," Corundum muttered, easily descending nine steps. "One could easily drop down into this little well, and jump up and out, in this gravity that hardly merits the name. But someone seems to have thought of everything or nearly. Little human precautions and comforts. Extra expense to keep men happier in what has to be lonely duty. Living quarters down here will be next to luxurious, I'll bet."

He was looking up, watching Janja descend into that claustrophobic trap. Descending stairs was strange, in the bulky spacesuit and in one-quarter gravity.

Corundum pressed another wall-mounted key, yellow. The trapdoor came down above them; behind them. Thank Aglii that the stairwell was well lit, in eye-eez turquoise!

Someone was cautious and wise indeed. The aerated, pressurized bubble, only slightly flexible, was first protection from oxygenless Dot. The "phone booth" was the second, a haven within a haven. The little chamber at the bottom of the stair was a third. The trapdoor, too, was an airlock, though there was no hiss or change of pressure when it closed. Precaution after precaution after precaution, adding up to failsafety.

Janja imagined the spinning of that big locking wheel above her head, a giant screw penning them underground, and tried not to feel trapped.

The wall before them was about three meters high and only about sixty sems wide. It grew a door about forty meters by a hundred eighty meters, which slid open to reveal more surprises.

"Come in, Captain," the squat, prognathous-jawed man said. He waved a big hand. He wore some sort of soft shoes and and an obviously lightweight coverall. It was open to the navel and he was hairless. He had a gut and would show a lot more gut on any normal-G planet. And Janja wasn't through being surprised.

Here were Dot's miners. The TMSMCo employees stood or sat all around the walls of the rectangular chamber, and standing must have been a matter of choice. None of these men was truly tall, or truly fat.

Walls and ceiling were beige. The floor was grass green, a high-piled carpet. The lighting was a lovely gold or muted yellow, bright without being bothersome. Three walls were mostly viewscreens, with banks of instruments and viewscopes and TP gloves at waist level of the seated men. Each faced his screen and not one of them looked around at the newcomers. Discipline could not have been so good, and they must always be delighted to greet those few visitors who came here. Thus they must have discussed, and decided. Coming up was a discussion and possible deal that was hardly straightforward. The decision, then, was to continue with work and let Aaron deal with the visitors who might be merchants or pirates. No one else would so much as glance around at them.

Janja wondered if she and Corundum really were

trusted. Were these men armed? Was each armed? Was the entire underground chamber perhaps covered by automatic or TP weaponry? She realized that she saw no living quarters, no bunks. There was at least one more chamber, then. Probably about half this many men were in it; they must work in staggered shifts.

Yes, she thought, *we are surely being monitored.*

Some of these "miners" sat with their faces fitted into shaped viewscopes. While they stared, their hands seemed to be working away at their instrument panels.

Others wore the weird telepresence helmets or coifs; TP-coifs. Some were manipulating wall-mounted circular mechanisms like old steering wheels. Others fingered keys and occasional toggles or levers of varying sizes and shapes, and the hands of some men were fitted into gauntlets. Telepresence gauntlets: TP-waldoes.

Janja realized that every one of them must have studied and practiced at length before coming up here. They were professional miners but hardly the burly, smudgy men one might expect. She would bet their knowledge embraced far more than sports scores and the Akima Mars series (starring Setsuyo Puma as Akima Mars: The Biggest Pair in the Universe!).

These men *were* mining. One way or another, each was manipulating a piece of machinery elsewhere on Dot, or in Dot. It and its "driver"-manipulator were TP-connected, electronically. The feedback on such devices was mutual. The men directed the equipment as if they rode it or pushed it, and yet better. Via TP, men were part of machines. Each was electronically present at the site of his mining activity, as part of the machine doing the mining. Each saw what his equipment "saw" and even felt changes of resistance in the portion of Dot he worked.

Some had to be digging. Some must be moving ore. Others must be operating or at least monitoring extracting/separating equipment. Maybe some were monitoring the others?

"I'm Aaron, Captain."

The man who had greeted them gave no other name or identification. He had no need. His preoccupied miners did not turn or so much as glance around. Corundum unhelmeted. Janja, as he had instructed her, did not. She was sexless and faceless in the bulky turquoise suit with the viewplate of one-way hyperplas.

"Captain Tojuna of Qalara, Aaron," Corundum said, when he had bared his head, and Janja was surprised still again. "But never mind the 'Captain' stuff. This is my aide—uh, Cinnabar."

"Your Mate?"

"Not capitalized, no. Ship's Mate is onboard, ready to offload some damned fine equipment you men need and are going to love, Aaron."

"We need it, yes. Uh—I think it may be best that I call you—ah—Captain Viking?" Aaron's expression was mildly arch, which was strange on that slab of a face centered with a nose that appeared to have survived a seismic disaster—barely.

Corundum showed him raised eyebrows. "Oh? And why is that?"

"We're all engineers here, Captain, true, but we do have various other areas of specialization and interest," Aaron said quietly, leaning a bit toward Corundum. "We are not cut off from the rest of the galaxy. Oh, we are *physically,* yes. But we have input, a library with anything available on Murph, since we're computerlinked with Murph; and we get the news. We try to stay current, you see."

Corundum nodded, looking polite but uncomprehending.

"You are unexpected, and the name and planet you gave sound a lot like another name, someone else from that same world. Someone rather . . . famous. And, ah, cautious. I see no reason for anyone else here to know your name or the name you've given, which is transparent, Captain—since you are about to offer me good equipment at a substantial discount, no questions asked."

The broad, shortish man looked levelly into Corundum's strange eyes, which were little more eyes than the TP cameras-viewers used by the men in this chamber. Janja held her breath. For some reason, Corundum had made this fellow believe that he was Jonuta. And now Corundum was nodding.

"It may just be a pleasure to do business with you, Aaron. You are empowered to negotiate purchases?"

"Pos. What are you hauling, Captain Viking?"

Corundum gave him a printout. Aaron looked at the list, at the pirate, at the faceless Janja. He nodded. He turned and strode to the four-faced computerminal in the chamber's center. With a glance at Janja, Corundum followed. She remained where she was. Aware of her facelessness. Aware of the weight of the stopper against her thigh. She watched interestedly and saw little. Just the backs of coveralled men, all concentrating on the work of their eyes and hands. It was new to her, as Dot was. New and fascinating, and yet dull.

Aaron held the paper not out to the side, but directly before him as he stood before the terminal.

"Economic adviser," he drawled. "I want some prices and a total."

Janja saw a picture—that is, a holographic simulation—appear on the screen. An oldish man, pretentiously bearded. He nodded to Aaron in a mixture of greeting and condescension, as if silently saying "All right, you've got me; what is it you want?" Aaron began reading off the serial numbers Sakbir had taken off the machinery of Captain Ota's cargo. The bearded, white-haired man sat nodding from the display, tapping some sort of electronic stylus against his teeth.

Janja realized that he was a program. Someone chosen—or invented—to anthropomorphize Aaron's "economic adviser." That he was also the simulacrum of a dead and still highly respected economist, Janja did not know.

"Please hold the total until I ask, *Myrzha* Sarcon," Aaron said, using what Janja had learned was a rather formal and semirespectful title for the program, whose name was Sarcon. Aaron turned to Corundum. "You heard?"

"I heard. I admit surprise that you have such a fine computer system here, Aaron."

"T.M.S.M. is no molecule-size company, Captain. Too, we are partially subsidized by Murph's government. It is lonely on Dot."

Corundum was nodding. One of the things he had learned on the way out here was that the government of Murph was almost an extension of T.M.S.M.-for-Mining. Hence part of the mining activity here was financed by the people of Murph, probably on the grounds that they benefited from TMSM's presence and contributions to the planetary economy and well-being. Strange things happened on some planets. Strange systems and situations existed, and stranger alliances. Corundum was aware of the theory that TGO did not *really* crack down on such men and Jonuta and so many others, because slavery was good for the galactic economy. So Murph's government was almost company controlled. So what? Companies tended to be run more intelligently than governments, anyhow.

"The main banks," Aaron was saying, "the central storage and processor, are down on Murph. We have a satellite data bank and a smallish peripheral processor. Naturally, data we have more frequent need to access is stored here. We also store lots and lots of holodrama tapes, several programs such as Errar Sarcon here, and other . . . entertainments. This terminal's capability gives us something to look at, think about, talk about. Someones to talk at besides each other." Aaron half-turned to gesture at one of the men at work.

"That's Sabusaku, in the yellow with the TP helmet and floppy sandals. In another year-Murph he will be well off—since none of us spends anything here. Through his off-hour studies using this terminal, he will also be a true expert in something called sam-you-rye. He wished to become expert and he has, right here. He wishes to teach. He will!"

"All from this fine audio-visio-multiprogram computerminal the TMSM Company provides," Corundum said, "*and* full linkage to the planet's main bank."

"Exactly—and the private display unit Sabusaku uses, in his turn. We have four available to us, with sound-sight inhibitors to make study a private matter. This is a crud job and we are all highly skilled experts, Captain Viking. TMSM takes good care of us."

"I have been impressed with its *precautions* on your behalf," Corundum said, leaning on the word that might apply to the man he was pretending to be—by allowing his "subterfuge" to be seen through. Doubtless Aaron was pleased with himself for having seen through the ruse; Captain Cautious just hadn't been cautious enough, this time! "And," Corundum said, with a tiny wry smile, "you stay current."

"Yes. When new data, even irrelevant shit, is available from anywhere off-Dot, off-Murph, out-of-system—anywhere in the galaxy—it's beamed up here and stored until we can view it. Some we keep. Most we wipe. Why store things we'll never access? Murphcomp Central is Dot's data storage vault. We feed up to Murph too, of course. Daily. We are also well guarded and defensed."

"I understand you, Aaron," Corundum said without a blink at the words and a repeat performance of Aaron's anomalous arch look, "and elect not to be insulted at the warning."

"Warning!" Aaron waved his arms and the printout from Jinni rippled with a rustling sound. "Oh no, Captain. Delighted to have visitors, always delighted.

And to have equipment that we have long wanted. I'm so familiar with some of that stuff I even recognize the serial numbers. It's also nice to be able to pay less for it, with less paperwork."

Within her helmet, Janja smiled. Paper hardly existed but the phrase persisted. More than ancient, Corundum had told her. Aaron meant that there would be no formal requisition orders and no red tape in dealing with this . . . merchant.

"No," Aaron said, "just sort of bragging, I guess. We know what we're lacking, Captain . . . Viking, and naturally we love the opportunity to brag about what we have. And will have! Now, Captain Viking. Your list shows no prices. Do you know them, or the aggregate value at current market?"

"I do not. I assume that *Myrzha* Sarcon does," Corundum said, though he did of course have another listing back on *Firedancer,* complete with prices and total privided by Jinni. These men had not had time to prepare lies for him. Why not pretend to be trusting, then, even naïve?

Besides, Corundum was neither Captain Cautious nor infallible.

A smile had lit Aaron's slab of a face. "Unless the price has changed in the past four em-ess," he said, pronouncing the usual verbal shortcut for "months standard." He was adding, "Give me the total market value of all those items, *Myrzha* Sarcon," even as he turned back to the display.

The program did, aloud, and seemed to inscribe the figure on the inside of the screen with that electronic "pen."

From inside her cerulean space helmet, Janja stared. So much! So many stells for mining equipment—millions of stellar credits!

"I accept that figure as accurate," Corundum said, with a glance at a miner who looked around from his wall-screen, with mild curiosity. His machine—perhaps kloms away, but not many, on little Dot!—must be shut down while he rested his eyes and neck.

Aaron said, "What's half of that figure, *Myrzha* Sarcon?"

"That," Corundum said, "I do not accept."

Aaron, gazing at the excellent representation of the dead economist, turned only his head. "Oh?"

"I offer a huge bargain, Aaron, at twenty-five percent off market value."

Aaron regarded the taller, darker, rangier man. "A bargain, true, if everything is intact and functioning perfectly—"

"We both assume it is or we would not be bothering. All is in its original crating. A scan will confirm that, and report intact seals, all the way from the manufacturer."

"But," Aaron went on as if he had been interrupted and had not heard "Captain Jonuta's" quietly confident reassurance, "what sort of bargain for you if I refuse to buy at three-quarters market value?"

Janja tried not to stiffen. Clever devil! She felt tension and wanted to up her suit's aircon a bit. She did not. Now what? She must remain still and silent while these two bargained. Would their pride and stubbornness make all this for nothing? Then what would Corundum do?

"A very bad bargain indeed, Aaron," he said with a sort of smile, "and a bad decision to come here with such merchandise."

"But what could you *do* with such a cargo of such expensive and specialized equipment, Captain . . . Viking?"

"If you are going to pause over the name *you* decided upon, Aaron, we may as well call me by name. If I could not find another, reasonable buyer, I would thank the powers and my past dealings that I'm no poor man who has to take a buyer's offer, and either dump it in space or aim it at a sun."

"All that equipment? Worth millions?"

Corundum shrugged.

Aaron regarded the pirate, who looked at his ease . . . and formidable, in the black spacesuit he had chosen for this occasion. Deliberately, his stopper's holster was not black. It called silent attention to itself, as did Corundum's calm face and emotionless optics. Aaron glanced at Janja, a faceless bulk in what some called sky blue. At last he looked at the screen.

"Sarcon" had long ago "written" half the original figure. It still comprised millions of stells.

"I offer half and the seller asks three-quarters, Sarcon, and he's independent, too. Think we should bargain?"

"Since you ask, Aaron," the program said, nodding (without saying "and since you have programmed me so"), "yes. If this buyer departs you have saved nothing and you two are not friends."

"Nor will the equipment you need," Corundum said softly, "be soon to arrive."

Aaron glanced at him. Yes. He had assumed that this "merchant" had hijacked machinery intended for Dot—probably en route to Dot. Hardly easy or customary, but anyone who thought Jonuta was a normal ordinary thief had rediscovered rust—in the circuitry of his own brain.

"Perhaps you'd best give us a figure for sixty percent of the market value, Sarcon."

"No sooner said than done, Aaron," the program said, and proved it.

"I'd like to see a figure ten percent higher than that, Honored Sarcon," Corundum said.

"You two will wear a poor overworked economist out," Sarcon said almost petulantly, and Corundum smiled.

"A superb program!"

"Thank you, Captain. Captain—" Now Aaron spoke to Corundum but looked at Janja's oneway viewplate. "Pardon me, but why does your poor aide remain helmeted? Our air is as superb as our programs."

"I will tell you quietly," Corundum said, and moved a step nearer. "My aide's face would not be wise to display on womanless Dot."

Aaron stared. "Ah. I—I see what you mean . . . that is, I don't *see*, but do understand. I appreciate your discretion but wish you hadn't told even me. Already I'm starting to prickle in the armpits." He looked the cerulean suit up and down, as if visualizing female contours within. "I am working now to say nothing . . . untoward." His sigh was both visible and audible. "I think we should strike a bargain and get you off Dot. Sarcon, show us the original market value of this spacefarer's cargo as listed."

"Shit," a voice said succinctly, but the speaker was across the room with his eyes as if glued to his contour-curved viewer. His reaction had to be something done—or not done—by the machine that was his responsibility.

"And now half that," Aaron said, looking at Janja, or rather at her suit. She saw his Adam's apple bob. She was very glad for her fabroprene suit.

"An ugly figure," Corundum commented.

"Oh, surely not," Aaron said. "Slim, certainly . . ."

Janja bit off her chuckle while Corundum dryly advised the other man that he had been referring to the monetary figure displayed behind Aaron.

"You see how I am distracted," Aaron said. "If the helmet were to be removed I might agree to the three-quarters figure."

"No," Corundum said softly. "No, Aaron, my friend. If the helmet were removed you would wish to see more. Eventually we would come to some trouble. You would end up dead and I've little doubt this chamber's defense systemry would atomize me. At that instant a light would go out on my ship and an alarm would sound. Then this installation would be destroyed."

Aaron looked at him for a long moment. Slowly, he

nodded. Deliberately, he turned his back on the pale blue spacesuit he now knew contained a woman.

"Sarcon, what is point six-six of the original sum?"

"Point six-six to infinity," Corundum immediately amended, for he had already decided that they would settle on a price of two-thirds market value.

Suddenly Aaron half-turned. "Sixty even, in pnamprum."

"Semi-refined," Corundum said at once. Aaron was offering payment in extremely valuable ore, and surely about to cheat his employer into the bargain. That put Corundum two up. When A cheated B to deal with C and C knew it, C had a hold on A. That hold meant power, a future call. "How many kilos is that?"

Blank-faced, Aaron told him.

"So few," the pirate said, while his heartbeat speeded. A fortune in a go-bag—again! Pnamprum was close to TZ in value with the redeeming virtue of being legal and instantly salable anywhere, to anyone with the cred. Still, to add to the Murpher's feeling of having bargained well, Corundum said, "Let's just add a half-kilo—"

Blank-faced, Aaron said, "No."

Captain Corundum heaved one of those great big sighs Janja had learned were artificial; pure drama. "Outbargained again," he murmured, as if it were so. "Ah, someday I shall learn! Someday I shall *truly* merit being called Captain Cau—" He stopped as if catching himself at the point of slipping, and now Aaron was absolutely sure that he was dealing with Jonuta. "But oh, what friends we shall be after this, Aaron! *Done*. Record it and effect it any way you wish, my friend."

8

When a fleet can incinerate a world,
I prefer that governments not have fast reflexes.
Dominic Flandry

They had transferred the crated, sealed machinery to the surface of Dot. It all had to be genuine and new. The guarantees were on tape inside each crate, which still bore the manufacturer's seals.

The spacesuited Aaron, with Janja and Corundum, had loaded the semirefined, blue-green pnamprum into *Firedancer*'s airlock. The 'lock had no trouble containing it. The ore massed that little! During the process Janja had been stumbled against and twice rearwardly fondled, by Aaron. She let it go. Corundum affected not to notice. There were no men on Murph's fourth moon and this idiot must not be taking the pill that did not just curb desire but virtually eliminated it.

Perhaps women, Janja mused, were less greed-driven than men, to accept such long employment. *Or too smart,* she thought, *cherm*ing Aaron's lust for her just because he knew she was female. For all the suit showed, Corundum might have been lying and Janja might have been male. Not to Aaron. Suggestion was sufficient. He doubtless imagined that the short bulky figure looked very female indeed.

"I sure do wish you'd invite me onboard for a drink to consummate our bargain, and to give me a glimpse of your charming aide at least, Captain Jonu—I mean Viking."

"Ah Aaron my friend, I fear that we—"

Corundum was interrupted by a siren: *Firedancer*'s. It was overridden by the sound of Hing's voice, hollow in the airlock:

"Two incoming spacers. One's a Janissary pardon me new model RT-Quad class Janissary, closing fast! Fast, *Captain!*"

"That has the sound of TGW to me," Corundum said. "Aaron, our business transaction is ended and I must be away. I suggest that you redshift."

"What?"

"It is difficult to believe that you are unconversant with spacefarers' slang, friend Aaron. I suggest that you return to your bubble, at the run."

The spacesuited mining boss provided a new surprise. He flipped his fingers and said, "No."

The moment Corundum drew his stopper, Janja did. Aaron looked into the snouts of two tub-pistols.

"We have transacted good business and are both happy, Aaron. I cannot imagine why you wish us to await the arrival of what seems to be a policer ship. Surely you did not somehow call for such; for if I thought that, you would not outlive the next two seconds. Farewell."

Aaron nodded, turned, and redshifted. He moved at a long-striding, semifloating lope back to the dome. *Firedancer*'s closing airlock occluded their view of him. Janja turned as Corundum did, holstering his stopper. The pressure gauge changed and the inner hatch opened. They entered *Firedancer* to find Sakbir standing ready, awaiting instructions. Corundum's helmet was off before Janja had hers undone. She resolved anew: *practice, practice.*

"The ore will travel just fine in the 'lock," Corundum said briskly. "Stand by for multi-G acceleration ASAP. Stand by defense systemry—and arm those guns, Sak."

Sakbir rushed away in one direction while Janja and Corundum hurried bulkily to the bridge. *TGW,* Janja reflected, calling up memories both artificially implanted and gained the hard way, from library master edutapes on Franji. TransGalactic Watch. The uniformed arm of TGO—The Gray Organization. *Sunmother's light! We are in trouble!* TGW *is the* competent *policer force!*

"Janja: buckle in," Corundum snapped as they joined Hing in the con-cabin. Shining instrumentation, blipping telits and blinking lights in several colors, constantly displayed updates on the oncoming spacecraft. There were two. "Hing, is that miner back inside his dome yet?"

"Back in! That flainer's already sending to those ships! He's telling on us and they are TGW, Captain, sure as starshine."

"Away!" Corundum snarled, too loudly, and Janja buckled herself in while the captain, spacesuited but without his helmet, slapped both keys that gave all control of *Firedancer* into his hands.

His gaze flashed over his console and read it as easily as another might read a book-display. Corundum's control panel was covered with clear plates of manufactured crystal, in various geometric shapes. The colors were to his specifications, designed in calibration with the abilities of his artificial eyes. There was the cold frozen flame of pale cobalt blue; a warm almost ethereal orange; a chill, pulsating lavender and radiant, translucent ultramarine composed more of pale blue than yellow; the "green" of traffic signals. Quartz-shining circles glowed with the luminous aura of white, faintly beige-tinged to soften it into glarelessness. And there were the hexagons, which lit hotly with the pure, intense crimson of danger and warning, blood and death. The paired vertical ovals flashed roseate only with the beat of words; communication incoming from outside the ship.

Blue and green and lavender twinkled and flashed as he began keying a sequence of inputs with swift-moving fingers. The console imitated that ancient superstition called a Christmas tree.

He was well practiced; he was more than experienced at hurried evasion and elusion. None was so foolish as to call Captain Corundum less than a master at ship handling and at escaping the figurative nets and fixing pins of . . . collectors. He depressed the keys smoothly, almost lovingly, and Jinni responded with instant electronic obedience. Its response and activity were signaled with flashes of flame yellow from thin horizontal quartz bars.

Two standing ovals flashed roseate and the strange voice that crackled into the cabin, which was the bridge on *Firedancer*, was about as friendly as the snout of a leveled stopper.

"You are guidelined to stand by for I.D. and interview. Remain in place."

" 'Interview,' " Corundum sneered, in a mutter. "That's policer-ese for 'search and harassment'!"

"Guideline" was not worth comment. It had meant "rule" or "order" for centuries, when it emanated from the authority of government or its enforcement arm, policers.

Janja was in communication with herself, acclimating herself. She was making her body-mind, the entire entity that was Janja, aware of the imminence of a lessened lack of weight to be followed by real weight. The pressure of acceleration and actuation of *Firedancer*'s grav-systemry were seconds away. Janja of Aglaya had more control of self, resulting from greater awareness of mind-body linkage and contact with her self, than these Galactics thought possible. *They,* a race different from hers, alien to hers. She had just convinced her self, her *entity,* that it did not really want to float and would soon be weightier, and should prepare for the effect of high velocity departure. Then the voice entered the con-cabin and Corundum and his SIPACUM yanked *Firedancer* off Dot's surface, all at once.

For that, Janja was not prepared.

The acceleration was not just sudden. It was almost instantaneous, the most massive she had ever experienced. Inconceivably mighty forces strove to hurl *Firedancer* into space and at the same time to squash the ship's biological components—the crew.

A frightening, horrible weight crushed Janja. She could not breathe because someone seemed to be standing on her chest. Her body swore that the weight was insupportable. After a few moments of panicky fighting back of panic, she began assuring her entity to the contrary. The weight had to be supported, to be borne; she had to breathe. The alternative was to be strangle-smothered, and she could not believe that Corundum had imparted that much lift. Suicide while attempting to escape was hardly productive, or Corundum's style!

Meanwhile two sirens were clamoring for attention in two separate and equally unpleasant voices and lights flashed all over the console, in six colors. Again the insistent voice commed its way into the cabin.

"Cut your power!" the ship-to-ship ordered. *"Your attempt is both useless and damning. You cannot elude two specialized ships! We must have words with you. We need not hold you long, provided you are honest traders."*

Janja reflected that since they were not honest traders, the reverse would be just as true: they would be held longer than long. Inertia was continuing to lean on her chest with mighty hands. At least it prevented any outcry that would have embarrassed her with her own weakness. While he was from a high-G planet, Corundum was still standing at his controls and Hing was fighting his way out of the captain's chair. The captain actuated his comm with his knee.

"Our business here on Dot is consummated and we read you as attackers," he snapped. "You have no authority to hold us."

"Freeze! Otherwise we freeze you—we do *have the authority!"*

"Put a tractor on us and you will be inconceivably sorry," Corundum snapped back.

"We call that bluff—now! Any attempt at making us 'inconceivably sorry,' pirate, will result in automatic activation of our defense system. Cease your threats and attempts at escape and I.D. yourself."

"I.D.—I haven't heard your identification, pirates!"

Janja had only an instant to reflect on an attacker's referring to threatening gunnery as "defense" and on a pirate's snarly name-calling of policers as pirates. The ship was straining, bucking, creaking, and lunging like a shell caught between contrary winds. No—like a tiny craft atop a waterspout, with winds blowing contrarily down at it!

She heard the groans and creaky complaints of plasteel and cyprium—monofilamental hydrogen bonded at the electron level and stronger than steel. Could the ship withstand the forces tugging at it, thrusting at it—in opposite directions? And if it could—for how long?

The console blazed hot with lights in orange and crimson, lavender and ultramarine, off-white and yellow, like an ever-changing chemical fire. Corundum's telits and warners seemed in the sweaty grip of hysteria.

Yet this new threat of *Firedancer*'s breaking up or being crushed by elemental forces had to share attention with Janja's other terror.

She was still laboring merely to breathe. How Hing was forcing himself from chair to floor was beyond her—at least with her limited experience—just as *rising* from that contoured chair was beyond his power. Corundum was forcefeeding power to impel his ship into space like a projectile while each of the oncoming spacers had hit them with a reversed tractor field, a pinner.

Dimly Janja was aware of the voice, and another; the crisp identification was of TransGalactic Watch and Murphspace Defense & Enforcement. TGW and MDE.

Firedancer struggled against the three forces. An obedient mustang, *Firedancer* wanted to obey her captain and computer and straining engines. They bade her jump up off Dot. The other ships applied hobbles of pure force. Their paired tractors-in-reverse struck from two directions to form a wedge with *Firedancer* at their apex.

The ship sat uncomfortably on a hot pin at the bottom of the V, and shuddered as it fought. The effect of the policers' fields should have been to pin the ship to Dot, an insect awaiting the collectors. But Corundum had imparted thrust, and the needly point blazing under *Firedancer* urged her upward to escape its hurtful prick. *Firedancer* danced on fire. They were pinned, but not on Dot. The ship danced helplessly, powerfully, just above the satellite's barren surface.

A bleeding Hing was inching along the floor. "Captainn," he got out, hoarsely. "Sit . . . Cap . . . tainn."

"Can't," Corundum grunted.

No one need ask why. If he unlocked his knees he would hit the floor in a second, struck down by massive power irresistible as sunstorm.

His fingers fought inertial force, prancing like spiders, tapping keys in a constantly changing pattern of attempts at evasive maneuvering. At the same time he muttered, gutturally throating out words of instruction to SIPACUM. He and his Jinni worked together as few men and machines were capable. The computer's narrow signal rectangles were a variable blur of flame-yellow light.

Firedancer sought to lunge upward and engines whined while hull, braces, and compartments groaned and creaked and made horrid rattling noises.

Fingers moved, keyed, moved, depressed another key or set of keys. *Firedancer* strove to obey. To dodge leftward, then to hurtle straight ahead along

Dot's shallow curve toward the indigo horizon that loomed so close. Corundum's fingers spidered and he muttered to his Jinni and *Firedancer* did her best to edge rightward, to hurtle upward. And all the while Janja only breathed, working at it, and thought how incredibly strong this man was. The strength of the spirit and the calves that held him erect while all this weight tried to press him flat!

And all the while that strange crisp voice threatened, bade, cited authority and regulations and "guidelines," ordered the straining ship to cease striving and freeze. The comm-signal ovals were a pair of constantly flashing beacons, their rosy light as warm as the words were cold.

"Brace," Corundum snarled, and let himself collapse into the chair behind it. He had only to unlock his knees. The crushing hand of inertia supplied the motion.

He slammed into the chair—as *Firedancer* slammed down onto Dot. He had left off striving and *allowed* his ship to be slammed down onto the satellite's surface by the policers' paired pinner beams. Pins, that now immobilized the insect. *Or the arachnid,* Janja thought, considering the way Corundum's fingers had looked on the keys.

Hing got himself to a position approaching safety. Janja felt her abdomen and chest pressing against her seatbelt. Corundum was examining a cassette, nodding, preparing to inslot it.

"Get flat, Hing," he said, in a small voice. He inslotted the guidance cassette.

Janja did not know which it was, what it instructed the ship to do. She learned only later. She heard the noises and felt the violent lurches, the return of massive weight. Corundum had made the next-to-last-ditch effort, the very last ditch being Forty Percent City.

The cassette he inslotted commanded SIPACUM and *Firedancer* to actuate every outwardly aimed weapon in a mad blaze of firepower; to lift off at the very limit of human ability to bear the acceleration—and at the same time to channel power into a traction field at the nearest spaceborne object.

That happened to be the MDE ship.

Convinced that she was dying as surely as if she lay beneath a herd of rampaging elephants, Janja heard yelling voices and knew none emanated from *Firedancer*. The attackers were thrown into confusion. At this moment only Corundum was sure of specific purpose.

His voice seemed a dying engine full of gravel, and it seemed to take a great part of infinity to form its command to Jinni.

"Cu-utt . . . trrra-a-acct-chun fff-fieeeelll . . ."

A moment later *Firedancer* continued to rush tornadically at the Murphspace policer ship, now pushed by acceleration but not pulled by its tractor field. Stars were points of light and more; the MDE ship was beginning to resemble a wall in space.

"Elu-u-ud-de . . . o-ob . . . jec . . . t-t . . ."

That was less easily accomplished, so close was the racing *Firedancer* to the other craft. Yet the command was carried out. In that violent, tight swerve away from fiery catastrophe. Janja blanked out, with an ugly sound in her ears. It was the sound of Hing's head striking something—whatever he had been hurled against.

Blasting weaponry had disrupted the policecrafts' fields while massive thrust had slammed *Firedancer* into space from a little satellite that had no gravitational pull to fight, and Corundum's tractor had made sure that his ship raced at the MDE spacer. A desperate burst from the TGW ship missed astern. It plowed into Dot's surface to mildly spectacular effect. At that, someone was mighty wide awake on the RT-Quad Janissary. Awake, and thinking rationally, and acting on it.

The Janissary began swinging, rapidly, as *Firedancer* rushed at the MDE craft. Onboard, the Murph crew must have been close to panic and frozen by it or nearly. They had also had a tractor beam on them while a madman raced toward them. They neither eluded nor activated defense systemry.

The TGW ship did . . .

And *Firedancer* obeyed Corundum's painfully rasped command to avoid crashing into the Murphspace craft. *Firedancer* made that violent, just-short-of-impossible swerve just as the TGW Janissary's weapons sent searing energy at her, unstoppable energy . . .

And the TGW ship destroyed the MDE one.

No one heard that destruction. No one heard anything other than oncomm yells, and a single scream. The flash of light was very bright. Stars seemed to dim as the Murphspace Defense & Enforcement spacer emulated a nova.

Then the yells ceased. The MDE spacer and her crew did not exist.

"Re-du-u-ussse p-ow . . . errr . . . two-oo z-zeer-r o-o-oh perr . . . cennnt . . ."

Spaceship *Firedancer* shuddered. Hing bounced off something else without a moan. Janja, almost conscious, felt an upward lurch and gasped a breath, for that had become possible again. Corundum's hands stretched forth again. He depressed, again, the keys that gave him control of the ship. On the console, the hot scarlet lights faded to orange and began winking out. Not all of them.

"Janja! Get that cassette out. Crew: Report!"

Bearcat's reply came weakly.

"Control of DS to you," Corundum told him, glancing at Janja, who wallowed loosely in her chair. "Stand by to fire. Janja!"

"Fi—Captain . . . yes, Captain." Bearcat; reluctant but efficient.

Corundum's hand swept out to hit a vertical rectangular key. The slot popped open and out came the course guidance cassette like a rude tongue. It had done its work. Janja stirred.

"Janja! Janja!"

"Captain?" Bearcat, wondering about Janja.

"Stand by DS! Stand by to fire!"

Janja heard. She snapped back fast and clawed herself into an erect sitting position. Mind and body melded, functioned. She was an entity, that fast.

"Janja! Janja! Inslot seven-zero. Inslot cassette seventy."

"Right, Captain."

At her voice and movements to obey, Corundum sighed audibly. Other matters wanted his attention; demanded his attention. The TGW ship was still there. He gave his attention to Jinni, to *Firedancer,* to TGW.

Janja found the proper course guidance cassette. She checked it to make sure—reddish waves were coming and going inside her head—and thrust it into its slot. Lights flashed. SIPACUM/Jinni was instructed to enter subspace at the first possible instant, with warning if possible. It was possible; this was one of those times when within seconds a bell dinged.

"Now, you rotten bastards," Corundum muttered. He completed his ship's arc, aimed it at the TGW craft, and braced. "Fire fire fire!" His voice was a shout.

Janja blinked. The TGW was onscreen—on several screens. It was not firing. It was not trying to give chase. It was as if everyone onboard was frozen in horror, the horror of having accidentally destroyed the other policercraft. Or perhaps someone was being relieved of command, or a suspected computer was being pulled. Whatever the case, *Firedancer* was seconds away from whipping them all along the Tachyon Trail and the enemy was not making anything like a hostile move, and Corundum had just ordered—

Bearcat fired and fired and fired and suddenly the TransGalactic Watch spacer was a sheet of yellow and then a ball of cornea-searing white and then it was no longer there, for almost at the instant of the Janissary's destruction *Firedancer* and everything onboard was converted to tachyons and was safe, "in subspace."

Just as safely as it would have been had Corundum not vindictively ordered the deaths of those crewmembers on the TGW spacer.

9

Nosce te ipsum: *"In order to know yourself, it is necessary to have gone through frequent alternations of happiness and unhappiness, and that's something you cannot give yourself."*

Stendhal

Just before its death off the satellite called Dot in System Aristarkos, TransGalactic Watch spacer # 809-QJ, got off a message via coherent lightbeam. An assortment of relay stations batted it on, zigging and zagging around the geothermal noise of the many, many enormous generators at galaxy center; those generators were called suns. The message fled along energy beams to *headquarters: TransGalactic Order.*

She was pretty, and pretty short, and her hair was a shocking shade of pale. It was pretty short, too. Her eyes were unbelievable. No one had eyes the color of twelve centimeters of water in a pan whose bottom was pale blue. No one caused children's eyes to be changed to such a hue and no one chose to be cell-dyed to that color. Hers had to be celldye, nevertheless. It was weird—and striking.

She wore black. The knitted shirt fitted snugly, with a stiffened stand-up collar once called mandarin. The ring-pull zipper was flashy, of silveron, and really worked. Its sem-wide silveron track ran most interestingly from collar to . . . a matter for conjecture. It flowed right down into the tight black stretch pants. Their belt was linked by a round silver buckle big as a Jarp's eye. Another ring-pull zipper ran down the front of each pant leg until it vanished into snug black front-zip boots. Platform soles and heels were of quiet-soft rubbron.

Pants and boots appeared to be of refulgent leather and were more likely of its manufactured look-alike, equhyde.

She could not be called white; no one could. She was, however, lighter of skin than anyone else in the lounge called the Loophole. A stopper was holstered on her right hip, lowish. It was slung there by means of an attention-demanding semicircle of silvery links. The silver flashed; the black leather or equhyde gleamed as ever such stuff did.

Her nails were unpainted. She wore no jewelry or makeup except around the eyes and to strengthen pale brows. She'd have been striking even if she were not in company with the tall lean man who also wore fitted black, and a crimson sash and a stopper.

His jumpsuit of stretch velvet was pocketed, as her clothing was not. (She wore a chocolate-colored pouch on her left hip.) In contrast with hers, his eyes were black as a pirate's reputation. A pair of hard, glittering onyxes set in his good-looking head.

He saw people he knew, in the sprawling bar called the Loophole, and he introduced her to them, Janja, he called her. They called him Captain, or Corundum, or both. More than one of the others also bore the title "captain."

The Loophole was a fascinating place. The walls were set with chunks of the planet's ancient scoria. They were the remains of dead volcanoes that were now stupendous slag piles. Once they had ruled Thebanis; now they reared in conical death to brood sullenly over past glory. Each piece of scoria was stucco-rough with a thousand thousand facets, and the ashy slag of them was jet- and green-tinged here and there with an impossible electric blue and dots of angry scarlet. A halo of ever-moving lights in the ceiling turned each ragged, pocked piece of slag into an individual light show, all atwinkle as if alive with multicolored iridescence.

At the long room's far end, two steps led up to another level. A fenced alcove. The porch-like area housed two big tables and a small one. Booths and couch and chairs surrounded them. More chairs were drawn up, with attendant noise.

The quite young couple at the smaller table soon decided to depart and find a place on the lower level. Corundum bought, for his friends. Drinks were extruded from the panel in the wall beside the table. On the couch beside Corundum, Janja tried to remember eight new names.

They talked and laughed and drank, telling stories and sharing reminiscences. The Loophole's spectrum of winking, living light turned the eye of each into a reflection of the stars, and flashed weirdly from the optics of Captain Corundum.

A number of other patrons in the Loophole bar in Raunch of planet Thebanis did little but listen while trying to appear not to be listening. Some of those people in the rear alcove were famous, or infamous. Listeners heard snatches of good stories and some ridiculous or plain dumb ones. They heard the names of faraway places and a dozen or more planets. They heard of the personally beheld light of stars they had never heard of. They heard allusions and shocking almost-statements about lawlessness and violence, but little of real substance. Nothing indicting. Even the proudest of law-flouters practiced some discretion.

"Aglay-ya, you said? Did you say Aglaya, Zhanzha?"

"I did. Can't you say 'Janja,' Dignis? Why do so many people have so much trouble pronouncing my name?"

"Must be because none of us ever went to Aglaya," fat Shieda said, and the others laughed as at a brilliant joke. Shieda immediately looked embarrassed, and he was not dissembling.

Shieda was a man who avoided making waves. The carnous man of the long ringleted hair and shining shirt of canary yellow was in the people business. Such men knew of Aglaya, which was Protected so poorly by policers obviously not really trying to put a stop to the business of trading in people. Shieda sold a goodly number of people, but he bought few. He was a slaver. He called Janja "Yanya" and his iridescent cerise sash erupted the dark grips of two stoppers.

Sluttish pink-haired Althis laughed so hard at his words that her mighty meaty jelly-jiggles of breast nearly churned their way out of her bodice, which appeared to be molded of frozen purple light and was cut very low. The better to display big meaty jelly-jiggly mounded warheads and a necklace of cerulean and chilly green stones that flashed and glittered like starfire. The necklace plunged into her cleavage, which was deep, dark, and roomy. It accommodated the necklace as if it could accommodate an arm. Doubtless it had, several. She wore eye-offending heliotrope pants tight enough to show a pimple. Nine elliptical cutouts ran down each outer leg. Neither of those pant legs would have formed a sash for Shieda. Althis was only a little taller than Janja, perhaps because Shankar's gravity was 1.39 standard. Her crystalline sandals propped her up on six-sem platforms with sixteen-sem heels. That was nearly the distance from her wristbone to her elbow.

Janja of Aglaya thought that Althis of Shankar was

a tacky whore ten minutes away from being badly overweight, and Shieda a thrice-overfed idiot. The ringed-planet tattoo on his cheek, in blue, added nothing. He was sipping at a tall plass of Alive, a Thebanian mineral water supposedly drawn straight from a long-deceased volcano, with a twist of errus and a bit of lemon. Althis's drink was a purple—well, lavender—concoction called an Aldebaran. That had been the name of an orange member of a binary, back before the stars had all been renamed, even those with Arabic names. It looked awful. Fitting, Janja thought.

She also thought that over-plump Dignis of Thebanis had the eyes of a rude fifteen-year-old and the instincts of a rutting swinger—the primate tree-dwellers of Aglaya. As for lean but paunchy Vettering—he was so ugly and truly ignorant, thinking himself clever as only an ignorant, cultureless peasant could, that he deserved none of his success.

(It was considerable. Vettering now commanded three spacers. They hauled things, some legal. He had begun as a fetch-and-carry for some years-dead captain and had shown an uncanny ability for being at the right place at the right time. Dressed like a Ghanji lord, Vettering did. Wore a little mustache that was a perpetual sneer. Althis was his woman and the necklace he had given her was real. Rahmanese sapphires and jade and the strange ice-emeralds of the world named Havoc. He wore a big bracelet just as gaudy and about as expensive. Diamonds, in two colors alternating: lemon, and the hue of Janja's eyes. Cloth-of-gold encrusted his wide-shouldered, laced-front vest in an Arabesque pattern that looked formless until one realized that it aureately spelled out "Vettering" again and again.)

The woman called Hellfire was known to be competent. The trouble was that she was a bitch and an obvious ex-gutterbrat from some back alley of Lanatia. Deadly competent, was Captain Hellfire. She too commanded a spacer. *Satana,* she called it. A "merchanter." Sure. The same kind of merchant as Corundum, that was thin, sharp-faced Hellfire with the hair and voice of brass.

Only the hair of her head was dyed or cell-dyed. Her thick brows and lashes remained their natural color, which was just as jet as her dangerous eyes.

This galactopolitan group contained a Jarp. If it had a name, no one used it; they all called it Raunchy and it obviously took no offense. It was as sweet-looking as all Jarps. Huge round eyes and almost pointed, elfin chin. It affected a very full-sleeved white blouse under a high, tight, brocaded jerkin or singlet of scarlet, black, gray, and grass green. And brown leather pants. Raunchy was the first Jarp Janja had seen that dressed to minimize its breasts. It hardly left off looking at her and she wished its big round eyeballs would fall out.

"They don't use as good a brand of Port in this as they do on Franji," Althis remarked, regarding her purplescent drink with hauteur.

The two locals were called Pacy and Pearl. Only they seemed not to be armed. (Not too pretty likely, in Raunch of Thebanis.) They were "with" Shieda, both of them. Except that Pearl was interested in the Jarp and apparently fascinated with Corundum. She did not have to keep her leg there, where it pressed his long black-sheathed one. Pacy's foudroyant black hair was pulled back to reveal really dainty ears from whose lobes depended five links, each, of delicate gold-hued chain. Pearl wore a blue Terasaki coil over her own hair, with almost matching cerulean lip make-up, and Theban dimple-scars. Pearl looked eighteen.

Ten of them at that rear-set table, and surely enough armament to stand off the entire local policer force, if need be, or even a gaggle of Thebanis's neo-fundamentalist flagellants—who were too much for the local policers.

Nine stoppers and the other thing Shieda wore; it fired explosive darts. Five knives that showed. Three rings big enough to cut. Dignis's was a double, and too obviously designed for striking blows rather than decoration. Too, Janja had no doubt that the long straight pin of Hellfire's replica of an ancient brooch, silver with a lovely multihued head of opal and shell, was a dagger. Probably poisoned. Corundum had already told her that Vettering never took off his gloves. They were loaded in the knuckles, both of them.

A charming group, and getting noisier on alcohol and a couple of other substances. Shieda had dropped a blue capsule in his otherwise harmless plass of Alive.

Janja was not charmed. She was a year off Aglaya and only a few months out of slavery. Nevertheless she felt socially conscious tonight, unaccountably superior. Slumming. Surrounded by slime.

Including Corundum?

She was beginning to think so.

(Shieda said something to Pearl and she answered with something he did not like and his stiffened fat thumb practically buried itself in the side of her breast. She lurched, paled, and subsided. No one said anything. Everyone affected not to notice. Shieda sipped. Pearl's leg drifted away from Corundum's. A moment later she compulsively finished her drink. Theban gin-'n'quinette.)

Corundum, Janja mused. Her companions began to fade as she went inside her head. That was the trouble. Corundum. She was no longer happy and she'd have been no happier in company considerably more couth. She could think sneerily of Althis as the woman of peasantly insufferable Vettering. His whore. Austerely, she could consider Pearl and Pacy as whores, too. Beginners. Local opportunists. Willing to do whatever Shieda wanted of them in return for what the seven-ringed wig-wearing bucket of lard could provide.

(Vettering was telling a story involving the momentous discovery of a "new" populated planet. His elaborate gestures attracted the eyes of the others. Corundum availed himself of the opportunity to slip a red into his and Janja's drinks. It was better than harmless; it was an antintoxicant. Clever, clever Corundum. Althis was rubbing Vettering's leg, high up. A-liens, Vettering kept saying, dragging out the first letter. A-liens. Galactoid. Felinoprimates. A-liens! It *was* momentous, highly important, and Janja pretended to be interested because she should be. She wasn't. Not just now. Her own thoughts wanted her.)

What, she mused, was Janja? Was she more or less than ship's girl of *Firedancer?* Sure, she was captain's girl. Corundum's woman. His exotic "white"-haired pet, fitted out by him in black to complement his standard onplanet attire. He wore her too, proudly. As a bauble in this murkily lit dive with its scoria-studded walls and mean-beat sawblade music or "music" and outlaw clientele.

What else am I? How am I better or more than Althis?

That thought was no source of cheer. Janja's happiness was in decline along with her self-esteem and her hopes.

She who had been Janjaheriohir of Aglaya had pride, much pride. She had retained it during her capture and imprisonment and her sexual use on Jonuta's ship—by his crew, not by Jonuta. (But on his orders. After she had so proudly challenged him and sneered at his rutting intent, he had cloaked himself in pride and *he* had foregone raping her.) She had remained relatively insouciant and definitely proud throughout her owned servitude to the former High Priest of Gri and his son, of Resh. She had kept her Aglayan pride, her Janjan pride, when she had fled and schemed and taken abuse and stolen and tricked and fought to get off Resh, and then off Franji. She had retained her pride when the library edutapes on Franji told her that her Aglaya was a barbarian world of no known value save for its big orchidlike flower, the phrillia. She schemed to leave Franji to get to Qalara. Qalara. For Qalara was all she had known about Jonuta, then. She had naïvely thought that since he was from there, she would find him there.

That seemed years ago, and it was across light-years. But only months had passed. . . .

She had been delighted, elated to join with Corundum against Jonuta. In quest of Jonuta. To search him out, and find him, and repay him for her murdered lover and her disrupted life and her slavery. To stop Jonuta forever!

Now the elation was gone, and even happiness, and her self-regard was staggering. Now she felt compromised. Her pride was become evanescent mist, because her conviction was, and her purpose. Joining Corundum had not been *necessity*. Staying with Corundum was not necessity, either. Never mind how much she enjoyed their times in bed—their hours and hours in bed. His "Primeval Princess" indeed!

Never mind her growing realization that this pirate was close to the opposite of her former owners, Sicuan and Chulucan of Resh, who had been genuine pathological sadists.

In quest of Qalara! In quest of Jonuta's death!

She had joined Corundum to further that purpose.

Her Purpose, which she might mentally capitalize. To go after their common enemy together and to rid the spaceways of Captain Cautious, dealer in people. She had looked upon it as an alliance almost holy. Righteous warriors with a Mission! An honorable name applied to a bond for the taking of vengeance that was truly justice.

Instead she had become Corundum's woman.

Corundum's Woman, and she was no longer so charmed by him. Oh, the genius and the courtliness remained. He had the manners and style of what he called the "court of the Sun King," and he remained charming. And charmed, too, with his Primeval Princess.

The trouble was that Corundum was not *driven* to seek out Jonuta.

The trouble was that they were not searching for Jonuta. And the trouble was that now Janja knew Corundum.

The charm was superficial. Like Jonuta his enemy, Corundum was an actor. He enjoyed the role of the smooth, sophisticated, courtly buccaneer. He enjoyed the knowledge that though some considered him effete, none could sneer at him, for he was competent.

His main attraction to Janja seemed to be her exoticism, and the bed. The bed remained his only attraction for her. His predilection for the haughty Primeval Princess game, of being dominated, was confined to the bed. He loved it when her thigh came up as if menacingly, saying that it looked like a wall of pink before his face. He loved her to lean it in, to crush his face to her vulva, her stash. Happily then he treated his Primeval Princess to the dexterity of a cleverly sweeping, swabbing tongue that soon had her moaning aloud and trembling uncontrollably while he might be fantasizing that he was being forced to this. It was easy for him to press his lips over the pink twig of her surgically sheathless clitoris and suck it rapidly in and out until she was practically screaming in pleasure. That gained him what he wanted, too: she clamped him between the pale-skinned towers of her thighs and ground her hips up at his face.

Few would have believed how he loved it, the grim pirate in the ebony clothing and the staring eyes that were not his! The sighing helpless woman, enslaved and enslaving all at once! Abandoning herself to the spasms and grinding her uttermost femininity up to his face. Her entire body contracted and every muscle flexed in purest, almost unbearable pleasure. Her juices flowed and her stomach was a flat plain taut as a Sekhari drumhead. He considered himself successful and lucky if she reached the point of being unable to bear it more, and of thrusting him from her. Of clambering panting up over him to shove him into position and impale herself on him and ride him, ride him, ride him, the Primeval Princess looking down on her smiling subjected male. . . .

("Not two, or four," Vettering was saying, gesturing, "but two whole rows of titties! No no, not all furry—they are developed from felines, cats, but they have evolved past the furry stage just as we did millions of years ago. Oh, some of *those* exotics will be turning up along the spaceways, you can bet your savings on that!")

Janja shook her head sharply and slugged down a good swallow of her drink. She realized that she had been staring without seeing, and that her eyes had been leveled at Hellfire. Hellfire was staring back and Janja wondered what the lean, long-legged woman thought of her glazed eyes.

"One supposes that you would not share the coordinates of this planet," Shieda was saying, "or even its sun . . . even if you knew it. . . ." And Vettering was laughing in friendly scorn, and Janja still was unable to be interested. Another populated planet found. Another race! Felines, developed to become erect humanoids or rather Galactoids. What did it have to do with her, or with Jonuta? Well, perhaps it did have something to do with him: was this to be another planet on the so-called Protected list? Eagerly pleading exosociologists were denied entry there, to study this new and truly alien culture . . . while it became a private game preserve for poaching dealers in people such as Jonuta and Shieda and others! Was that the fate of this world, this people that Vettering would not name or locate? Another Aglaya? What could Janja do? How could it concern her? Could she change the spaceways entire, when not even TGO could or would?

She closed out Vettering and Shieda and Hellfire's eyes. She closed out the table and the Loophole again, and returned within herself. Within the entity called Janja-once-Janjaheriohir that was so aware of its wholeness and of all its components.

She returned to her doubts, her troubles, her

thoughts of Corundum. Not as lover! As Corundum! Pirate, trickster, charmer, ally, killer.

He was a pirate, and he enjoyed it.

He was a killer who enjoyed killing.

True, his slaying of Ota could be termed murder but could not quite be called in cold blood. On the other hand, that slaying had excited him, aroused him, as he had soon proven. It was an *unnecessary killing.* Ota had been ranting. Blowing off steam. He had been no threat to Corundum and probably none to the crew-members he threatened, not really. The merchant after all had been carrying the highly illegal tetrazombase that had put so many stells into Corundum's hands. (So much buying power credited to his I.D., more literally. And more literally still: his I.D.'s, plural.)

And those two policer ships . . . !

There was that horror, yes. It made gooseflesh rise on Janja's skin. The kill on the TGW ship had been unnecessary. It had been Corundum's pleasure. Yet that incident followed so much else, all of Corundum's ingenious plotting and trickery. Clever, clever Corundum!

Janja had not known that her concept of *getting* Jonuta was more straightforward than Corundum's. Her "plan" was to search for the slaver, follow him if necessary, hound him if possible, and find and trap him. Then, she had merely assumed without really thinking about it—then she would kill him. Jonuta was not honorable. Many individuals would be better off were he dead. The spaceways would profit by his death. To kill him, therefore, could not be a dishonorable or immoral act.

(*But would it be honorable?* Never mind! That was back in the gray area again. Evil gave unto Good unto Evil out of which came Good.)

Now it was plain to her that such was not the plan of Captain Corundum. He was seldom so straightforward. Indeed, he must consider her "plan" naïve!

No one could doubt that his mind was excellent.

Obviously he could have pursued many other occupations, accomplished much, to profit with respect and even honor. He chose not to. Piracy pleased him. He preferred the danger, the constant thrill of illegality, the role he played, and the constant need for crafty maneuvering. Shrewdness and elaborate plotting pleased him and deviousness pleased him more—therein lay his great source of delight. Greater, Janja suspected, than orgasm. She remembered the labyrinth of guile, of cross and double-cross, that he had described to her with regard to the business of Ota and the TZ that Ota had carried.

Maybe all those twists and manipulations he had detailed—in bed—were reality and perhaps they were fiction. But how he had enjoyed telling it! How he had enjoyed Janja's reactions, her admiration of his genius.

Devious, clever Corundum!

On Dot, he had not called himself Jonuta. Instead he had deliberately chosen the transparent "Tojuna of Qalara" alias, and pretended a couple of additional slips as well. That way Aaron had the ego-boosting pleasure of believing he had caught out Jonuta in an attempt to conceal his identity. How clever Aaron felt! He had worked it out; the pirate had not denied; therefore Aaron was sure that "Tojuna" was Captain Cautious: Jonuta!

Could he have thought I was that overblown Kenowa? Well . . . in that bulky spacesuit . . . and if he had never really seen *Kenowa, the cow . . .*

Aaron must long since have advised more than one investigator that it had been Jonuta of *Coronet* who had come to Dot, concealing his identity while bearing new, needed factory-sealed equipment. He had dealt with TMSMCo through Aaron, who had made a superb cred-saving bargain with the outlaw.

(But—might Aaron not now be in trouble? His trading pnamprum was illegal. Could Aaron cover that, or was he by now another victim of Corundum? —fired or even indicted, for cheating his employers?)

Two policers had come arushing. Called in by Aaron? Called in by someone else, while Aaron left with the supposed Jonuta and his aide? It did not matter. Both were destroyed with all hands. Their quarry, the man Aaron had dealt with, had escaped.

Corundum had contrived to make Jonuta guilty of the destruction of both a Murphspace policer and a TGWatch ship!

Was that to be Corundum's way? Did he intend to stay away from Jonuta, to let TGW/TGO do his work for him? Their own proper work, really, but never mind that—Janja wanted Jonuta herself. It was personal and she wanted to end it personally. And, wasn't TGO the enemy? The Gray Organization! Huge, secretive superpolicers of the spaceways! With all the honor and morals of—of Corundum, Janja realized, and the realization hit hard.

(". . . sitting there looking so blank-faced?" Vettering asked.)

("Oh," Corundum said smoothly, thumping Janja's leg with his, "she's always this way on a second drink. She sort of . . . goes away for a while. She will be back." Clever, devious Corundum, covering Janja's obvious preoccupation. He went on smoothly, "Hellfire, I understand that you recently had to play some serious hide-and-seek with that revolving collapstar out near Jorvas's Star?")

Gray, more gray. Corundum is betraying a fellow outlaw and enemy of TGO, Janja was thinking, ignoring the others and not registering what they were saying. *Double treachery—he's helping their mutual enemy!*

And the way he did it! That policer ship . . . all those people—in cold blood!

By now Janja knew that the standard crew of the new RT-Quad class Janissary, the spacer favored by TGO's uniformed arm, the TGW, was nine. Nine persons. Human beings. Dead—unnecessarily. They had been in shock and indecision, having accidentally blown away the local system's policer craft. *Firedancer*'s escape was assured. Unnecessarily, in the very act of escaping totally unscathed, Captain Corundum had killed nine people. Because he enjoyed it . . . and because it was a fine way to damn Jonuta.

The deaths of those TGW crewmembers constituted murder, a mass murder. Yet, again, as in the case of Ota, it was not *quite* cold-blooded. There was or had been an extreme emergency, which Corundum had met brilliantly. Not quite cold-blooded, then. Calculated, yes. Also unnecessary, and therefore doubly evil.

And Corundum had enjoyed it.

Clever, clever Corundum's mind and stopper remained set on Fry.

This was dealing with Jonuta?—gaining vengeance on Jonuta?—removing the slaver Captain Cautious from the spaceways?

Hing, she thought. Yes, there was Hing. He'd had a broken arm, several broken fingers, obvious internal injuries, and a messily cracked skull. They had done what they could find for him and left him on Front, in a hospital. Hing would survive, Corundum had sorrowfully reported on returning to the ship, but Hing's would be a long convalescence. They would have to find another crewmember.

Yes, very well, but—why had they not remained on Front? Why had they lifted so rapidly, dodged the Demonhole, and come zooming here to Thebanis? Why not have zipped directly from Dot to Outreach, which was near? Hing was a comrade! Or here to Thebanis, which was as close to Murph and Dot as Front was—and without the necessity of avoiding one of the hugest collapsed stars—formerly "Black Hole" and now collapstar—in the galaxy? Thebanis! Gods of space (if any truly existed), what was Thebanis? Everything red and luridly, disconcertingly double-shadowed under the light of its angry red giant of a sun and its pale companion? What idiot had decided to colonize this dreary world covered with its myriad of ugly old fumaroles and gigantic volcanic cones, standing over the planet like the watchful sentinels of inimical gods?

From the way Corundum now referred to his loyal Hing in the past tense, Janja suspected that Hing was not in hospital on Front at all, and would never recover or even convalesce. She suspected that Corundum had killed him, or had him killed, on Front. Only he and Hing had left the ship there. A live Hing might talk, mightn't he?

There was no use bringing the matter up to Corundum. She was sure of nothing. He could laugh at her suspicions, or be nervous about her afterward, even if she was careful. She would have to accept whatever he told her—having let him know that she doubted him. She would not.

(She was only peripherally aware that the cold eyes of too-thin Hellfire seemed trying to burn a hole through her black zip-front, into her right breast. Why? Did the skinny bony-faced woman fancy Corundum? Did she perceive Janja as a rival, or some sort of threat?)

Somewhere, Jonuta continues; business as usual, with or without TGO/TGW after him, she reflected bitterly, *while Corundum also smugly continues with business as usual. The business of piracy and the killing he enjoys. A slag-decorated bar in a skungy spaceport town called Raunch! And now he has an exotic whore by his side—"Zhanzha" or "Yanya" or "Jonja" —They will persist in mispronouncing it—to share his thievery and his murderous triumph and his bed. Me.*

Good and evil, black and white! *Look at me. Hair and skin They call "white" because They're all dark . . . and these black clothes. So dramatic. Corundum-colored clothing! I felt so superior in my knowledge that They were the ancient black-for-Evil and I the lily-white of Good!* She remembered learning that contrary colors could not mix; that black and white could not mix and that gray was thus impossible.

And I believed it. Even then I was becoming gray. Being changed by Them into a mix of Good and Evil. Their evil. Even then I was becoming more like Them. And now?

Now I am a pirate, and less than a pirate.

I am Captain Corundum's pet, his whore.

Hail Pacy, Pearl, Althis . . . my sister whores!

10

. . . the difficulty is to render physical violence irrelevant, which is the only hope of any human being.

Germaine Greer

Janja focused her eyes and stared at her unsavory companions in this unsavory place. No, that was an exaggeration. Pacy and Pearl were just girls, children, thinking they were doing well. Janja remembered the remark of a blowzy acquaintance of Corundum's, weeks ago on Ghanj when Janja's wardrobe was being bought. "You get sucked in," Trevvy said wisely, "by sucking 'em off."

Just now it was a Heaven High that Shieda and Pacy were sucking, sharing. His lips around the cigarette were like fat worms, the kind that grope about all ugly and stupid when a big log or stone is overturned. Orange, red-haired Raunchy's huge ebony eyes seemed to be giving Corundum—or Janja, *or both of us?*—looks about as subtle as this damned bom-boom-bom-screeee-wah "music," or as subtle as Althis's decolletage.

"This roun's on me," Dignis said, practically sniffing Hellfire's crotch. "Stannard—*stan-darrd*—Theban hos-p'tality."

Dignis, Dealer in Anything, was not the only native Theban present. Pearl and Pacy were locals. Their hospitality, however, had nothing to do with buying drinks and mind-affecting smokes. They carried it with them just as Dignis did, but not in the form of an I.D. credcard.

Chain-earringed Pacy wore a little blue blouse of wetcloth, a product of Thebanis, and those nipples could not be real. Her skirt covered her abdomen and little else. Janja, who was not seated opposite the girl, knew that her underpants were an obscene tongue-pink. Her wrists were decorated with the paint-on jewelry currently popular here. Pearl wore a ridiculously revealing, totally nonutilitarian bra that consisted mostly of straps—red straps. And a long, long red skirt. It was tight enough to appear painted on. Slit to the hip and laced up that side, from the knee. She had her little finger in her mouth—red—and looked positively watery of eye. Pearl did have a cute navel.

Somewhere off down there in the bluish, "music"-swirled murk, someone yelled in anger. Someone else cursed and was punched with that unmistakable meaty sound of fist impacting flesh. Someone hit the floor. Janja did not look around. In the mirror behind Hellfire she did see the cybernetic bouncer come around the bar, fast. It had a face. On silent rollers, it made for the scene of the altercation, although that seemed to have been settled by the participants. By one of them, anyhow.

"Anybody over here got the time?"

The voice came from Janja's left and just behind her; she sat with her back to the Loophole's main room. She did not turn.

"On what planet?" Shieda asked, looking past Janja at the newcomer, and he giggled. So did Pacy, Pearl, and Dignis, and even Corundum smiled. Shieda flipped his fingers and looked self-conscious.

Hellfire did not. "Screw off, traffic-watcher. You so-secret undercover policers give me the crawling fobbies."

"Awww—listen here now . . ."

Janja glanced sidewise without appearing to, and saw that the stranger stood almost beside her. Janja watched Hellfire. Hellfire looked at the man, and she looked mean. She leaned well onto her right hip, resembling someone forcing a fart. That was not her purpose, Janja knew. Hellfire was hoisting her left hip to clear her holster. Her hand swung down that way and Janja felt a blasting cherm of intended violence.

Her left hand swung out, bending, ramming back. The elbow connected and she grunted. As the elbow's connection was with the man's crotch, he made a far uglier sound. Janja whipped her arm back at the same time as Hellfire's stopper cleared its holster. The man was bent almost double. His head was just beside the edge of the table, just beside Janja's hand. With a swift jerky movement she gave him the side of her fist in the ear.

"Shit," Hellfire said, while the man fell noisily.

Hellfire gave Janja a look, and for just a moment Janja looked into the stopper's snout. Then it practically leaped back into its holster. Beside their silent table, the man was on the floor, still trying to maintain the fetal position with both hands to his crotch. Only now did Janja look over at him. He was a nice enough looking fellow, a bit seedy, and big. Also, at present, ludicrous.

And here came the bouncer, rushing on those silent rollers. Sensors apprised it of the steps and it lifted nicely. Its "face" blinked and it spoke. The voice was perfectly human, deliberately and almost ludicrously tough-guy.

"What seems to be th' trouble here, fokes?"

"I . . . fell down—" the man on the floor said, with effort.

"He fell down," Janja said. "Must have been the steps. Looks drunk to me."

The robot assimilated that, and its "head" section swiveled toward the luckless man. "We mix good drinks here, bud. Maybe you had one or three too many. We also like a nice quiet place here. Good night."

The bouncer waited while the man got himself up, wincing and making a face. He flashed a look at Janja, who had probably saved his life. He made another face and tried not to grab himself as he departed. The bouncer's top section did a 180 to watch him before turning noiselessly back toward the table. Someone with a nice sense of humor had furnished it with a strong, slab-shaped, stubbly face.

"Sorry, fokes. Hope you don't hold this against th' Loophole. How 'bout a half-price round?"

"Nice idea," Shieda said wheezily, smiling. "Nice place you run here, bouncer."

"Call me Rocky. Your last round is on record. Same upcoming." And the cyber-bouncer departed. It navigated the two steps beautifully and settled to the floor to move silently away toward the bar at the far end of the Loophole.

Janja watched Hellfire almost smile, and relax or work at it. She knew the man had redshifted. He must have been an undercover policer at that, since he hadn't even bothered to deny it and had spoken quickly to avoid any sort of inquiry. Then Hellfire's gaze moved, in a twitch, and Janja was staring into her eyes. They were the same color as the tabletops in the Loophole. Mahogney, it was called.

"You sure scared off that little mouse-turd, Hellfire," Dignis said, high-voiced, and he giggled.

Hellfire blasted him with a glance and returned her searching stare to Janja's eyes. Janja had prevented her from using her stopper to make the man dance—or worse.

"You can protect me anytime," Vettering said, and several others chuckled, while Janja and Hellfire stared into each other's eyes.

"I've seen that mouse-turd before," Pacy said. "You know, now that I think about it, he must *be* an undercover nipper!" She was looking at Hellfire, who was looking at Janja. Looking mean.

"How'd you know that, Captain Hellfire?" That from Raunchy, who was looking at Janja looking at Hellfire who looked only at Janja, and continued.

The table went quiet again. Eyes rolled. Away across the main room someone finished a joke and several people laughed alcoholically. No one laughed up on the alcove at the rear.

Hellfire spoke. "What're you looking at, Cloud-top?"

Janja saw challenge, heard and recognized challenge. Hellfire had confronted the man and had meant to give him a jolt with her too-ready stopper. She'd have enjoyed it. Janja had interfered. Alcohol was in the way, but Janja chermed more than challenge—what? She ignored it.

"Looking at? I'm looking at the woman who recognized a policer and had him scared off with a look and a gesture before I had to go and interfere, Captain Prass-top." She glanced at the others, hearing a couple of gasps. "Sorry I made a fuss and attracted attention, jackoes." She looked back at Hellfire. "You can call me Janja, Hellfire. How *did* you know that escaper from a cesspool was a—what is it you call 'em here, Pacy—nippers?"

Pacy smiled and started to reply and Pearl calmly reached across herself to pop her palm over her friend's mouth.

After another long silent moment, Hellfire wrapped her left hand around her mug of Pale, an almost calorie-free ale. Hellfire was left-handed or ambidextrous, Janja had already noted. She smiled lopsidedly, on the left side of her mouth. That wide mouth, thin lips, and staring eyes made it an unwholesome grimace.

"I *smelled* him," she said, "and you can call me Prass-top, Janjy!"

The laughter at their table was so unnaturally loud and uproarious that others in the Loophole stopped to stare, nervously or angrily or merely curiously. The cyber-bouncer eased back toward the half-score of patrons, but did not come all the way to the alcove. These people were known to be well-off, big spenders, and dangerous. The volume disc set into their tabletop was chastisement enough. Its sound-sensors reacted to the laughter by blinking silver-blue to advise that their noise level was out of line.

Janja winked and lifted her own drink in silent salute to the thinner woman. Hellfire returned the gesture; they drank.

The wall plate beside the table's other end was extruding new drinks. At half price, of course.

Janja had been leaning back and she had never moved. Now she crossed her legs. Her right calf bulged atop her left knee, the black fabric gleaming almost white. Hellfire regarded that leg with appreciation.

"How'd you get to be captain, Hellfire?"

Again silence cloaked the table and again eyes rolled. The others knew the answer. Hellfire's deep-set mahogany eyes rolled, too, at Captain Corundum. Tension rolled in like heavy fog.

"Killed my captain," Hellfire said, and again glanced at Janja's captain.

After an interval that seemed to drag on for a couple of weeks-standard, Janja said, "Oh."

And after another time, Hellfire spoke. Her voice was the antithesis of her name. Her voice had the quality of one who speaks from a hypnotic fog.

"I was computrician on a good ship. After a lot of months in space, the captain decided that I looked almost like a woman. Then he decided to try me and see." She flipped her fingers. "I don't like men, Janjy. Not as sex partners, I mean. If I decided to, it'd be *me* deciding, and *I'd* do the choosing." She continued to gaze at the blond exotic who had been a slave. As a woman who prefers women stares at a woman?

Janja was blinking in disconcert. "Oh," she began badly, and whether advertently or in-, Raunchy came galloping to the rescue.

"How about Jarps, Captain Hellfire?"

Someone sniggered. Two someones, Pacy and Dignis. Janja, on whose leg Corundum's hand now territorially lay, stared at Pacy. Hellfire shot Dignis one of her looks, from those dangerous eyes.

I wonder if her stopper's set on Three, Janja thought, suddenly reminded of Corundum. *I'll bet she loves to kill, too. Odd. There* is *something sexually interesting about her, despite her . . . being the way she is. A dynamism, or something. What do you call it when some people have something like electromagnetism?* She had a flash of Jonuta, and dispelled that image from her mind with some anger.

And Raunchy had just asked Hellfire if she "liked" Jarps. And the tension remained. It was interesting, this tension and this conversation. More electromagnetism.

Hellfire looked at Raunchy. "Well, I know enough not to use the term 'Sunflower,' " she said, using the common word for Jarp-lover. "Otherwise—who's going to laugh at me if I admit I don't know?—I've never had any experience with a Jarp."

"No one at all," Corundum quietly answered.

"Who's going to laugh," the Jarp said, fiddling with its translation helmet, "if I admit that I've never had any experience with a spacer captain who prefers its own sex?"

The gathering laughed rowdily again and Vettering slapped the tabletop. The sensor-disc imbedded there warned them with a brighter flash than last time. Even laughing, though, Captain Hellfire was looking at Janja.

"Jarps, it is said," Janja began innocently, "can be all things to all people. I have enjoyed the . . . company of a Jarp. Otherwise, I am not all things, but ever a woman to a man." She flipped her fingers; *their gesture,* learned from Kenowa on *Coronet* and seen a hundred times since. "Merely the old heterosexual bias."

"A pity," Hellfire said, and her eyes seemed to have gone luminous.

"Some men," Corundum said most quietly, "doubtless feel the same way about you, Hellfire."

She stared at him and new tension formed. *Aglii's light,* Janja thought, *she challenges everyone always! He was paying her a compliment.* A glance around the table and a little reflection, though, led Janja to another observation. *Stow that. There are ten of us here and not one of us is totally comfortable or at ease with self or in role; unchallengably sure of itself. Unless maybe Althis is . . . the cow.*

Corundum spoke easily, almost softly. "Come, Captain Hellfire, stare not at evil Corundum, black-clad pirate of the spaceways. He has lusted after you for years and years and still pays compliments when they are merited."

His hand had closed on Janja's leg. It turned, and it hurt. She showed nothing, or thought she did not. Corundum, she knew, was steeled. It was not his gunhand that tensed on Janja's leg. That hand was free, and it was not on the table. His brain and stopper had one setting: Fry.

Hellfire threw back her head and laughed. "Sure," she said, licking her lips and banging down her mug. (The table's sound-disc flashed testily.) "Oh sure."

The willowy woman rose, sinuous as an orange-maned Aglayan nightprowler. She looked at the Jarp. "Past my bedtime, mates. Thanks for the drinks—enjoyed the company and all that. Be wary and keep your DS clean and oiled. I hope I see you all again this side of the Forty Percent Trail. How raunchy are you, Raunchy?"

The Jarp rose. It was a dozen sems taller than the pirate with the brass-dyed hair, and almost as lean of hip. Its lemur eyes stared at Janja.

"Raunchy," it said, "always raunchy. Isn't that what they say about all us Jarps? Janja, the Jarp you—got to know. Was it a slave, on Resh?"

Janja was startled at this mention of Whistle, but she replied at once. "Yes."

"It is happy now, with a fellow Jarp. It is now on the ship of one Captain Jonuta, with his Jarp crew-member of some years' standing. You did them both a good turn, Janja—and a good turn for lots of others as well." Raunchy bowed, rather ceremoniously, to the doubly startled Janja. Its long fingers adjusted the system of straps that composed its translation helmet. It emitted a swift sequence of whistles, and readjusted the helmet. "I give you a blessing of Jarpi," it said. "And to all, a good night."

It moved to Hellfire, who started to swing and head for the door on long wiry legs, then paused. She walked out with Raunchy, side by side. The couple was stared at, naturally. Still, it wasn't as if a choice Theban female was going off with one of those damned orange strangies.

Most of those on the other side of the law, however successful and arrogant and proudly challenging, learned or cultivated some discretion. Most. Sometimes. Thus no one at the table in the Loophole's rear spoke until Hellfire and Raunchy were out the door and gone for sure.

"That," Althis said, addressing herself to her smoke, "is about as unlikely a couple as I could've thought of. And jackoes, I've thought of some odd ones, believe it!"

Dignis tittered and Vettering gave Althis a proprietary caress.

"I cannot understan' how a fee-male can love a

woo-man better'n men," Pearl said, tiny beside huge Shieda, who had as much teat as Pearl and Hellfire combined.

Janja smiled and lifted her plass. "I suppose I can't, either, but a Jarp is, after all, a compromise! Besides, *I* can't understand what women see in about ninety-eight percent of *men!*"

While she drank, Vettering said, "Present company excluded, of course."

Before Janja could make a dangerous reply, Corundum spoke. "Don't be silly, Vett. Who could prefer Corundum? Janja is his captive, you know." And he smiled.

Pearl and Pacy, oddly, looked uncomfortable. Perhaps they thought it just possible that the dark and somberly clad man spoke truth, smile or no. Perhaps they noticed Janja's squared jaw and compressed lips.

Althis's glance shifted restlessly from Janja to Corundum to Vettering to tabletop. And back to Janja. She licked her lips in a nervous gesture. The prospect of trouble among them made her worse than uncomfortable, and it showed. She thought of the perfect placating words:

"How smart you and me are then, Janja, to have found our men from among the other two percent!"

It wasn't the perfect thing to say. Janja's lips paled still more. She had just acted strongly with that presumed policer, and the adrenaline was still working in her. Too, she had the example (and admiration?) of Hellfire, an obviously strong woman and her own person despite her problems, also obvious. Abruptly Janja turned to face Corundum. The ring of her zipper pull flashed silver. Pale eyes met the cool cybernetic gaze of his optics, dead on.

"Janja is *not* your captive, Captain Corundum. She is your aide, your crewmember, your ally, remember? Janja is not your captive, or your whore!"

Once again that table of ten and now eight accommodated an extra guest: tension. Once again, they greeted its presence with silence. They were an unpredictable group. A violent person had left them, with Raunchy. Others, given to violence and driven by ego, remained. Even multikilogram Shieda, his fingers tucked like a family of rock-grubs into Pearl's nonutilitarian bra of red straps, froze. He pretended interest in his drink while secretly watching Corundum. Corundum was perhaps the most unpredictable element present. Althis looked ready to wring her hands or cry.

Corundum looked mildly at Janja, and seconds dragged by like minutes or kilometers. A pan of fulminate of mercury balanced on two fingers above concrete. She did not glance down or away.

"Oh my dear, my dear," he said at last, quiet of voice and charming, oh so Corundumly charming. "I know all that! I meant nothing by what I said. Vettering knows that." His hand moved, but did not quite touch her.

"Vett, old friend: this woman was foully stolen from her own lovely 'Protected' world by that dung-worm, Jonuta. He peddled her on Resh to a pair of sadists. She was slave. She was used and misused, buggered and tortured. And she freed herself. You know of the deaths of that old sow Sicuan and his son Chulucan . . . behold her they mistreated!" Corundum's gesture was flowing and dramatic. "Behold their killer! Somehow, she got herself to Franji. There Corundum met her . . . when she tricked him! Me, Corundum! With Corundum's stopper she fried that slimy lizard of Jonuta's, Srih."

"She?" Vettering was staring and pointing. Astonished, eyes large. He had forgotten Althis. *"You?"*

"She! Of *course* you are not Corundum's captive or his hust, Janja! Fortunate is Corundum to attain her favors now and again. Corundum's aide—aye! Crewmember—nay! Partner and *ally,* as she said. Ah no, Corundum meant no insult, Janja, for you are my Primeval Princess!"

"Tao's fuckin' toenails," Althis muttered, reaching for another Heaven High. "This is heavy!"

Pacy looked at Pearl, glancing only briefly at the pale slugs she seemed to be wearing in her bra, which the two of them knew was called a "strap-titser." She did not speak aloud, despite her alcohol-glazed eyes. She only mouthed the words, silently: *Prime-evil Prin-cess?!*

Janja felt the coolth where Corundum's hand had left her leg.

She realized that she did not miss it.

She also knew a certain feeling of dread. Not quite fear. Cool Corundum! Cool, charming, contained Corundum . . . actor. Devious, clever Corundum, so cleverly covering, preserving.

She had to fight not to smile as, while picking up her drink, she reached up with her other hand and drew the shining ring of her zipper all the way down to her belt. Under the snug black shirt she wore only Janja.

Her pleasant smile caressed Althis on its way to Vettering. "So hot in here, don't you think, Captain Vettering?"

"Warm," he repeated automatically, staring while he nodded automatically. Fascinated by her, now that he knew about her.

"Couldn't be the alcohol," Dignis said, with a nervous giggle.

Janja smiled, then let her gaze and smile drift back toward Althis. Althis put her head with its broad face on one side, looking into those eyes of mist and ice. Hard as blue lace agates, weren't they, with less blue in them. Janja was sure that Althis's next action was deliberate; the voluptuous woman wanted the small blond to see her gaze fall into the open front of the black shirt. There stood Janja's tight untrembling breasts with their high gravity musculature, looking positively snowy framed by the fabric of Corundum black. And, compared with Althis's chest, childish.

With her eyes fixed there Althis said, "Vett . . . remember Ahizna?" and Janja wondered what in the Cold Hell the woman was talking about.

Janja jerked her head toward Corundum and slid a hand along his black-velveted thigh. "Did you put anti-intoxicant in this drink?"

His hand came onto hers and he gave his head a single shake. His lips only seemed to be considering a smile.

She retracted her hand. "Oh," she said. "Good." And she drank deeply.

"Of course," Vettering was saying to Althis, ignoring the facts that Pearl was rubbing Shieda's crotch while he palpated her breast while Pacy stared at Janja and tried to disguise her obvious awe and admiration.

Althis looked at her Vettering and, somehow, swelled even more the mighty beige jelly-jiggles of her warheads. Her look was questioning. Vettering, with a very small smile, nodded. Janja tried to cherm what lay behind those signals and failed. She had just dumped more alcohol into her system and she had made no effort to reduce its effects. That was an ability They did not have and did not know she possessed. They used drugs, along with the natural substance riboflavin. She had the feeling that somehow they were discussing her. Althis had made a suggestion, hadn't she, and Vettering had agreed or acquiesced?

"We're all staying at the same hotel," Althis said. "Why don't we head that way before this dive closes down?"

Once, Janja was thinking, *with someone called Ahizna or someplace called Ahizna, these two joined two others for some four-way salaciousness. Now they are ready to try it again, with Corundum and me. With me, and Corundum incidentally!* Her eyes flicked to another. *And Pacy would love to make it a fivesome!*

And I? Yes, I'm excited. Undoubtedly spurred by the example of Hellfire who challenges everybody and takes nothing from anybody, I challenged Corundum, confronted Corundum in public. And he backed down! At least publicly, for these people.

That was exciting. It was even sexually exciting. It built her confidence and ego and self-esteem. It made her want to celebrate, and sex was the ultimate celebration. Centuries and millennia had not changed that.

With Vettering and Althis?

Sunmother's Light—no!

With Pacy, her stash speaking through her eyes?

Why, she's only a child!

She felt Corundum's optics directed at the side of her face. Knowledge of him gained by their intimacy enabled her to cherm his feelings. His excitement, his suppressed violence, his sensual glow, his . . . something else. Alcohol intervened and supervened. Alcohol dulled the senses, They said, and Janja had six senses. They were right. Her ability to cherm was dulled.

With a grunt and various jiggles of flesh, Shieda moved. He sent out an arm like a thick pseudopod. It extended along Pearl's back, and Pacy's back, and his hand dropped onto Pacy's wetcloth-clad chest, onto the lump that simply could not be the real nipple of such a youngster.

"We are more than ready to redshift this place," Shieda said. "Aren't we, troops?" (Pacy gasped and her eyes rolled loosely.)

All dutiful, mindful of duty and future, his girlish "troops" assured him they were. *No one sold them into slavery,* Janja mused; *they sell themselves.*

The servoplate in the wall began to flash. Corundum frowned at it, bent to it. He depressed the single horizontal bar that opened the comm.

"Pray apprise us of the meaning of this signal."

"With pardons, a message for someone called Cloudtop."

All of them stared at the panel, and then Pacy and Dignis tittered. Althis smiled. Vettering sat back, stretching his legs, gazing at Janja with his brows up.

"Cloud-top," Corundum pronounced, tight of lip, "is here. What is the message?"

"With dozens of pardons," the human voice said in the way of Thebanis, *"the message can be taken only at the bar."*

Silence and frowns. Janja flipped her fingers. "How convenient! I have to recycle a couple of drinks anyhow."

"So have *I!"* Althis said, moving.

Janja, seated on the outside, was on her feet. "Oh—if Corundum is ready to leave, I am."

She and Althis descended the two steps and moved through the big blue-murk room. Only half its tables and booths were occupied, now. The two women were appraised, but no one said anything. Behind them, just in case, Vettering had stood and was staring at their backs. He was very visible, as he intended to be. A call to the comm might just be a trick, a trap. Vettering knew why Althis wanted a few minutes alone with Janja and he was far from displeased. He was prepared for trouble, just the same.

"Go ahead, Althis," Janja said, when they reached the bar, which was only partly automated and presided over by a very human young male. Nice-looking. "I'll be with you in a moment." She looked questioningly at the bartender.

He was regarding her, a woman all agleam in snug black and looking supple as a serpent. He gave her a little smile and a slight wag of his head. "You're Cloud-top, all right—ma'am. Right over there. The booth privatizes automatically."

Janja walked to the booth. Althis's choice was limited to waiting or going ahead to the Loophole's relief station. She bit her lip, felt pressure on her bladder, and made her way to the door while Janja entered the booth. Hear-see inhibitors engaged when she buttoned the comm and the booth's open entry seemed to become an opaque, soundproof wall to everyone outside.

"Cloud-top here."

"Prass-top here, Janjy. You people still there, hmm? Raunchy and I are enjoying a last Pale and a look-see out over the city—Raunchy swears it's named after her, of course—and we wanted you to know you have friends in Mod 754 of the Thebanis Mahal."

"Thanks, Hellfire. We're staying there too."

"Oh, I know. In 879. Here comes the click."

The comm said *click.* Janja gazed thoughtfully at it for a moment. She smiled just a little. She had noticed how Hellfire applied the female pronoun to Raunchy. Probably automatic, Janja decided, buttoning off the phone. A Jarp was an *it.** Most Jarps were quick to remind others of that fact. Janja turned and stepped out of the booth, glanced about, and headed for the door marked HERN.

"Rest" rooms, Janja had learned, had not changed much across the hundreds of years. That was a finger-flipper to her; there were no such facilities on pastoral Aglaya. The Aglayan euphemism translated as "the bushes" as in "I have to go to the bushes."

As she entered, Althis was just coming out of a stall. They nodded without speaking and Janja entered the adjacent one.

She soon emerged to actuate the foot-switch to cleanse her hands radiantly. Althis stood waiting.

"Nothing like a good pressure release to make a woman feel like a girl again, hmmm?"

Janja nodded. Words seemed called for, ridiculously. She said one: "Right."

"Say Janje, me and Vett would love to have yourself and Corundum join ourselves in a few minutes for a little . . . party." She chuckled. "Actually I think it's you Vett and myself are both taken with, but we can't leave out Corundum, huh!"

"That's what Ahizna means to you two, isn't it," Janja said, turning to the door.

* Actually the third, genderless pronoun, not the fourth one for things: "it." There is unfortunately no English equivalent, "they" being plural only.

"Uh—pos. You caught all that, huh. You're too fast, Janja, just too fast!" The tone was admiring and placating, not quite fawning. "We—"

"I'm afraid Ahizna is not on Thebanis tonight, Althis."

"Oh. Uh. You mean, uh, Vett and myself don't interest you, huh." She followed Janja out, watching that small blond head shake.

"No, Althis. That's not what I said. It's not—ah—something I want to do, that's all."

"You don't like Vett?"

O Aglii, has this creature no sense of self, no matter how often she misemploys the word myself? Janja said, "It just isn't something I want to do, Althis. That's all. Really."

"Um. Well, uh—what if [illegible]
stay alongside the other wo[illegible]
to the rear of the Loophole [illegible]
—uh, you're not going to [illegible]

Janja shook her head.

"Hey, Janja, quit rushing, we aren't enemies and I'm not begging, f'r Tao's sake, I just—well, what if Corundum and Vettering are talking right now and Corundum *does* want to?"

Janja almost stopped. She turned her head to look into Althis's eyes, and she kept her expression pleasant. "That won't matter to me, Althis."

"Tao's balls, you are really something Janje, you know that?"

Oh sure, Janja thought, moving on back to the others. *I'm really something, all right. The trouble is I don't know what and I'm no longer sure who.*

11

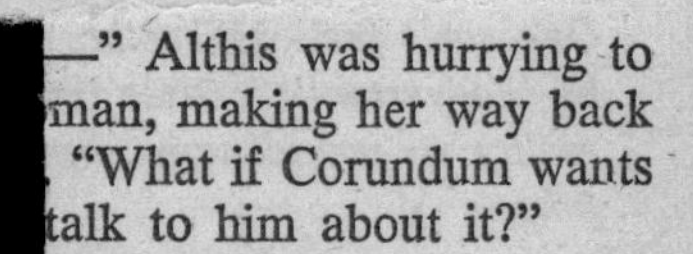
—" Althis was hurrying to
man, making her way back
"What if Corundum wants
talk to him about it?"

Vettering and Corundum had not been discussing the invitation to a mini-orgy because Vettering was still standing, watchfully waiting. Janja merely glanced at him. She assumed his questioning look would be met by a headshake from Althis, and that would be that. She was right.

She turned to smile at Althis. Janja winked. After a time, Althis smiled back. Yes. That was sensible. Practicality really should rule. Let sensation and its call just sort of wander off by itself into the more primitive area of the brain. Just a thought. Lightly, the larger woman gave Janja's forearm an understanding squeeze. No hard feelings. It was obvious that Althis worried a lot about hard feelings.

"It's a night," Corundum said, and Janja arrested herself in the act of settling into her seat. Corundum was making the *beau geste* of feeding his I.D. card into the wall panel to his right. The slot gulped the card and had it back in less than forty seconds. That swiftly the bill was settled, while Dignis and Shieda made spluttering noises about being cheated out of paying.

"Pacy," Shieda said abruptly, squeezing so that she winced, "do let us bring Dignis up to our suite for a nightcap."

Janja smiled. How nice for Dignis. If he could stay awake with his considerable load, he was going to get to share Shieda's wealth of just-post-nubile flesh and willingness! She felt nothing for the girls, who looked accepting if unenthusiastic. They chose their actions. They were as much in charge of their lives as anyone else.

As much as I am, Janja thought in some revelation, as Corundum rose to stand beside her. She remembered the words of the philosopher Gaier: "When I was younger, I used to look like me." And she considered a modification: "When I was younger, I used to like me." Her mouth tightened.

The Thebanis Mahal hotel was three and a half blocks distant and at least three of Thebanis's moons were visible. Maybe four; Janja was not sure about that point of light. They walked. Only an army would have molested such a group. Janja asked about the point of light, but Dignis was having a hard enough time just walking, without answering ethereal questions. Pacy said she thought it was a star. Pearl said she thought it was Flicka, the planet's sixth moon. Flicka was the seventh, Pacy thought. Some people talked too much, a wheezing Shieda observed.

"Oh, it *is* a lovely night," Althis said with enthusiasm, ever anxious to allay anything approaching strife. "Let's stay another day, sweetering. I'd love to have dinner tomorrow night in that open restaurant on top of the Commerce Tower!"

Dignis concentrated on walking, aided by Pacy. Shieda puffed along with an arm around Pearl, leaning on her a bit, and his other hand in Pacy's. Janja and Corundum walked ahead, saying nothing. Vettering didn't answer Althis. A police cyberpatrol car went by, all green and shining silvery aluminic. People stepped aside for the group of eight led by the armed couple in black, and they stared after Janja, wondering if her hair and pallor could be real.

In the hotel, Shieda elected to wait for the next elevator. The Thebanis Mahal had no anti-gee chutes. Janja and Corundum bade Vettering and Althis good night and got off on Eight. They walked down the hall in silence. The door of 879, its electronic lock reset to his standard I.D. credcard, opened. Corundum entered and did a little checking anyhow, while Janja closed the door. He went into the bathroom.

Janja realized that she had just braced the Loophole bartender, walked several blocks and through the lobby with her breasts exposed as if advertising. She rolled her eyes upward and forgot it. She was thinking. Her thoughts generated a prickling in her armpits and a tightness of her scalp. She decided. She pulled the zipper all the way up just as Corundum emerged from the bathroom.

"Well, Primeval Princess—"

"Althis and Vettering wanted a four-way sexaria and I told her no."

He paused, letting her know he had noticed the interruption, before he nodded. "Good. We—"

"I think I'll go down and have a last quiet sip of Pale or something," she said casually.

It was not casual. O Aglii, it was not casual! It was a first, Janja's saying that she was not going to do something without him on her own, and they both knew it and the significance of it. He was captain, and experienced and knowledgeable, and he was Corundum. He was senior and he always decided. For that reason she had phrased the enormity of her statement as she had, softening it. She watched his jaw work.

"Up," he said quietly, mildly. "The hotel bar is up. The astrobubble on top."

"Up, then." She gazed at the copse of slate-colored trees on the holographically pastoral wall, and she kept her expression wide open.

He stood regarding her. "Is it correct to assume that you imply but merely did not say the word . . . *alone?*"

She forced herself to swing her gaze back to him. It was an enormous step, and it might be right off a cliff. She took it. "Pos."

Looking at her almost expressionlessly, he nodded. Then he walked over to pass a hand over the panel that drew the drapes. The view from that window was rotten, anyhow.

"The door cannot be left unlocked," he said, "and it opens only for the card of Corundum, who is going to bed."

This was getting consummately meaningful. Maybe she had stepped off a cliff. He had said it quietly, flatly, with his back to her. He had just told her that if she left she could not get back into the module. She had no intention of asking to borrow his card.

"Are you certain that you are not... just tired, Janja?"

She heard him, and she understood his meaning. She had been challenged, and now he gave her opportunity to reconsider without loss of face. She heard the formality of her name, too.

Janja maintained her strength. "No. I need to think a little, Emery." Deliberately she used her private name for him. "To settle down a little."

"Umm."

Gnawing at her lip, she waited. He was not going to say anything else, she realized. She watched him move his hand again. The drapes reopened. He was not even going to ask about that call for "Cloud-top." Its origin was obvious. She fidgeted, wondering. Far from comfortable or happy. Giving herself a chance to reconsider, as he had done.

No. Then she realized there was something she did not know. She must ask. She considered that for a moment, then moved to put her hand on the door.

"Emery."

"Yes?"

He did not turn. Staring out at Raunch, or pretending to do. *No more happy or comfortable than I,* Janja realized. That helped a little. *But I thought he was so mature and sophisticated! We communicate no better than . . . than most married couples!*

A new thought inveigled its way into her consciousness: *or stern father and willful daughter?*

"Are you telling me not to come back, Emery—in the morning?"

"Suggesting that you reconsider leaving," he said, clipping the wings of her choices. "Otherwise—no, of course not. It is not what you are suggesting, surely. Not this way, on little more than a whim, the tick of the moment. That fellow Starnik is meeting me here for breakfast, at ten-hundred Thebanistime. Corun . . . I should prefer that you be here then, too. Then, and after, and after that as well."

Janja was elated. *He means always,* she mused, *though he doesn't say it. He is saying go and have your fling, Primeval Princess, and come back* . . . home. With no threats and no suggestion even of talking about it, now or tomorrow. Stiff as a board or a stern father. And yet he had switched from "Corundum" to "I," deliberately softening. She made a softening gesture, too:

"The bar closes at three, local time, doesn't it?"

"Yes. By then Corundum will be long asleep."

His words closed the door. That was that, then. She could stay, or she could go and stay gone. Until morning. He insisted that this be a major decision, and action. Corundum: a hard substance often used as an abrasive.

"I'll see you for breakfast then, Corundum."

She left. Quickly, before he could turn or say

something else. The door closed behind her and she glanced back at it. Then she went down the meadow-land carpet of the bright-lit corridor, to the elevators. After passing a hand over the UP plate she waited, thinking, staring at nothing, chewing the inside of her cheek. She felt a little *frisson*. Her armpits were not just prickly, they were damp. She was taking a tremendous step, heavily freighted with import. She could recall it; she could go back and knock on the door. Now. Swiftly. Before he got into bed. Alone. Now—

No.

Primeval Princess had been strong and he had accepted it, up to a point. She must; she had to continue strong. Otherwise she was just a girl. Corundum's girl.

The elevator door opened. A very straight-looking couple stood inside, almost as if at attention. Their glances slid over her and slid off like oil. They were the sort who did not meet eyes, who did not stare even at the surprising and stareworthy. *A couple who does/do not communicate,* she thought, joining them on the elevator.

She watched them off at the Tenth, rode on up to the top, got off, and was just in time to catch the other elevator going down, with a group of noisy people. Locals, here only for a night out atop Raunch, looking down on Raunch. They were paired. They looked, but no one said anything to her or sought to flirt with the blond exotic in the snug black clothing.

They stated no floor, meaning they intended to go all the way down. And thence home to their pair-bonded beds, doubtless.

"Excuse me." She leaned to the plate, murmured "Six," and got off there, feeling silly in her secretiveness, opening the stairwell door and walking up to Seven. She saw no one. She heard voices emanating from a couple of modules as she walked along the meadow-carpeted corridor. Her heartbeat was not much short of lightspeed when she reached 754. She paused there, all prickly anew. Her heart thuttered while she looked at the door.

She took a few deep breaths, rolled her neck five times left, five times right, gave herself a few silent instructions about settling down. And she knocked.

Silence. She waited. Just as she knocked again, a voice called from the other side of the door:

"Who is it?"

"Cloud-top."

Silence. She waited, getting less comfortable by the second—or more uncomfortable, rather.

The door opened. "Come in, Janjy," Hellfire said.

The room was dark. Janja entered slowly and the light came on in a flash of illumination, hot blue, and she was staring at Hellfire, naked, thin-not-skinny, wiry. Tattooed or body-painted or cell-dyed at navel and nipples. Legs apart. Stopper in hand.

It was pointed at Janja.

Behind her the door closed. She glanced around, not wheeling because she was mindful of the gun. Raunchy stood beside the door. Also naked, weirdly blue-lit orange. Nice wide-set breasts were almost perfect cones and a growth below that more resembled an impossibly enlarged clitoris than a small penis. Below, almost concealed, a small vaginal opening. There was, after all, only so much room down there. Raunchy's hips were mighty lean—but then so were Hellfire's, and Janja's hardly formed a voluptuous cradle for the rocking of men. Raunchy's nakedness was emphasized by its lack of translator helmet and, of course, body hair.

The Jarp, too, held a stopper. This one, too, was pointed at Janja.

Aglii's Light and Hands—it was a trap! I've been a fool, a fool, I am a fool—it was a trap!

"Take her stopper, Raunchy." Hellfire's tone was not flat, but excited.

"T'l-ldleew'eetl!" the Jarp said, just behind Janja. Her stopper was whipped out of its holster while she was still in shock.

Hellfire gestured with her left hand. Hellfire's hairless pubis was shockingly protuberant, her legs obviously strong. Her stomach seemed nonexistent and her navel shockingly surrounded by a sunburst in orange-outlined gold that was little different from her own color. A child could have covered those hard-looking breasts with its hands. The aureoles were gold-and-blue dotted. Nipples like raisins.

"Gimme."

Raunchy stalked past Janja, who even in her shock appreciated the look of those tight boyishly round buttocks, set intriguingly, anomalously in from a woman's svelte hips. It handed Hellfire both stoppers and turned to face Janja. It smiled.

"The door's locked," Hellfire said. "You've been kidnaped, Janjy." She waggled her stopper and her breast on that side tightened visibly. "Strip."

Janja swallowed hard. "No."

"Wha—strip, bitch! I've got a stopper on you!"

"You want me naked, *Captain* Prass-top, come strip me."

"Aw come on, Janjy, dammit, go along with the game!" Hellfire said almost pleadingly and then, in a different voice, *"Strip,* you beautiful cloud-haired stash!"

Now a confused Janja obeyed. Zippers made their *wheep* noises. (That had been improved out of zippers long ago, which had then been replaced by Velcro and molecular bonding. When zippers returned, consumer demand soon resulted in a return of the *wheeep!* or *zzzip!* sound. Five or seven years ago seams had returned to hose, too, and remained popular on over half the worlds of the galaxy.)

Hardly happy, Janja at last stood naked under the weird blue lighting, facing her naked captors.

So much for independence, she thought bitterly. *Corundum, Corundum . . . maybe I am just a silly little stash who needs a keeper! Now I* am *a captive, but not yours, my loving Emery!*

Still, she was watching for her chance. Others had tried this, and received grievous shocks. Something approaching a berserker fighter lurked beneath the taut skin and powerful muscles necessarily developed on a high-gravity planet.

Then Hellfire walked, tight-assed, to the typically Theban dresser, which was ridiculously encrusted with gingerbread. She opened a drawer, dumped the three stoppers inside. All three, yes. She turned back with a grin like a big neon-mnemonic sign.

"Now you're our sex prisoner for the night, heh-heh, and are you ever going to get and give a lotta heh-heh loving, you doll! Oh, are we glad you came! Oh are you going to come! Huh, Raunchy?"

"Ldl-leet'l!"

Janja's legs went weak as they seized her, laughing, and she realized that it had indeed been a game, and happiness soared with all the added force of relief.

Hellfire was right, too. She got a lot of loving, and gave, too, while thrills leaped and pulsed through her like the rippling flare of a luxichord's light-music.

She groaned at the flickering of tongues and the stroking and probing, tweaking and scissoring of fingers, at deep deep kisses at mouth and belly and breasts and mouth. Her hips arched and surged automatically and her lips and fingers and tongue were powerless not to move, to find, to explore, to give and strive, to love. Moans and groans became sobbing cries and high-voiced outcries.

Hellfire watched with fascination, way over an hour later, when Raunchy assumed the male role and Janja clamped it to her so that Aglayan and Jarp wallowed in thrusting sexual embrace and Hellfire did not know that she was watching two aliens, not just one. Janja was not exactly stuffed, but she was definitely sliced, and the movements and straining were mutual.

After that it was the three of them again, wrecking the bed, with Raunchy a "her" again, and then . . .

12

The sky over Velynda was stained pink, lavender, cinnabar, and an electric blue. Shadows were black. Some shaded into indigo. Jonuta glanced edgewise at the weary old primary sun of Franji, now a ball sliced in half and laid flat side down on the horizon. Its dark mate was small and pale and sullen; asleep or moribund. Jonuta could look directly at it.

This system was a binary, as most were; a few more than half the suns in the galaxy had smaller, paler companions. Most were B-2 suns. The double stars were mated for life. Two separate cults on Franji maintained that this was clearly part of Booda's Plan For All In The Universe, BOOPFAITU. They argued accordingly that humans were meant to mate for life. Others pointed out with just as much logic that it could as well be said that Booda intended such a fate for only a few over half of His children. Too, they demanded to know whether one mate was also "meant to be" so small and pale and hardly significant, so overshone by the other. The absolutist fundamentalists were not amused.

Leaning on the rail of the hotel balcony, Jonuta glanced over to the west. There, where darkness crept stealthily, other suns showed bright along with those lights that were not stars. A crescent moon, barren, was a silvered pink that would grow more and more eerie as the planet slid over its warming suns and the solitary moon slid forth in transitory triumph.

Hellpit, many kilometers from Velynda, showed the long-ago fate of a second moon.

As night claimed Franji's sky, other lights burned brighter and brighter, too. Comsats One through Six; Powersats One and Three. Monitor Beta and Franjistation Prime, closer than the moon in geosynchronous orbit. Larger than the moon in appearance and yet, coincidentally, almost the same diameter. Booda made the one—or Allah, or Primover, or She, or Tao or Theba or Tiwan, depending upon which Franjese was speaking—and mortal humans had made the others.

By whatever name, gods or God made suns and their satellite planets and the planets' satellite moons; and, too, God made humankind: mortals, Galactics.

Galactics made and hung Comsats and Powersats and Defensats and Franjistations and the slender tethers that linked the latter physically with the planet. Mortal Galactics, not being gods or God, had to start from scratch. God or gods had no cause to be proud. Pride was for His or Her or Its creations. They were Galactics, the children of the Earth, the Thingmakers.

Janja called these spacefarers Them, and Thingmakers. It had not occurred to her that God—Aglii, in her language, and female—had also made *things*. Suns and planets and trees and stones; flowers and mountains and rivers; and strivers made of bone and flesh.

Now one of those strivers stood on the balcony outside his suite in the Hotel Royal Franjis, gazing at sunset on Franji.

Franji is beautiful at dusk, Jonuta thought. *Here at this hour and the hour to come, or on the far side when dusk kisses and colors it all pink and copper and sanguine, it is beautiful.*

Qalara is home, and beloved. It is part of me and in my blood, a mystical matter. That's why I love it. But I can be content on Franji.

He wore clothing of Franji's capital, for only so would he come down onto this planet. His ship nuzzled the vast wheel of a space station above. *Coronet* was docked there; electromagnetically coupled. Now it was being scanned and nurtured by two great segmented leads like vast intravenous tubes. *Coronet* was here for a physical exam. The ship's captain was a most cautious man, and proud of that caution. And alive because of it.

Captain Jonuta's collarless shirt resembled a tunic and he wore it outside his waistband, Franji style, like a tunic. Its three-quarter sleeves were cuffed. There were four pockets and shoulder straps no longer called epaulettes or even epaulets (and serving no purpose beyond decoration). The shirt was white and the buttons were spheres the silvered pink of Franji's moon. His trousers, cut to blouse at the bottom and called blousars, were the color of the dark Franjese whiskey made from native maize: berbun. Soft-soled shoes of openwork scrim were popular among the leisured class of Franji, this year-Franji. Jonuta's were of a beige lighter than his skin.

Too recently a law had been passed prohibiting people from going publicly armed in Velynda, and so a special holographic mini-projector disguised the stopper on Jonuta's right hip. It appeared to be an insy bag—for the carrying of incidentals—of Saipese lizardskin. They were not quite in fashion among the wealthy of Franji, but Jonuta's identity here could afford to wear the eclectic and exotic.

On Franji he was Haj Seablood, party-loving heir to something-or-other, a fortune, and a transplant here from . . . where was it? Ghanj, perhaps, where there was Real Nobility? Or was it distant Shankar, with its strange god, whatsHisname?—or had Haj ever said, really?

No matter. He was Haj Seablood, well traveled and a loosecard. Fun to be with and around. He was well liked. That big woman with all the wigs was always with him, but everyone knew he got laid. The big woman was hardly as aristocratic as he, that was obvious. But nice. Oh yes, she was nice enough, though a bit daunting with all that chest, don't you know.

(Her name was of course Kenowa and she of course accompanied him into the Royal Franjis in Velynda of Franji.)

She checked in wearing a long flowing Franjisari of darkish heather green woven with metallic threads, cuprous. And a rope-sling "belt," loose, and a truly voluminous cloak of old-blood red. The sari was not even décolleté. Or not meant to be; on Kenowa, about any garment showed cleavage unless it was genuinely high collared.

Her cloak-matching wig was cut to reveal ornate earrings of two metals and three colors. The center stone was blood-hued and blinked steadily off and on, deep in its depths.

Those pendants and the cloak and chest-taut sari drew attention from her lower body. That was deliberate and studied. Kenowa had gained weight again and was sensitive of extra meat at her middle, and of swollen haunches. Her body's delight in enlarging itself was a curse and a lifelong battle. Depending on where her womanly rhythm and her circadian rhythm were at the moment, Kenowa could eat a pound of food and gain two pounds of weight, always between bosom and vulva. At least she was a woman who cared, and who knew how to disguise extra weight without looking like a woman hiding extra weight.

Franji's .73 gravity was nice. It helped. Indeed there were only two aspects of this planet with its warmth and its double shadows in black and purple that Kenowa did not like: one was the women, and their continuing, constant hanker for Jonuta/Haj. The other was the fact that here only the lower classes wore those

had drag-carried her, addicted and hurting, screaming and resisting, out of a low bar in Sopur. He had hauled her all the way to his spaceship. There he had just as forcibly "overseen" her kicking the EF habit. Naturally, she loved him. And naturally she was an unreconstructable romantic. She would spread for him, kill for him, suffer for him, hold her buttocks open for him, even sell her body for him, if need be.

Once she'd have done all those things for the next EF fix. Jonuta was a far preferable addiction. Too, EF would have killed her. Jonuta had saved her life, then.

Tonight, her suggestion was simply that he go out onto the balcony and occupy himself with Franji's suns-set. He would return to the suite only when he heard the wake-up alarm.

Jonuta agreed readily. He knew that she would prepare herself and a titillatingly interesting scenario—a Change.

Jonuta's imagination encompassed chicanery, planning, and the getting out of scrapes without violence. He did entertain normal male erotic fantasies, but those were in his mind. Kenowa was less analytical and less imaginative—except in the area of eroticism. Kenowa took fantasies out of holos and the mind and put them into the bedchamber where they belonged.

Only a few "nights" ago, on *Coronet,* he had entered his cabin to the startling and exciting sight of no less than Setsuyo Puma languidly awaiting him, on his bed.

A hyperstar because of the Akima Mars series of holomovies popular all along the spaceways. Setsuyo Puma. And a hyperstar because of her hyperdeveloped chest. Unsubtly touted as "The Biggest Pair in the Universe!," 'tsuyo Pumo stood 175 sems tall and measured a quite incredible 134E-100-64.* Her presence in Jonuta's bed was Kenowa's most clever use of holoprojection, a new high for her.

* 53E-25-40 at five feet nine inches.

Jonuta appreciated it. Both he and Kenowa appreciated the result. Secret Agent Akima Mars was magnificently loved, mauled, mouthed, stuffed, plumbed, and fondled off after.

Kenowa was hardly brilliant. She was wise enough to know herself, and what excited her. She was wise enough to know that men did need their titillation and their variety, which she called their Changes, even if the Change was an illusion. Having seen the audience-delighting amorous and rather masochistic secret agent Akima Mars in his bed, Jonuta *knew* she was there. As he joined her, she wisely pitchdarked the cabin. The illusion was preserved; now he saw behind his eyes what he had "seen" in the light. His memory saw what his eyes did not, and it became a memorable occasion. Jonuta's toenails did their best to ruin the sheet while Kenowa would have sworn he was in her past the cervix and nudging the floor of her stomach. Considerably later, his fondling her off took less than a minute. Later she told him that was her second time, that night.

A bit later still he snarled, "Now get your warheads and overblown hust's body out of here, Setsuyo, and send me my Kenowa!" And in the darkness he slapped the backside of his sprawled bedmate.

"You . . . win, slaver darling," she gasped, and in the darkness "Setsuyo Puma/Akima Mars" departed. Jonuta imparted a bit of light to the cabin just before Kenowa entered to find her grinning man waiting with arms opened wide.

When they awoke, it was for herself that Kenowa received what she'd got last night, as Setsuyo Puma.

And so tonight Jonuta willingly watched the suns-set from a balcony overlooking Velynda while Kenowa prepared herself and their suite for another Change. He focused his mind to think about Jonuta because his brain treacherously wanted to think about Janja, who lingered in his memory still, to fascinate him. What a Jonutan woman was that barbarian! But he did not really want to think about the bitch. (Kenowa's unfortunate attempt, months ago, at diverting and pleasing him by making herself resemble Janja had been short-lived. *That* pallid little wig was gone forever.)

By now he knew that here on Franji Janja had an I.D. as Tachi-Linshin 810244204TR for Resh, credless former wife of one Tachi, merchant captain. Tachi existed. There was no Tachi-Linshin, and Tachi had never been married to anyone. She had managed to escape Resh on the merchant spacer of Captain Tachi, because her fellow Aglayan, Whitey, was a member of that ship's crew.

This Jonuta knew about Janja. He wanted to know more, and yet he wanted most sincerely—or most sincerely thought he wanted—to forget her. And so, while Kenowa prepared, he thought about Kislar Jonuta, and Haj Seablood, and his other identities.

13

Nothing is more varied than the pleasures of love, although they are always the same.

Anne de Lanclos

His Franjese friends knew little about Haj Seablood other than that he had a fine home and apparently limitless funding and traveled a lot. Calls to that fine home, far from the capital, usually reached only cyber-answers and recordings. The callers left regrets plus their best wishes and invitations. They did not think of him as mysterious.

Those society friends of the wealthy Seablood did not know that he was also Eri Haddad, of the planet Jasbir.

Eri Haddad accumulated interest here in a large account at the Franji State Bank & Transfer. A *large* account. The I.D. for Eri Haddad's account was the retinal print of the infamous but glamorous figure of the spaceways, Kislar Jonuta of Qalara. No one at the Franji State B & T knew that. No one had reason to check Eri Haddad. (There had indeed been an Eri Haddad of Jasbir. He was both clean and dead. Financial institutions were not motivated to question the business and bona fides of major and thus profitable depositors. Franji State B & T had no reason to go checking the retinal prints against the Galactic Master Databank—which may or may not have existed. . . . Could it exist? The galaxy was a prodigiously, an inconceivably vast entity. There were many, many stars in the cosmos. And planets. And people. And I.D.'s. Few, however, were stellar depositors in financial institutions. Those who were formed the backbones of banks.)

The I.D. card of the late, clean Eri Haddad had come into the possession of Captain Cautious as part of a business transaction on still another planet.

Then there was Panish. Panish was another world on which Jonuta maintained two fat backup accounts for possible emergency or retirement use. He was also heavily invested in a fund based on the overall economy or Gross Planetary Product of Panish. A package of Crescent Emeralds awaited him there too, the price of one female. (They came from Terasaki, a world where Jonuta was about as welcome as vomit in freefall.)

Captain Jonuta could have had a fleet, or bought a government. Indeed he could have bought any of several planets, not to mention Arsane er-Jorvistor and other such men he dealt with.

Success in his line of work, Captain Jonuta had said, demanded caution, genius, and luck. After those came the factors he claimed to consider less important:

Continuous information from sources kept happy by thorough oiling;

Fine equipment;

A willingness to accept an unimpressive, even smallish percentage of profit—constantly.

He saw to the third by investing so much in the first and second . . . along with caution, genius, and luck.

His seemingly ungreedy methods had paid. Profits accumulated and piled up until they might have bought the contents of Ali Baba's cave. Jonuta minimized the appearance of such real, stellar wealth while maximizing its usefulness and its distribution. Had not the Booda said, "Wise is he who entrusts not all his bites to one meal and not all his bytes to one databank?"

Jonuta put the golden eggs of his fortune into many baskets. He also maintained a massively expensive backup computry system just seconds from online status. Only Januta knew what he was worth, in the stellar purchasing credits called stells more often than SPC or creds. Jonuta's "mate," SIPACUM, did not know. The backup computer did. The information could be accessed only by someone who knew all the cred-backed identities of Captain Cautious. Even then, such a resourceful genius was likely to be blown to bits, not bytes, by SIPACUM's defense circuitry and attached explosive.

Only Jonuta knew all the cred-backed identities of Captain Jonuta.

He carried in his head the key words that bade SIPACUM release its set of code phrases—without self-destructing. A specific rearrangement of those phrases, with the interpolation of three more phrases out of Jonuta's head, bade SIPACUM II yield up the information he might eventually require. Not his financial standing. Not his worth. SIPACUM II "knew" only where the investments were, and under what identities. Both Jonuta and SIPACUM II knew that the chances of someone else's obtaining just that information, all of it, were on the order of 7^{13}. Jonuta judged that to be a sufficient hedge to merit being called "impossible." The system was Jonuta. All the records could be accessed only by Jonuta, and that only laboriously.

Should he ever decide to cash in everything, more than a year-standard would be required, even with communication by tachyon beam.

There was more.

(The last visible sun of Franji was almost gone now, leaving a rosy wash in the darkening sky. Noise rose from the city of Velynda, whose population was about fifteen thousand, with a daily workforce approaching twenty-five thousand. The bright green shafts of the elevated tubeway system arabesqued against the sky, full of outbound bureaucrats and agents of enterprise.)

Various favors were owed him on various planets. They were ancillary to agreements all along the spaceways, throughout the galaxy. Gaining such favors, due on call, was part of the trading style of Captain Cautious.

He was owed several on Jasbir, where he had still another I.D. His investment there was sufficient to finance four months of living based on the economy then current. Even if it underwent considerable change, he would have the financing for a well-funded hiding out.

On his homeworld of Qalara, Jonuta was hardly unknown and in fact no minor figure. Local boy had made good—very good. Kislar Jonuta maintained Qalaran citizenship. His Qalaran investments remained major despite his withdrawal of several. He took that step after the messy attempt on his life there, and he saw to it that it was well publicized. The Kenuta Investment Consortium of Qalara (Ltd.) was almost solely Jonuta's. He maintained a large luxurious apartment in the capital, Norcross.

And he was a major (stellar) backer of the galaxy-renowned Hakimit Medical Center. It was a cautious man's superlative form of insurance. Even Kenowa did not know about his very special secret project at HMC, although in a way it had been her suggestion.

Nor did anyone know that the speculator in Sekhari Minerals, Jone Shuttlesteader, was Kislar Jonuta.

Only TGO had the power and (maybe) the capability to learn enough (maybe) to break Jonuta. And TGO had not. The Gray Organization's purpose was to maintain order in the galaxy. Order was preserved by good trade and a healthy overall economy. Slavery fed such a sprawling, ungoverned economy, and propped it. Slaver Jonuta had not *had* to work for years and years.

Jonuta, however, liked to work. What fun was play, except after one had worked, dared, risked, accomplished?

These things he reviewed under the twinkling astral lights that clustered thick in the sky of Velynda, on Franji. And he heard the bong-bong of the wake-up alarm he and Kenowa took onplanet with them, everywhere. Leaning on the suite's balcony rail, Jonuta smiled. Kenowa had readied this night's Change. The evening was about to debouch into debauchery.

With a last glance up at the luminous, star-studded sky, he turned and re-entered the Sultana Suite where she awaited.

The suite's main room was aglow with a roseate light that was almost luminous. It was not eerie, even though it tinged the walls and every object in shades of pink and red. The effect was sensuous. Jonuta moved through that sex-hued room to the bedroom, where there was no direct light; the pink glow bled in from the sitting room.

He stepped through the doorway—and halted. The smile left his face. He was staring into the muzzle of a stopper.

"Do come in, Captain Cautious. So you are caught at last."

He recognized that sneering voice. He did not recognize the speaker. He knew the uniform. It was that of TransGalactic Watch. It clung to the curves and indentations of a more than attractive woman. Every seam and button of the uniform seemed ready to burst with the ripeness of her. Nevelcro closures must have been hanging on as desperately as a kitten dangling from a limb.

Jonuta elevated his hands.

"May I ask who my captor is?"

"Indeed you may," the only just familiar voice said. "I am Brevet-major Shariella 118-99-793SR."

He showed her a restrained smile. "Shariella" was a name right out of a torn-bodice holodrama. He took that as a clue, since the sneering, slightly disguised voice was familiar. He wondered if the uniform and long curling masses of black hair were real or holo-proj. In the sensual dimness of the pink light that seemed to warm the room while turning it into a sort of fantasyland, he could not be sure.

"And about to be full Condor-major, too, once you've brought me in, hmm? What is the charge, Brevet-major?"

"Never mind that shit, Jonuta." She stepped back a pace, and aside. She gestured. "Precede me out the door."

Jonuta swallowed. The adrenaline burst triggered by the initial shock was dissipating. Now he went prickly again. He was right, wasn't he? *This* is *tonight's Change, isn't it?*

He walked to the door, past her. He lowered a hand to the opener plate, pivoted, clamped the gun hand—the right—in his and thrust it straight up, and gave the uniformed woman a short, sharp, three-bent-fingers jab in the left breast.

She grunted. The stopper fell to the carpet. He used her upraised arm as if they were dancing. She had no choice but to move with it, turning her back to him. He didn't bother swinging his right arm around her. Instead he grasped her upper arm, set a knee against her prominent and taut-pantsed backside, and shoved, hard. He let go with both hands.

With a distressed sound, she was catapulted a meter or so forward to bring up against the side of the bed. She sprawled upon it. Just as she was turning over, Jonuta was upon her. She and the bed bounced.

His grab for her stiffly standing collar brought him only the feel of skin. He ran his hand down until the fingers slid into fabric, and he yanked. Cloth tore. He assumed it was something old. Cloth came off in his hand, but the uniform remained undamaged. She sputtered and tried to knee him and he jammed his own knee straight in between her legs. All the way. It impacted with a jolt that brought a throaty gasp from the brevet-major. He jiggled the knee while his hand clamped down on the bulge of a uniformed breast, hard. Again he felt no uniform. The unsupported warhead was indifferently covered with a silken fabric thin as epidermis.

"Stop resisting, Bitch-major Shariella, or I'll twist this mass of meat right off your chest. Titsy slut, aren't you?"

"You . . . dog! Don't even think of raping me!"

"Of course not. Rape is a thoughtless act."

He'd had enough of the uniform he could see but not tear or remove, since it was a projection. A hand came at him but gave him plenty of time to notice and slap its wrist. Not hard, but she squeaked and the hand flopped. He pawed her. Silken fabric and skin. He found the projector at her waist, naturally, disguising itself as a TGW standard issue holster.

"No—wait . . ."

She didn't want him to kill the holo. All right. "I'm going to punch you and knock you half-senseless," he said, and aimed a blow at her chin that didn't quite land. She went limp while he kneed himself back off the bed with a lurch. He pounced to the doorway connecting the rooms and closed the door. End roseate light. The room was almost dark; the wan glow of a Franjese moon and several distant suns—all larger than points, here close to galaxy center—crept in through the window.

He clamped an ankle and pulled her off the bed. The impact was not silent and neither was Kenowa.

"Hush, Shariella," he bade her, jerking the ankle high while he opened his pants. "Your ass is definitely padded enough to protect you from the floor, Trans-Galactic Witch! It's a wonder you didn't bounce!"

"Oh! Dog!"

"You said that." He kicked away his shoes and his pants. He was not amazed that his penis had both thickened and lengthened. His woman knew her man. And she knew herself. She was one of the few who were fortunate enough to realize their sexual fantasies—without danger or consequence. Otherwise all of this would be horrible, both inhuman and subhuman. "Your vocabulary seems limited, Brev-slut. Sheltered life?"

"Blackguard! Varlet! CIA! Spittle of an unclean Crusader!"

"Better," he said, recognizing a few old-fashioned terms straight from her 'dramas. "But . . . sticks and stones, TGW bitch. Going to take me in, were you! Hmp—here, let's get you . . . turned . . . *over!*" He did that, with her on the suite's rich carpeting.

After that he made loud whistling-rushing noises with his belt, while he used his left hand to land awkward slaps on the upturned buttocks of his "captive." She squealed, kicked, pleaded, pretended to be hurt, and began promising to Do Anything, ANYthing.

"Glad to hear it," he said into the almost-darkness. "Maybe I won't kill you, then. For awhile. You *are* the sexiest TGWatcher I ever saw."

"Ohhh nooo," she said, in a tiny voice. His hand wasn't slapping the mound he could see now. He was rubbing it, lovingly, with a circular motion.

"You mean you'd rather be killed than meet a Fate Worse than Death?" He reached around to palpate her breast.

"No—I mean . . . fiend! How can you be so cruel? How can you be so—so . . . *male?!*"

"Must be in the genes. Now you have only to turn over, get up onto your knees, and get your tongue and lips to work on me." He paused one beat before adding, "Whore." (Kenowa liked the word. Had not Vardis Fisher written that a woman would rather be called a whore than a fat-ass, and been confirmed by his wife?)

"I'm *not!* Y—"

"You will be before you leave here."

"No! I won't touch your nasty slicer with my mouth, you—owww!"

So she had decided she hadn't received quite enough on the upturned ass, eh? Well, he'd give her some more. Kenowa well knew the neural connection between the buttocks and the genitals, male or female . . . aside from the psychological reasons for her enjoyment.

"Oww! I'll do it, *oh!* I'll *do* it, monsterowww!"

"Sorry," he said. "That's only nine. I decided that you need twenty. With the buckle end of my belt, of course."

He rushed the buckle through the air and struck the bed while his off hand slapped her tensing cheek. She squirmed and affected agony.

"Theba's mercy—you'll bruise my poor, uh, me!"

"Bruise! Hmp! I'll draw blood, wench! We Crusaders know how to treat you sexy bitchy Saracen sluts!"

And he gave her the other ten slaps, medium hard, meanwhile making a lot of noise with the belt. He was not, after all, either a conquering Crusader of old or a Gorean—Jonuta liked women.

Then she licked and sucked while her eminently malleable, manipulable warheads were manipulated and palpated with much much attention to their erected tips. And eventually the poor groaning moaning (and thoroughly interiorly wet) TGW brevet-major was sprawled on the unyielding floor, however thickly carpeted, being cruelly raped. It was marvelous. The sound of flesh slapping flesh rose in the room as he rocked in her cradle, and the odor of sexuality rose around them like a curling mist.

Both of them became quaking, sighing moaning prisoners of carnal passion. The relentless pounding of his sinewy body raised libidinous joy to an extravagant peak of arousal and need.

"Take . . . this . . . deep . . . TGW . . . whore!"

"Oh yes," she breathed, and was inwardly sprayed.

A bit later, before she began to rub herself while he pressured her nipples, Kenowa turned off the stern TGW holoproj and removed the belt whose holster contained the toes-to-neck projector. The long, long curly wig she retained. Both of them liked it, as both of them had far more than liked Kenowa's latest Change scenario.

14

DESTRUCTN OF OUR SHIP OFF MURPH INTOLERABL. JONUTA MUST BE PUNISHD. READ: RUINED. INITIATE FULL COMPUTR SRCH & SCAN OF HIS AFFAIRS. ACCESS ALL AVL. DATA + ANCILLARY E.G. POSSIBLE INFORMATN. OPERATION CLAMP TO BE INITIATED IMMEDIATELY. END

Message received & amplification requested. What command to personnel & ships re: Jonuta?

ZERO COMMAND TO SHIPS & PERS. RE: J. DO NOT REPT ZERO ATTEMPT TO ATTACK, KILL, OR ATTEMPT TO ARREST. NO CONTACT. PREFER HE ZERO KNOWLEDGE OF OUR MOVING. OPERATION CLAMP IS TO CLAMP & CRUSH, ECONOMICALLY & SPIRITUALLY. CONFIRM. END

Confirmed. OPERATION CLAMP initiated this date.

Top Secret Exchange: TGO

It began when they flew out over Haj Seablood's mansion, far from Velynda. It was not there. It no longer existed. There was plenty of rubble, slag, and the horrific shapes of tortured structural materials. There was no mansion.

There had been an explosion, Jonuta saw with stricken eyes. The ensuing fire had burned hot and without attention. Some power failure must have prevented the automatic fire-control systemry from doing its work. Perhaps it had been destroyed in the explosion, which would surely never be explained. There was nothing left. Only that saddest of sights, rubble and char and impossibly ugly, surreal twistings of a few unconsumed materials.

Haj Seablood was burned out. He did not land the handsome little yellow and blue craft, its gay colors now garish, obscene in the presence of disaster and hideousness. He did not land because he did not want to. He could not. He was grieving.

"I loved that place," Jonuta said softly, in a dull voice, and he said nothing else.

His jaw was tight against words and grief, all the way back to Velynda. Kenowa shared his anguish and his silence. All there was to say were the ridiculous clichés people said at such times, and she would not mouthe such things to Jonuta. They would talk later.

He did not even consider arson or a bomb, until the second blow crashed down.

There was nothing in Haj Seablood's account.

It was then that he had the first new feeling, deep in the pit of his stomach, that was beyond grief. A plot . . . ? But no, it had to be some sort of mistake. As Seablood, he knew the president of the Franji State Bank & Transfer, and he could damned well accost her. He did.

There was no mistake. Computer storage and no less than two human employees provided the information and the documents. Without formality, Haj Seablood had quietly withdrawn every stell, to the stell, simply by using his I.D. to effect a transfer to an account at Vanguard, a planetary money market.

"I did no such thing, Fara."

The eyes of Farathis Littel, president, Franji State B & T, were anguished.

"I believe you, Haj. But—you see the copies. It was all done in an orderly and even casual manner. I did not even know about it until later. The account was not formally closed, you see. Just emptied."

"Looted," said the man in her office: Haj Seablood, suddenly unwealthy.

She heaved a sigh. "Looted. Brilliantly and—well. When I discovered the heavy transfer, I checked. When I found it was your account, I tried to contact you. You were offplanet. There is a message out at the house."

"There is no house, Fara. It's . . . rubble. Burned out. After an explosion."

"Oh, Haj!" Her commiseration was genuine. Bank presidents were human, especially with social contacts. Especially with big depositors. That would have to change, if he was ruined. But right now she was able to share some portion of his anguish. Right now he remained human. Haj Seablood *couldn't* be wiped out.

His stomach was churning. There were things he wanted to do. Calls he wanted to make. Fear was rising.

"It . . . it was insured?"

"You know where it was, Farathis." Of course. She had been there. Socially. "The house was paid for, and way out there insurance was twice the cost of taxes. I spent more thousands and thousands putting in warning systems and cybernetic decombusters and fire-suppressants. *Two* systems, separate. Obviously they failed. No, I didn't have insurance. It's a total loss. And it's impossible." He stabbed a finger at the printouts on her desk. "As impossible as this."

"Let—let me call Theb Arortis over at Vanguard. Do you know him?"

"No." And he added bitterly, "I wish I did. Looks as if I'd better wish I'd had my account with Vanguard all along. It won't be there, Fara."

"Oh, *Haj,*" she said, trying to combine commiseration with a tone of accusation, and she made the call.

He was right. The account with Vanguard had been of brief duration. No one at Vanguard had met Haj Seablood. He had opened a smallish account by phone, sans visual. He had transferred in the huge amount from FSB&T. And he had called and had it sent to him, by voucher. That was that. The account was inactive. It was also empty, and would be automatically closed at the next auditing period, unless there was activity.

There would be no activity. Jonuta was sure of that. And what was he to do? Call the policers? Sure. Someone had cleaned out Haj Seablood, and they would investigate, and offplanet the message would go, and . . . how long until Haj Seablood's real identity was known?

"No, Farathis," he told her, while her hand lay on the bank's direct comm line to the police. "I have resources."

"Haj, you've been *robbed!* Someone . . . you've got to . . . what will you let me do for you?"

He rose, shaking his head. "Nothing, Fara. Thank you. I have resources."

She rose also, a woman of about fifty, apparent-age about twenty-six, figure carefully slim yet imposing. "Haj—"

"Get back to work, Fara, dammit! I am hurting and there is nothing you can do—but I've *got* to!" And he left her.

He could not get to a public comm fast enough. Nearly everything on Franji was government owned, which explained high taxation and inefficiency. Financial institutions, though heavily regulated and constantly snooped upon, remained publicly owned, which on Franji was called "privately owned," since the euphemism for government ownership was "publicly owned." Using the Eri Haddad I.D. and no visual, he called Velyndabank, for direct access to the account of Eri Haddad: his account.

The message came onscreen and it was a big knuckly fist slamming into his stomach.

ACCOUNT UNDER INVESTIGATION. PLEASE APPEAR PERSONALLY TO VERIFY I.D.

They've got me. Someone knows about Seablood and Haddad, too. I've been burned out and looted. Maybe it's Franjese confiscation. I doubt it. This was too efficient for government work. They'd still be talking about it, planning and arguing about just how to go about robbing me—to "confiscate" my property. Or they'd have botched some aspect of it so that the bumbling governmental hand would be obvious. It isn't. All this has been handled smoothly—hideously smoothly. It's not even possible, not using an I.D. and going through the bank's computers and safeguards to get my Seablood account! No. Someone else. Who? Someone knows about Eri Haddad. A dead man, with an active account on Franji. Do they know whose retina print his is, too?

Probably.

This time his sinking feeling was almost physical illness, because he was coming onto the only possible answer. *Corundum? Ridiculous. No individual has this kind of resources and ability.* No, the answer was obvious, and it sent fear crawling slimily even into Captain Cautious. It had to be TGO. TransGalactic Order. TGO: The Gray Organization. Preserving "order" through any means. Doing good by doing evil. Justifying the means by the end achieved.

Nor would an outlaw be making protests or trying to fight!

The new thought hit him. In this case there was probably a tap on the account. An alarm had probably gone off somewhere the moment he had used his Haddad card to access the account at Velyndabank. An agent or agents were probably already scrambling to converge on this public comm booth.

Jonuta left it.

Jonuta was ruined on Franji. He was nobody and nothing on Franji. Haj Seablood had nothing. Luggage in a hotel, and a few memberships. A few stell notes for use as tips. That was the extent of Haj Seablood on Franji. Eri Haddad had never existed and still did not—and now he had nothing. Kislar Jonuta had a ship and crew docked above—and he hadn't even the stells to pay the hotel or the fare up to Franjistation.

He had been tracked and found and hit expertly, hit hard. Now he fled, hunted and fearful. And trying to think.

Resourceful Captain Cautious was an outlaw. An outlaw could not protest, institute legal action, make pleas as others could. He must take, and take, and depend on himself, and find ways to escape and to abide and survive. And, perhaps, to fight back.

Captain Cautious had not been cautious enough. Now he could not even be cool. Panic sought to seize him and he tried to elude it, to fight it off—while fleeing almost in panic. Fleeing that comm booth in a city where he was next to penniless, he tried to think.

By the time he reached the Royal Franjis he had regained enough control to think with something approaching rationality. He had not been caught or, to his knowledge, spotted and followed. He was ruined—and yet new confidence surged, for he had realized that he was still not without resources, on Franji.

Less than a year ago he had set up a just-in-case here, for Kenowa.

"Some people just can't seem to like me," he had told her, with a very small smile. "If one of them succeeds in taking me out, I want you retired more than comfortably. It's my pride, of course," he had added, as if embarrassed by her glistening eyes and gratitude. He had set it all up while feeling guilty about his foolishness, the liaison with Countess Reesapantarii. "Countess Squeezer" and Haj had met at a party and spent the next several days-Franji—and nights, oh yes the nights—together. And, of course, the time had come when he took leave of her and returned to Kenowa . . . after setting her up with a false-I.D. retirement, here on Franji. Just in case. Under that other name, Kenowa had a nice piece of an apt-complex here, and an interest-bearing credaccount. Her Franjese I.D. card was stashed. Both he and she knew where. All she had to do was use the card. She could decide for herself whether to continue to use that I.D., to become that person—if ever necessity arose.

Necessity had arisen, but not because Captain Jonuta had been taken out. Someone was after him in another way, and had done a superb job of it. However . . .

He was nervous entering the hotel, and worked not to show it. Nothing happened. He and Kenowa did not check out. The need to move was too great to give her time to weep for him, for them, even with all he told her. They left the Royal Franjis together and went together to take possession of that card, and a bit of its cred. The card was in a permabox, permanently paid for, in the depository in the Citizens' Bureau. That's what the Franjese government called it, anyhow. Jonuta liked the idea of letting the government watch over Kenowa's property for him. No one could open this drawer—safely—but Kenowa, or Jonuta. In the public hall that was always brightly lit with alarms and guards at the doors, he watched her open the permabox. It was empty.

15

Remember, things always look darkest
just before they go totally black.
Roger Dennis

Coronet rode the spaceways.

Bleak was "close" to Franji, and so was Front. But on each of those planets Jonuta had only enough cred to enable him to visit without cash or trade goods. The SIPACUM computer he called First Mate, along with his own course guidance cassette, were directing *Coronet* to Jasbir.

Jasbir, where slavery was entirely legal. Where Badakeacorp could not keep up with demand for its interactive calculators. Jasbir, source of the mini-holo-projectors used so imaginatively by Captain Jonuta. Where the slaver Jonuta was welcome and TGO was not. Jasbir, where the slaver Jonuta had investments sufficient to finance four months' princely living.

On Jasbir he was owed various favors-on-call, too, by no less than three individuals.

Coronet rode the spaceways, on course for Jasbir.

Jonuta had not bothered trying to collect on the

favors owed him by the Franjese. He did not want to hear their replies—or chance violent ones. The seeming sorcerous instrument of his ruination seemed to know everything, to have thought of everything. To be capable of accomplishing anything and everything. In that case he had no friends left on Franji, and no favors owing. None that would be admitted or paid, anyhow.

He was forced to write off Franji, where he had been someone, his Haj Seablood persona unpenetrated; and where he had enough wealth to buy another ship and outfit it as expensively as *Coronet*. And where an act of love had set Kenowa up for life, just in case.

Gone. Gone.

Why? That is, it was not that the slaver Jonuta had not merited interference and worse. The point was, assume that it was TGO. And the question followed naturally: Why *now?*

Why not last year, or last month, or two or five or eleven years-standard ago? Why not next year or two or six years-standard hence? That was it, aside from the anguish of his massive loss. Why . . . *now?*

It was not a question of what had he done. It was a question of what had he done recently, that was so ghastly? What had triggered this expert and horribly effective attack? An attack that was all the more crushing because it was indirect, multiple, and thorough.

(When he and Kenowa discovered that the permabox had been—impossibly—entered and robbed, that she had no I.D. on Franji, that all he had set up for her was gone, too . . . then he had had the horrible thought. *Coronet!* Suppose—O Booda no, no, not the ship, not beloved *Coronet,* the perfect ship! Not that too. Not after all these years of laboriously and hyper-expensively outfitting and equipping it. Not *Coronet!* Not until later did he consider the awful prospect of being stranded on Franji, without funds, cred, or friends. Naked! His first thoughts were all of the ship itself. Its loss would be unsupportable. He had to find out or try to prevent any pirating of it, and he had to do it *then*. Never mind the bill at the Royal Franjis. Never mind their possessions there. They hadn't the means of settling the charge for the Sultana Suite anyhow. He had rushed to the Franjistation terminal. There he deliberately used the Haj Seablood card—knowing it would be respected, and that the charge would never be settled—and got them ferried up to the station. *Coronet* was there. *Coronet,* Sakyo, Shig, Sweetface, that damned Tweedle-dee; all were fine. They had no notion of the disaster that had befallen their captain and perhaps themselves. Ready to defend if necessary, he had settled the bill for *Coronet*'s thorough checking, using a bit of cargo he preferred not to part with. That was necessary to gain clearance to depart, which he requested immediately. His skin prickled . . . and he had been cleared at once. All precautions were unnecessary. *Coronet* whipped away from Franjistation, and into deep space. Then, out amid the star-spattered indigo, Jonuta's adrenaline high evaporated and he began sagging into . . . what he had become.)

Why *now?*

Jonuta agonized over that. He brooded while *Coronet* plunged toward Jasbir. In less than a day-standard he somehow took on an underfed appearance. He looked unrested, older, even smaller. He worked with his Mate constantly. Inputting SIPACUM with recent acts and possibilities, gaining computer estimates of possible consequences and probabilities. He hovered over the con, over SIPACUM, and he kept at it like a man possessed by some demonic force. Anguish festered in him. Anger boiled in him, exuded from him, exploded from him. He was no fit company for anyone. He was not Jonuta, not the Jonuta anyone knew. The others of *Coronet* tried to understand, to make allowances. They tried.

Already there had been trouble on *Coronet;* tension, before the visit to Franji. Now it was worse.

The captain had no sympathy for his long-time crew-member and companion from Jarpi. The captain was short with Sakyo and Kenowa and Shig, but he was worse than short with Sweetface. Always it was because of the Jarp's half-wit companion.

When this ever-distracted new Jonuta wanted something, he wanted it five minutes ago, no matter who was on duty or off and no matter what activity he interrupted. When he was preoccupied with his constant postulating of *why*, he was more than distracted. Nothing was important enough to merit interrupting his thoughts, his endless brooding and working or "working" with SIPACUM. Let the interrupter beware!

That was not Jonuta. Worse, it was not Captain Cautious. Kenowa feared the consequences of a possible in-space confrontation by another ship. The most competent eluder and trickster along the spaceways was gone, to be replaced by this new person wearing Jonuta's body with the new dark rings under the eyes. The gaunt, staring eyes.

He chewed them all, and Sweetface received the brunt.

Sweetface was railed at, accused, cursed, blamed (because of Tweedle-dee) for everything from "tardiness to the con-cabin" to "inattention to the con" to the glitch in the waste recycler to a stray comet that must have been on a million year-standard cycle. And *Coronet* rushed on toward Jasbir, a ship about as happy as H.M.S. *Bounty*.

Then Jonuta went too far, naturally.

Sweetface could understand or try to, could make allowances and take more than it should or thought possible. But then Jonuta came upon Tweedle-dee when he was rushing along the ship's tunnel. He yelled his order for "her" to get out of his way. The confused Jarp froze. Jonuta shoved it, banging it into the bulkhead, and stormed on his way. And he had gone too far.

Sweetface was a humanized Jarp. The residents of Jarpi were all territorial and interprotective to begin with. Those who had long interacted with humans were doubly so. In love or long infatuation, territoriality and protectiveness were magnified unto exaggeration. Sweetface had become exaggeratedly, ridiculously protective. It resembled the daughter or son willing to insult and break with the parent because of slight to the offspring's intended. Whether attributed to biology or psychology, it was a strong force. Sweetface went seeking his captain.

"Well?" the glowering travesty of Jonuta snarled. "Do it!"

"Tle'e-wheet'l p'l—"

"And turn on your damned fuckin' translator, you ignorant fuckin' *Jarp!*"

Sweetface did. It spoke formally. "I am no more ignorant than I ever was, *Captain.* You are distracted and don't realize it. I do not understand your urging me to 'do it,' Captain."

"You came at me looking all mean and protective to—what? To hit me? Bang me around a little or a lot? Use your stopper on me?"

Sweetface stared from enormous black eyes set in a strangely sweet, elfin-chinned face. "I cannot imagine either of us striking the other, *Captain.*"

Neither could Jonuta, but he was committed, and he managed not to show any remorse.

"That is not why I came here—angry, true. Angry with justification, Captain. This is no happy ship and I am no happy Jarp. Now Tweedle-dee is as miserable as—you, Captain. Tweedle-dee has tried. I have tried. I feel great empathy—and sympathy—for you, and wish I could help you. My great hope is that all is well for my captain and old friend on Jasbir and Panish and on Qalara."

"Well then? I don't want your damned effing sympathy and I don't need to be told that Tweedle-*dumb* is a miserable creature, a miserable excuse! You're blinded by infatu—"

Jonuta stopped. He had not lost all control. Jonuta, Captain Cautious, still existed in him. He heard himself, and he curbed himself. He saw the Jarp's reaction.

Sweetface stood stiff as rigor mortis, but its eyes were far from moribund. They were full of fire. The scarlet hair and bright orange skin suddenly reminded Jonuta of a volcano. He rediscovered his own sense and broke off, but he did not apologize. He never knew whether it might have changed anything, had he apologized and tried to start this conversation anew.

"I will not know about Panish and Qalara, Captain. Please compute our settlement. I leave *Coronet* on Jasbir, and I leave you."

"Leave—me?!"

"Yes, Captain."

"For—for that—for Tweedle-dee?"

"Has Captain Jonuta really never been in love?"

Jonuta stared at the Jarp, feeling that question as he'd have felt a blood-drawing pinch. "You . . . really . . ."

Sweetface nodded. "What I have said is truth and final, by the penis of my mother and the breasts of my father. My chosen companion—of Jarpi—and I will take no more from you, human. We part, Captain Jonuta, and I wish you nothing but well."

"You—you—" (Sweetface stared, for it had never seen Jonuta come even close to sputtering, before now) "—you expect a recommendation from me after *this?*"

"No, Captain Jonuta. I expect settlement and a printout of my record and competence, my rating. I do not expect to tell anyone what ship I have served on, if I can avoid it."

Jonuta's mental state led him to misinterpret, and to interrupt. "Shame, Sweetface?" he asked, lifting the corner of his lip.

"Never, Captain Jonuta! I don't wish to be questioned, or suspected, or used in some way against you. I wish to be no source of possible betrayal to you. You thought of that long ago, when you logged me as second mate on spacer *Skylark,* and registered that ship."

"It exists only as a computer memory!"

"Yes. It should not be hard for me. I don't expect to be recognized, after all. All us Jarps look alike to you humans, don't we?"

And Sweetface saluted, most formally, and left its captain's presence.

Jonuta did nothing about it. He could have done, perhaps successfully. He did not. Instead he plunged deeper into anguish, understandable self-pity, and the not understandable blaming of others. He began to move in a dangerous and ugly direction: from having made the ship's computer his best friend to making it his only friend.

Kenowa anguished with him and for him, but not in his company. He was almost the old Jonuta with her, in private. Almost. The difference reminded her of what had been. Next would come his "Don't look at me that way!" and that would be that for the two of them, again. And like as not he would head for his true friend and confidant. First mate, *Coronet:* SIPACUM. Together, they resumed seeking the answer to the question of *Why Now.*

Coronet fled past the eternal beacons of suns toward the one its guidance cassette singled out as destination. Huygens, around which turned Jasbir, like a bumblebee on a string. And within *Coronet* was no happy person. One of them grimly accessed the record of his Jarp crewmember, and with his nonhuman ship's mate he arrived at what Sweetface was owed.

The amount was impressive.

It was hideously so, to a man who had just lost a fortune.

Then they swept in past Huygens and within its system, and slowed to a crawl. Now they were within easy communication range.

When the message came that he was not welcome on Jasbir, or even at Jasbirstation, Jonuta went into something approaching shock.

"Panish," Kenowa later suggested. Carefully, diffidently. Jonuta was hardly Jonuta anymore. Anything might offend or anger him or worse.

"No," he snarled. "They'll have got to me there, too! No! Set course for Front! I haven't relaxed in the good old Black Hole Bar for years!"

Because Front was a nothing planet with ankle-high development, Kenowa thought. But she found the cassette and, checking it twice because her eyes were misting, inslotted it. *Coronet* revectored and rushed toward the planet named Front.

16

Detached reflection cannot be demanded in the presence of an upraised knife.
Oliver Wendell Holmes

The morning after that sex-filled night on Thebanis, Janja went up to Thebanistation to bid farewell to Hellfire. And Raunchy, who had just joined the crew of Hellfire's ship, *Satana.*

"You might's well do the same, Janjy," Hellfire said, but Janja only smiled.

Maybe it was a wistful smile. Maybe she wanted to go along with the golden-ocher woman with the brass-hued hair—and with Raunchy. And maybe even more than that she wanted to part with Corundum. It was just that she lacked either the guts or the cruelty to abandon him without a word.

They had done no real talking, Janja and Hellfire of Lanatia. Hellfire knew now that her words were just words, that Janja was not lesbian and would not be leaving the eminent not to mention wealthy Captain Corundum. She had little hint of the problem that had widened from a crack between Corundum and Janja to a crevasse, and no idea of Janja's disillusionment.

Yet as they whirred off Thebanis, seasoned spacefarers bemoaning the pits of their stomachs as the shuttle rushed them straight up, Janja was wishing that she could merely walk aboard *Satana* and bid Thebanis and Corundum good-bye—long distance.

"Raunchy," Hellfire said thoughtfully.

"Um?"

"On *Satana* you call me 'Captain,' Raunchy."

"Didn't need to tell me that, Captain."

Hellfire nodded. She didn't say she was sorry. Janja knew two slavers now, and three pirates. All were independent and proud unto arrogance. Yet Corundum, she thought, was more a gentleman than Jonuta or Vettering or Hellfire or Shieda.

So what makes me so stupid that I want to get away from him?

Raunchy was rubbing away at her thigh and she neither objected nor responded. She was busy thinking. Nothing was accomplished by it, and it was unpleasant to boot.

The shuttle emerged into the center of the torus like a pop-up toy. The space station's gigantic airlock closed beneath them, a just-in-case measure against possible breach and airout. The shuttle door hissed open. They and the other passengers emerged into the enormous circle of Thebanis Space Operations Center: Thebanistation. It was brightly lit and alive with voices and color in Degas splashes and just plain noise. The hubbub of many voices in many accents. A busy place the size of a small city, full of civil servants and factors and spacefarers coming and going to and from the coming and going ships. Up here, fashion didn't exist. No one planet's fashion, at any rate.

Hellfire turned to Janja. Was there warmth in those deep-set, dangerous eyes that seemed jet until bright light showed their mahogany?

"Well, Janjy, I— Why don't you come and see *Satana?*"

That was a nice idea. The would enable Janja to put off her return for a while longer. It was childish, she thought, this wishing she didn't have to return to Corundum. They'd have to talk. Last night she had faced him and braced him, and even known elation at his acceptance of her independence, even her public challenge. But last night was last night, with pride and Hellfire's example helping, and alcohol. Now . . .

Now it was a bright unalcoholic day, down on Thebanis.

"I'll ride around to your ship with you, yes. I'd love to see your *Satana.*"

"No need to ride the perimeter crawler," Hellfire said, indicating a direction with a nod of her head. "*Satana*'s only a few meters from the end of this spoke."

They walked along Spoke H, broad as a city street, from the station's apex to its perimeter. All along it were berths; many housed ships that were outside the station's enclosure. A spacer was nosing in now, just over there, clearly visible through the transparent wall along Franjistation's circumference.

The three walked to Captain Hellfire's ship, the "merchanter" with the name that fitted no merchantship. The flames of Hades and the queen of Hades. Hellfire and *Satana.* Raunchy should change its name to something more infernal, Janja mused, because her mind was jumping all about like an unchained pup, avoiding any thought of Corundum and her very real problem.

A bit of fondling and simpy face-making took place on that short last walk, all of them remembering a marvelous night. And then they were there, too soon.

Satana nuzzled the rim of the station, in berth 19. An umbilical tunnel, a collapsible ramp, connected the ship to the station. Like a huge hollowed grub worm, the tunnel was sealed to the spacer's open outer airlock. And *Satana* was neither sleek nor beautiful.

She was an old ram-scoop, the duck-billed platypus of the spaceways.

Even the fresh-looking paint job, a rather dull orange combined with pink, could not add beauty to such a shape. Janja looked at the ungainly monster and made polite noises. She was hardly seeing *Satana* and she certainly wasn't thinking about it. She was thinking helplessly that Raunchy and Hellfire would be doing plenty of fondling, what Hellfire called "lickin' and stickin'," and that she had just enjoyed her last fondle with the mildly attractive consummately sexy pair. To a ninety-eight-plus probability factor, anyhow. The galaxy was big. It was vastly, incredibly, inconceivably big. The odds were that she'd never see these two again.

Maybe I'll hear about it and maybe I won't, when this unstable and ever-challenging woman is blown away because she's unstable and forever challenging, volatile as fulminate of mercury. And maybe I'll hear about it months or years-ess later.

Only an idiot would be standing here wishing she could accompany such a captain, Janja, you idiot! She's a walking deathwish.

"She's a good ship," Hellfire said, looking rather maternally upon her *Satana*. "A good ole ship. Want to come onboard a minute, Cloud-top?"

"Don't dare," Janja said. "Last night I innocently went to a hotel module on just such an invitation, just a sweet li'l innocent cloud-topped gurl. And I got kidnaped and lost my vir-ginn-itteee. I wouldn't dare go on that ship with you. What if I got k-kidnaped into s-sp-*space?*"

She stared at *Satana* and at Hellfire, making her eyes as wide and innocent as she could. It used to be easier.

It didn't work too well anymore, but Hellfire laughed.

"What? *kid*-nap! An honest dull ole merchanter captain like me is?"

"Oh stop." Janja chuckled. "I get sick easily!"

"So do I, girls. Ooops—*freeze*. You're covered."

They stared at him. He had been waiting in the airlock, and now came partway down the covered ramp. They were covered, all right. The man, coveralled as a cargo handler and wearing a stationworker's badge, was playing Lone Ranger with a stopper in each hand.

"Just come along into the tunnel here and lead the way into this dull ole merchant spacer, *Captain Hellfire*. The same for you two sluts. We need to have some conversation."

"Shaitan's balls! It's the traffic watcher from the Loophole, last night!"

"So right, Captain Hellfire," he said, waggling the rightward stopper. "You were right about me last night, too. Ho-ho good for you. Also too bad for you—we've got a positive make on you from two people on the little Delventine colony raid. Five weeks ago tomorrow you hit 'em, remember? Half their supplies and all their personals stolen, and two zapped?" His eyes flicked to Janja. "And today I won't be getting within reach of your talented left arm, Janja of Aglaya. Leaving Corundum or just visiting?"

"My my," Hellfire said, while Janja's stomach tightened up like a big fist. "He knows us, too! Too bad we don't give a snot about your name or I.D., jacko. Do you know Sweetface here, too?"

"I—"

"Never mind," Hellfire went on, cutting him off while Janja marveled that the woman knew the name of Jonuta's Jarp crewmember. "We are all three armed, jacko. Think you can—" And this time he interrupted.

"I'm authorized. And you are who you are and what you are. This is what is called dead to rights, and I am making an arrest. My stoppers're set on Fry. You resist arrest and you're fried, and good riddance. Understand? Say a wrong word to these two, make a wrong move, and you are molecules, *Captain* Hellfire. That is *scattered* molecules, you understand." He hefted the cylinder in his right hand. "And this one stays aimed right at you, just you. Don't do anything silly, Whitey and Orangey, or she gets roasted, toasted, and turned to dust motes right before your eyeballs."

"Lord, you aren't nice at all, jacko."

"You have a rep, Hellfire. If I tried a little niceness with you or let down m'guard, I'd never live to get back into uniform. Now let's board your ship."

Janja's brain had begun to function again. *Onboard* Satana? *With all three of us, plus whatever other crew-members are there? Why? What does he want?*

"What? Not going to show me some I.D.? I've got rights!"

"No you haven't, Hellfire." His voice had lost all its easy jocularity and so had his face.

"Going to show those guys some I.D.?" Hellfire persisted, nodding to her right, past Janja and Raunchy, whose long fingers kept twitching. Neither of them turned to look at no one.

Neither did the Lone Ranger. He kept staring at Hellfire. So did the muzzle of his stopper. Nasty little tubes! Janja had been hit with one, what seemed a hundred or so years-standard ago on Jonuta's ship. Just the first or second setting. She remembered. It was awful.

"Shit," Hellfire distinctly and succinctly said, and began to walk toward him, into the umbilical tunnel. A giant worm; a mortuary's cupola on a slant. He stood warily, right-hand stopper leveled at the wiry, lean woman. She began ascending. He glanced, only glanced, at Janja and Raunchy.

"Follow." The leftward stopper waggled.

Raunchy shook its head. "No. Not me."

"Freeze, Hellfire, and stay friz. I really am authorized, Jarp. Follow Hellfire, or I take her down. It's all the same to me."

No it isn't, Janja thought, *or he'd have done it al-*

ready. What does he want? Parley? Blackmail? Steal the ship once we've led him inside?

"Hey, come on, Raunchy," Hellfire called, "I'm too young and sexy to be fried."

Moving slowly, Raunchy stepped past Janja to enter the tunnel.

Janja did not move slowly. She drew while Raunchy blocked the man from her view and thus her from his. Raunchy took another step, onto the ramp, and another, and there was the man again and Janja squeezed the cylinder's grip. With an "uh!" their accoster stiffened and began to dance loosely. Two seconds later Hellfire had drawn and fried him. A few seconds after that, since she held, he was scattered components, mote-size.

From somewhere down along the inner perimeter of the wheel, someone yelled. Janja glanced that way, then charged into the tunnel.

"He must've had friends. They saw my stopper."

The three of them rushed up the claustrophobic length of the tunnel and into *Satana*'s airlock. No one said a word, but Raunchy and Janja both leveled their stoppers down along the ramp while Hellfire coded open the inner lock. Then it was open, and they backed after her into the ship.

"Stand out of the way," Hellfire snapped. "Leave the lock open. Just be invisible." She fingered the comm box mounted beside the airlock, gone all professional and seemingly as competent as her reputation. Her eyes showed nothing approaching panic. "Quindy!"

Janja stared across the open port. "Why?"

"If those were friends of his you saw, they might well just charge right in and up the ramp after us. If they don't, if they tell Station Control or Security instead, we're in trouble. Otherwise we'll hear their footsteps clomping up the umbilical tunnel. You pivot into the opening, see, squatting as you come around, and you squeeze. That's it. You might just change the setting on your stopper, Janjy. And thanks, Cloud-top. You've got a good head and you sure do know how to act."

Just as Raunchy said, "But we can't just—" a woman came arunning, from within the ship. She was astonishingly black, astonishingly good-looking. She wore low-slung, bright red pants that were tight above and loose below; a stopper and a red halter, and enormous loops of earrings, pink and silver. Her hair was a massy loose mane of bright yellow although her eyebrows were straight black lines, and her halter bounced.

She acknowledged the call professionally: "Captain!"

"Trouble, Quindy. These two are with us. Order ignition and *request* clearance to depart, calmly and politely as you can."

"You're the captain, Captain. You do that and I'll do this."

"Dam' good idea, Quindy—since Control would want to jaw about releasing *Satana* to you, anyhow." Janja kept her frown inside her head. *Hadn't Hellfire even thought of that? Was she panicky? She was going on: "Footsteps means bandits. Stop 'em."*

She started moving and Janja stopped her with a "Captain." As Hellfire turned back, looking agitated at being held up, yet attentive, Janja spoke quickly. "I think he wasn't a policer and the others probably aren't. If they were three policers, why bring us into the ship and why weren't they closer? I think he wanted to blackmail you—or, once we got him inside, kill us, use you to get *Satana* in space—and kill you too."

"Good thinking, Janja. No time to digest it now. Raunchy, I heard you say 'But we can't' or somesuch. Stand away, then. Quindy, Janja—you've got it." And this time Hellfire wheeled and ran into her ship.

Janja stared after her, then at Quindy. Janja felt caught on a roller coaster. Everything was rushing. There wasn't time to consider anything. A man was dead with no corpus delicti, and more might be coming, and only she seemed to be thinking, and she was involved and onboard—

She heard the footsteps. More than two feet's worth, trotting. From opposite sides of the open port she and Quindy looked at each other. Quindy had her stopper in her hand. The intensely black woman's eyes bored like drills.

"You know what to do, Whitey?" Quindy's voice was only just audible.

Janja nodded. "On your signal, Goldie," she mouthed.

The liquid black eyes flickered. Then, *"Now."*

They pivoted toward each other, into the open mouth of the port. Each went into a squat as she swung to face down into the enclosed ramp. Quindy assumed a two-handed grip on her stopper. Janja had a flashing glimpse of two people, oncoming. Both had stoppers out. The woman was uniformed. That attracted the eyes and Janja squeezed, at her. Unfortunately, so did Quindy.

That way the Franjistation Security officer was reduced to atoms—by Quindy's stopper, since Janja hadn't changed the setting on hers—while the man had time to squeeze his weapon. Janja felt a blow and then a ghastly continuing shock was tingling through every nerve in her body, ice and fire on and on, and she twitched and jerked and went spastic and half-rose and kept twitching loosely. A yelling Quindy was frying the man while Janja was flopping backward, absolutely helpless, falling, hitting her head against the unyielding pasteel of the bulkhead behind her, seeing a million colors in living color, and then nothing.

17

. . . stability isn't nearly so spectacular as instability. And being contented has none of the glamor of a good fight against misfortune, none of the picturesqueness of a struggle with temptation. . . . Happiness is never grand.

Aldous Huxley

"We'll let Sweetface and *it* off on Front," Jonuta said, "and get off it as fast as we can. Sak and Shig understand. There should be something on Front for Sweetface. I left it there long ago, a nice improbable place! Surely they didn't get that too. They can *not* be infallible!"

"But Jone—on *Front?*"

"Oh, I'll give Sweets the choice of going on with us, if it wants to." Jonuta shrugged and peeled open his coat to stand in a sweat-absorbing, short-sleeved, collarless shirt. He touched it. "Dam'! This is Panishi cotton, you know? *Panish!*" He shook his head. "Wide-open Panish, and *I* am no longer welcome there!"

Kenowa did not want him to continue with that line

of thought. She returned to his previous words: "And . . . and after Front? Then what?" She had to force herself to ask, because she was afraid to ask.

"Then we set course for Qalara, Kenny." He stood at his con, and everything was on automatic, and fine. "They can't have got to me on Qalara!"

Her head snapped up at that mention of the planet of his birth. Too, he had not called her Kenny since Franji. She nodded. "And . . . and then? Retirement, on Qalara?"

He looked at her and she saw that Captain Jonuta's eyes were clear and sharp and full of life. "Retire! Hell no! We get ourselves together, find some good Qalarans as crew, and head for deare olde Aglaya and some white-haired merchandise. Hell, Kenny, we can't retire now, and it isn't as if we have to start again. We're just continuing with business as usual. The only way the bastards can stop me is with a stopper!" He stood for a moment wearing a thoughtful, almost whimsical expression. Then, "And maybe not even with a stopper! I'll explain that once we're on Qalara."

Kenowa would have preferred that he had decided to retire, to put all danger and strife behind him. Yet she was elated and tears spewed. "Oh Jone! You're *back!*" And she flung her arms around her man.

"Back?" he said, holding her. "No . . . but by Booda's eyeballs, I'm on the comeback trail, Kenny. They can rob me, stagger me, try to ruin and smash me, but by Booda they can't crush me. Those bastards can't keep a good man down."

Weeping and laughing all at once, she clung to him and was held, and clung to. Then she felt his arousal, and she was even more elated.

"Damn! You sexy slut—did you have to get me all excited just now? SIPACUM has everything in control and I was about to hand you the con and go get some rest."

"That's all right, darling. Just sit down here in the

captain's chair for a change, Captain, and let's see what this sexy slut can arrange."

Sinisterly black-clad, Corundum saw Starnik out once they had completed their information exchange and negotiations. It was well after eleven, Franjitime. The pirate went over to the window. Shoulders back, hands clamped behind his back, he stared down at the city called Raunch. He had just learned that his deception out on Dot, combined with his destruction of that TGW spacer, had indeed served its purpose. Corundum had brought down on Jonuta the wrath of TGO.

Yet Corundum was not smiling in happiness.

"So, Primeval Princess," he muttered, grim of face and of voice. "You did not come back after all, eh? With that scrawny lesbian hust Hellfire, I have no doubt. Just the sort of volatile careless *girl* to get herself blown away before she ever sees the age of thirty. Well Janja, well. This is unworthy of you and of Corundum. How can Captain Corundum hold up his head among those who aggrandize themselves by considering themselves his peers? I shall find you, 'Cloud-top.' If I must cover half the galaxy to accomplish it. And then, my dear little ungrateful barbarian, we shall take *proper* leave of each other!"

Janja blinked open her eyes and saw mistily. Her mouth was unbearably dry. She realized the reason: she was lying flat on her back. The mist swam and coalesced and she was looking up into a lean, longish, sharpish face with pronounced bones. A sharp salient and hollows without plains or rondure, that face. Black holes of eyes like collapstars.

"Well, Cloud-top. A hell of a beginning for you, onboard *Satana!* You'll not be awakening all coddled and cuddly in the captain's cabin *every* day-ess, you know!"

"Hell . . . Hellfire?" Janja put up a quivery hand to touch that face. Though Hellfire's complexion was almost golden, the hand looked very pale against her skin. "I think . . . I think I thought I was dead."

"Nah. You took a rectaboosted jolt of stopper setting number Two. No policer's stopper, I think. And a nice lump on the back of your fluff-top head. You couldn't control your muscles when you tried to get up, and you fell backward. You are alive, Janjy. We're alive and *Satana*'s alive, and they are not. Quindy zapped 'em both and uncoupled us while I was getting clearance from Station Control." Hellfire set a finger against Janja's nose and looked stern. "You didn't reset your stopper on Three, my foolish Janjy. That's disobeying captain's orders."

Janja was still rocky, and more interested in feeling warm and safe than in feeling guilty. "S-sorry, Captain."

"Sorry! I'd say you're sorry. Begin your new berth by disobeying captain's orders. Disciplinary action called for. A whipping? Severe nipple-biting? Stopper-stuffing? No sex at all until we reach Front, in a few days-ess? Well, we'll see."

Janja didn't see the lopsided grin. "Uh—"

"Meanwhile, welcome aboard *Satana,* Janja Cloudtop. We're in space, but you certainly weren't kidnaped! We could hardly put you off after what we had to do, and this is where you want to be anyhow, isn't it?"

"Yes."

So how do you earn your keep on my ship? What are your skills? Aside from several I know about, I mean? Bar-fighting and wonderfully fast action against that policer or so-called policer—twice—and a good working brain. And of course your bed skills I am familiar and happy with."

Janja squeezed her eyes shut. It was done. From peace and love on "barbarian" and "Protected" Aglaya to captivity on *Coronet* to slavery on Resh to killer and penniless fugitive on Franji to spaceship *Firedancer* with Corundum (and never mind her status) to Thebanis to spaceship *Satana,* with Hellfire. And Raunchy.

And what was her status now?

Delighted, for starters. She was off Thebanis and away from Corundum, and she hadn't had to have that agonizing conversation with him—or worse—perhaps discovering that No One Leaves Corundum. And she hadn't really had to decide, either. She was happy.

And she replied. "I—I have learned more than you would believe about ships and engines and SIPACUM. I can almost qualify for mate. And . . . I've learned a few tricks from one of the greatest pirates of the spaceways."

"Hmmm!" Hellfire's black brows rose and her eyes were bright. "I'll bet you have, at that!"

Flat on her back and still shaky, Janja only just managed to keep her hands off her captain. "I think even Captain Hellfire will welcome some of Corundum's ingenuity."

Hellfire stared down at her, musing. Then she laughed. Setting her hands against Janja's breasts to thrust herself off the bed, she stood. Janja gasped.

"No doubt. Oh Janjy! We are on our way! Within a year-standard or three we'll own the flaining spaceways and people will wonder who Vettering and Corundum *were!*"

your damned translator dammit!" had never been deadly serious, nor had Sweetface's habit of occasionally patting Jonuta's small tight butt. Now, however, the idiot was really attached to Tweedle-dee—who really was an idiot—and her/its defense and pleasure. Sweetface resented being denied access to Franji's surface. The objection had developed into a serious altercation of words and loud voices.

Coronet's crew always remained off Franji, dammit. That was, dammit, a standard *Coronet*/Jonuta rule. Haj Seablood was careful of his identity. He was, after all, Captain Cautious.

In the Sultana Suite Haj and his big woman—she was Dulcinea on Franji, because she loved the name of that character in one of her beloved capture/rip bodice-and-everything-else/rape/love-forever holodramas—had discussed that altercation and the growing Sweetface Problem, and then Jonuta wanted to be rid of that subject. He made a suggestion. Kenowa smilingly acquiesced and made a countersuggestion. Or perhaps a parallel one. . . .

Kenowa's suggestion stemmed from her hobby, which was absorption with her collection of holodrama tapes. She added constantly to that cache of reactive-cassettes of what had once been called truconfessions or bodice rippers. (Female pornography, Jonuta called both related genres. Kenowa merely flipped her fingers. Sticks and stones! No laws had ever been passed to prohibit such melodramas! Few candidates for office had ever pandered to the bigot element by crusading against them or even condemning them. Those few who did had been females, who understood their concealed carnal appeal. They lost elections, too, in proof that women of all ages were more devoted to their pornography than males.)

Kenowa had never been a slave . . . to owners.

Kenowa had once been a slave to the swiftly addictive eroflor.

Kenowa owed her very existence to the man who

tall blue or lavender wigs popular all along the spaceways. They were called Terasaki coils and Kenowa loved them.

Her high-teased coiffure this time was the yellow beige of a big gun's stock. The silver flask at her left hip was not a silver flask or even a stylish purse. Kenowa, too, wore a holoproj-disguised stopper.

Their appearance alone had assured Jonuta's and Kenowa's welcome at the Royal Franjis. Then the assistant manager had come out smiling, to greet Jonuta by (false) name while appreciatively conning Kenowa's cleavage flanked by the happy brass-hued hills of her chest. She was aware of that; she stood close up to the desk, leaning forward a little.

The asst-mgr made apologies. The Jasbiri ambassador was in the Nirvana Suite. Good old Haj Seablood graciously accepted the inconvenience, and the Sultana Suite. His luggage was 'chuted straight up, along with Kenowa's four large bags and a box, also large.

Jonuta and Kenowa followed a bit less swiftly, on the liftplate. They entered the Sultana to find it mostly pink and green, and exchanged a twisty-faced look. They toyed with the neons and holocontrols until they had created an environment with hues to their liking, along with two nicer "paintings." *All pink later,* Kenowa thought, also thinking of the few things she had brought along for Jonuta's and her mutual delectation. He did not know about them.

Two hours later they had soni-showered and eaten —in the suite, whose furnishings were suitably opulent, if not fabulous—while being videotape-updated on events Franjese. There was no hint of the shock in store for Haj Seablood.

Once they had broken that helpful telecomm-link to Franjicentral, they discussed the most recent argument with Sweetface.

For years the Jarp and its captain had gotten along very well indeed. Jonuta's constant "Sweetface turn on